I0555632

AN ANGEL'S KISS

By

Vincent Cobb

Email: vincent_cobb@yahoo.co.uk
Web Site: www.vincentcobb.co.uk

AN M-Y BOOKS SOFTBACK

© Copyright 2012
Vincent Cobb

The right of **Vincent Cobb** to be identified as the author of
this work has been asserted by him in accordance with the
Copyright, Designs and Patents Act 1988

All Rights Reserved

No reproduction, copy or transmission of this publication
may be made without written permission.
No paragraph of this publication may be reproduced, copied or transmitted
save with the written permission or in accordance with the provisions of the
Copyright Act 1956 (as amended).

Any person who does any unauthorised act in relation
to this publication may be liable to criminal prosecution and civil claims for
damage.

A CIP catalogue record for this title is
available from the British Library

ISBN 978-1-909271-01-2

**Published by
M-Y Books
187 Ware Road
Hertford
Herts SG13 7EQ**

www.m-ybooks.co.uk

This story is for Pat, my wife, and for Bernie, my eldest daughter, who never believed I could write a love story.

CHAPTER ONE

Tom Metzler had recently graduated with honours from Harvard Law School and had been recruited directly from College into the Law Firm of Harrison and Freedman, of Lexington Avenue, New York: one of the largest of the New York legal firms they employed upwards of two hundred lawyers and sixty partners. It was a prized appointment, offered to only the top two from his class, and, with hard work and diligence, could lead one day to a Partnership.

Tom was twenty-five years of age, of average build, top of his class in the good-looking department with fair hair and lazy blue eyes, which disguised a razor sharp intellect. He had an air of arrogance about him that was characteristic of his youth and his educational achievements. His casual business suit easily portrayed him as an up and coming legal recruit with some way to go before he achieved his overall career goals, yet inside he felt, at times, very lonely. Sometimes, especially late at night after yet another evening spent poring over legal papers, he longed to enjoy the glittering nightlife of New York City, socialising with his peers and flirting with the pretty women he regularly noticed.

In reality he worked twelve hours a day, often six days a week, to fulfil his quota. He was absolutely exhausted when he staggered out of the building each night, with only enough energy to eat before stumbling into bed in a state of near collapse. On the occasions when females did attract his eye he was too weary to take it any further. One of the legal assistants recently asked him out to dinner with her; she was quite beautiful in her own way and Tom was certainly tempted to take her up on her offer. However, his stuttering attempts to liaise with her had ended in disaster and he was fast developing a reputation in the office as a legal drone. Smarting from the

1

encounter and embarrassed by his lack of social skills he had shrugged philosophically, and immersed himself further in his work.

So now, here he was, alone in the City of London completing an assignment to deliver a legal brief, together with an affidavit, to the Justices Temple in the City of London where it was required for an international fraud trial pending at the Old Bailey. Hand delivery was not unusual for high profile cases, even though it was 1988; some papers were just too valuable to be consigned to airfreight. In this case, one of the defendants was an American citizen and the affidavit Tom was entrusted with confirmed that he had previously been involved in a similar scandal in the US. Art Neston, one of the senior litigation partners at Harrison and Freedman, had specifically chosen him for the task, and Tom was determined to be as efficient as possible.

In addition to the thrill of being singled out for an assignment by a man he respected, Tom was making the most of his first time in England. The chambers in London were covering all expenses and he had flown business-class enjoying the free champagne and in-flight entertainment before arriving at a top London hotel in Park Lane where he was now staying. Delighted to be in London, he crammed in as much sightseeing as he could, visiting galleries and museums and seeing streets and buildings that he recognised from movies. Already the Christmas lights were up and the shops were ablaze with seasonal colour enticing people to come in from the cold grey streets to spend money. The only disappointment was that, as usual, he had no one to share the experience with.

Briskly striding through narrow streets it took some time for Tom to identify which of the old buildings he was supposed to be delivering the paperwork to. The Temples, off Fleet Street, were in what appeared to be a maze of derelict properties that could have dated back to before the great fire of London; very ancient leaning towers with narrow staircases led up to antiquated offices that housed some of the best legal brains in the UK. Finally locating the office he required, Tom received the Notarised Receipt from the duty solicitor and briefly met the Counsel who was heading the Prosecution team, who consigned the document to his sealed briefcase.

Regretful that his duties were now complete, but determined to visit London again one day, Tom looked over the arrangements made for his return to New York the following evening on the Pan-Am schedule from Heathrow Airport. Realising that he had the remainder of the day to do as he wished his spirits lifted. Fighting the temptation to spend the afternoon lying on the bed, resting before the journey, Tom decided to visit The Natural History Museum in South Kensington where they were displaying archaeological fossils from the Jurassic period. He grabbed a taxi from opposite the Queen's Bench Division, stopping to drop his briefcase off at the Hilton Hotel where he was staying on the way.

The Natural History Museum was fairly quiet that afternoon – it was mid-week in December, quite close to Christmas, and the weather was threatening a heavy downpour. It occurred to Tom that had he been in New York he might have been in the middle of a snowstorm.

The only curious incident in the museum was a woman who appeared to be eying him with an intensity that made him feel uncomfortable. She was dressed in a skirt that fell just below her knees, a beige cashmere polo neck and a tailored jacket that highlighted her slender waist. Glancing at her, he could see that her classic clothes belied her youth; she was about his own age. Another covert look and he realised that she was spectacularly beautiful, with penetrating eyes that seemed to change colour as he glanced into them. Drawn again and again to her when he finally allowed his eyes to meet hers she appeared to undress him, psychologically. Had he been asked to describe her he would have been confused because there was nothing he could really identify; he wasn't even sure whether she was brunette or blonde. All he did know was that he was dazzled by her steady gaze and that her beauty took his breath away.

He glanced down again, flushing slightly, and trying to conceal his interest swiftly moved on through the exhibition. The beautiful stranger persistently followed him from to room. Confused, he was on the point of either confronting her or asking her out when she disappeared: almost as if she had suddenly become invisible. He shook his head, a little disappointedly, and continued with his visit, but the experience with the beautiful stranger had unsettled him.

Tom was a typical product of his social background. His family had sculptured his whole life since his early days at preparatory school. His father and his grandfather before him were senior partners in one of the largest law firms in New York and his indisputable destiny was to follow in the family's footsteps. The family prided itself on logic and clear thinking and this made it unimaginable that Tom would allow himself to become involved in a random romance, even with someone who was so mystically alluring. Shaking his head, Tom decided he would forget the beautiful stranger, return to the hotel, have an early dinner, and perhaps explore the cities nightlife. He caught a taxi just as the rain began to fall and the heavens opened.

CHAPTER TWO

He was still shaking his head after he returned to his room and took a shower. Even though he kept telling himself to forget the incident he couldn't help speculating. What on earth could the woman want from him? This was his first time in London but perhaps she knew him from Freedman's. He didn't think so, particularly as he had not long joined the firm and hardly knew anybody there. Anyway, he told himself, he was hardly likely to forget someone as stunning as her. Towel drying his blond hair and splashing on his favourite CK One aftershave, he swiftly dressed in beige chinos, a striped shirt and loafers before abruptly turning off the Christmas songs merrily blasting from the radio and leaving the room.

It was still too early to dine, so he sat at the bar with a cocktail and wondered which of the shows he should take in. The Phantom of the Opera had good reviews and had just opened on Broadway. Alternatively he had not yet found time to see Rain Man, which everyone was still raving about, so maybe the cinema was a better choice. He picked up a nearby Evening Standard, scanning the entertainment pages for inspiration, when a woman caught his eye. Shocked, he looked again, sure it was the same woman who had scrutinised him so intently in the museum. She was sitting a few stools away from him, nursing a glass of champagne and half smiling as if they were acquainted. She had changed and was now dressed in a satin evening dress which clung to her feminine curves. Glossy hair piled on top of her head, soft tendrils framing her delicate face and perfectly made up she looked dressed for a night out at the theatre. From time to time she brushed away a lock of her hair that fell in front of her eyes in a mannerism that was wholly her own. Moving closer, he recognised the distinctive

5

aroma of sweet roses he had smelt earlier; it seemed to permeate from within her body.

'Do I know you?' he enquired politely, but with a tremble in his voice. 'Only you seem to know who I am.'

'You're Tom Metzler – from New York.' The strange woman replied lightly.

It wasn't a question; it was more of a statement.

He frowned. This was becoming quite bizarre.

'You've lost me. You seem to know who I am – have we met somewhere? New York, perhaps? Do you know Freedman's, the law firm on Lexington Avenue?'

Still smiling gently, she didn't say a word, but opened her purse and took out what seemed to be travel documents and handed them across to him.

'These are your revised flight arrangements for tomorrow. I've booked you on the TWA Flight for New York departing at eleven in the morning. You need to be there at about nine-thirty. You'll also find a pseudonym on the ticket together with a passport in the same name for when you arrive in New York.'

Tom took the papers from her and viewed her with dismay.

'I… I don't understand,' he said, surprised. 'What's this all about? I saw you in the Museum, did you follow me? Look, I've no idea who you are but you obviously know me! And now you're presenting me with travel documents for a flight, which I have no intention of catching, in an unfamiliar name – and you've given me a false passport. What's going on?'

In response she leaned over to him, placed a hand on his arm and in a soft voice whispered, 'I can't give you an explanation, not just yet anyway. You have your ticket, you have your passport, you'll catch the TWA flight as arranged and everything will be revealed to you when you arrive in New

York. In the meantime, please give me your Pan Am ticket and your passport.'

'But… who are you?' he stammered as, unhesitatingly, he handed them over to her. It surprised him even more when he discovered he had the documents with him; he was sure he had left them in his room.

'You don't need to know who I am. Just make the flight.'

Tom was still in shock. He checked the ticket she had given him and saw it was First Class in the name of a Mr. T. Heaton. Puzzled he opened the well-worn passport; it was in the same name as the ticket and an unfamiliar face stared out at him. The passport certainly seemed valid but he doubted he would pass inspection at immigration in New York given the stranger in the photograph. Ready to question the obvious he was shocked to see that once again she had mysteriously vanished.

'What the hell is all this about?' he puzzled aloud, as his mind struggled to make sense of everything. A stunningly beautiful stranger spots him in a London Museum, then presumably follows him back to the hotel and delivers a first class TWA ticket for a flight to New York tomorrow morning in a false name, with no explanation. Whichever way he explained it to himself it was ridiculous. How could she know his name? He didn't know anyone in London, other than the Counsel at the Chambers, so it made sense that she must have some connection with his firm in New York. But that didn't explain why she had changed his Pan Am flight to an early morning departure. Finally, just how was he supposed to get home with a pseudonym and false papers?

In desperation he considered contacting Art Neston at Freedman's to ask if he had something to do with it but, checking his watch, realised he would already have left for the day. Inspired, he went to Reception and asked the desk clerk to call Pan Am, desperate for a stranger to confirm that the strange woman had not actually deleted him from their manifest for tomorrow's departure. She hadn't. The desk clerk smilingly reassured him that there was a booking in his name: Mr. Tom Metzler, Business Class. Momentarily relieved, he gasped as he realised that he might be booked onto that flight, but he no longer had a valid ticket. Neither, it crossed his mind, did he have a passport. At least not one in the right name.

Muttering his thanks to the now confused receptionist, he crossed the lobby to the lift and escaped to his room. He really needed to think about this. Grabbing a bottle of Scotch from the mini bar, he rifled through his paperwork, aghast to discover that his itinerary had been altered, and his schedule from the travel agent changed. It was now typed over with instructions that was booked with TWA in the morning in that name on the new passport. He shook his head. Could he possibly have made a mistake? Or had he dreamt everything that had happened to him? He lay down on the bed trying to rationalise what had just happened. First the beautiful stranger had appeared seemingly from nowhere, then she had greeted him by name and then, even more amazingly, she had demanded his travel documentation, which he had handed over. She had then, without giving any reason, said that his plans had changed and he would now be travelling on the TWA flight in the morning. After that she had disappeared. Tom ran it over and over in his head, like a video on re-wind, but no matter how many times he played the scene he couldn't make any sense of it.

The next thing he heard was the telephone ringing with a seven a.m. alarm call. Waking grudgingly, the taste of stale alcohol souring his breath, Tom scowled. He was pretty sure he hadn't booked an early morning call. He struggled out of bed, still trying to come to terms with the dramatic circumstances that had literally overtaken him. He undressed quickly, took a shower, automatically packed his bag and checked out of the hotel to step into a waiting cab, which he hadn't ordered, for the journey to the airport. He was still in a daydream. He barely remembered he hadn't eaten the previous night – it didn't seem important at the present.

His confused state continued when he checked-in at Heathrow; no one queried his alias, either on the ticket or in his passport, and finally he boarded the TWA plane. For some reason, which he didn't try to fathom out, he felt a sense of intense loneliness this morning. Almost as though he had encountered a missing part of him and then it had suddenly been withdrawn.

A few moments after take-off he closed his eyes trying to forget the circumstances that had led him to this situation; his confusion, his headache, even his loneliness, he pushed to the back of his mind, and remembered nothing until the announcement from the flight deck that they were on their descent to Kennedy Airport. No one had disturbed him during the long journey. No one had offered him a drink, nor was there any mention of food. It was almost as though he was a ghost.

It was noon, Eastern Seaboard Time when he disembarked and caught a cab into downtown New York; he was still bewildered by the rapidity of events that had happened to him. He was even more bewildered by clearing immigration without even a question. He remembered rubbing his face with his hands as the Custom's official checked his documentation, and welcomed him to New York without a second glance.

When eventually he arrived at Freedman's, everyone appeared to ignore him; Mr. Neston's secretary gave him the impression he didn't exist. He also realised he had misplaced his briefcase with the receipted affidavit in it.

'Are you surprised to see me?' he asked the receptionist, Jenny.

Finally he caught her eye.

'How can I help you sir, do I know you?' she enquired.

Tom was stunned at the question. He was about to reply when one of the other secretaries came rushing into the office, her face drained of colour.

'Have you heard?' she said in a hysterical voice. 'We've just had a Reuters news flash,'

'Hmm. Heard what?'

'The Pan Am flight from London's just crashed in Scotland! They don't know the cause yet, but they think it was a bomb.'

'Jesus!' Jenny exclaimed. 'Tom Metzler was on that flight! Are there... I mean, are there any survivors?'

Tom sat down heavily by Jenny's desk, overcome by shock as the news hit him. The conversation between the two secretaries seemed to blur into a dissembled clutter of white noise, they were obviously discussing the accident but he was unable to take it in. He felt himself trembling, his hands began to shake and suddenly he felt overwhelmingly nauseous. He needed the toilet quickly and, rising from the chair, he dashed from the room.

In the lavatories, his head swam with unspoken thoughts as he retched violently. Pan Am Flight 103 was the flight he was supposed to have been flying back on from London but somehow that mysterious woman had changed his itinerary from the Pan Am flight to the TWA. He threw up again in the toilet. Whatever had happened to him; the bizarre change of flights, the new passport, it seemed that destiny in the shape of an ethereal woman had intervened. In reality he should be dead.

He stayed there for some time, leaning his burning forehead head against the cool white tiles, desperately trying to reconcile himself with his escape from the tragedy. Still shaking, he straightened up – there was no way he could go back into the office and confront the secretaries. His head hadn't yet cleared from the incidents in London and now he was being forced to confront some kind of miracle, because that was the only explanation he could put on it. Why had it happened? That was the only word that came to him. Why? Why? Why?

It was beginning to sleet when he left the office, spots of rain with snow mixed in; there would probably be snow later that night. Trudging back to his apartment through the damp weather without an overcoat, his thoughts continued to spin. There was nothing special about him, 'I mean if I were some kind of a mathematical genius I could understand it,' he mused, 'but a lawyer? Who the hell would want to save a fucking lawyer?'

Tom lived in a bed-sit off Sixty-Fifth Street; it was only one room, aside from a compact kitchen/diner, but very convenient for the law firm's offices. Opening his front door, he staggered across the room and flung himself on the bed, too weak to consider that he hadn't eaten anything for more than twenty-four hours. Groping around on the floor, his hand found a half-consumed bottle of whisky and he swiftly removed the screw top and drank a few mouthfuls of the burning liquor. Better to let the mystery disappear in a wave of alcohol, he decided, rather than try to interpret it. In any event there was no one he could ask who could help him.

CHAPTER THREE

'We're missing a soul.'

'How do you mean? We can't lose a soul'

'I'm telling you, we're one short from the accident. We should have two hundred and fifty-eight souls onboard, plus eleven who died on the ground. And we have one missing. Check it yourself.'

'No – I'll take your word for it. So, how could it have just disappeared?'

'It's that Imogene woman. I bet she was involved in it somehow. I'll check the list again and see if I can find the name of the missing person.'

'But why would Imogene be involved? I mean, what has she got to do with the PAN AM accident?'

'Nothing. Other than to anticipate the event; one of her charges was on board. She was advised simply to monitor the departure of the souls. But she's done this before, you know - avoided what should have been a tragic accident. And you know what happened in that circumstance?'

'Yeah, I remember. Thanks to her we now have to watch that man throughout his lifetime in case a "time-paradox" occurs. I don't want to get involved in that again!'

'Well, if I'm right and it is her again, I'll get permission for her to do the monitoring this time. She's not going to get away with it again.'

'I bet she thought she could play the same game with us... you know, allow it to happen and then leave the disasters for us to sort out. Have you checked the name yet?'

'Yes. It's an American... a twenty-two year old American. She changed his flight details... moved him off the Pan Am flight and onto an earlier one on the same day.'

'What's his name?'

'It was a Mr Tom Metzler, young lawyer from New York. Only now his name is Heaton – Tom Heaton.'

'Is he Jewish?'

'How do I know? And what difference does it make if he is?'

'Well, I just thought she might have picked him out to lay some blame on him… that's what she did the last time.'

'Even if she did, it's not going to work. This time we'll be ready for her…'

Imogene was suddenly aware of a feeling of trepidation. She knew she had done wrong in deciding the American was too young to die – especially in the horrifying circumstances of a mid-air disaster. But something told her that this time she wasn't going to be able to walk away from it and leave the clearing up to the others.

'Why did you do it?' she was asked.

'Because I thought he was too young,' she replied. 'I've watched over him since birth and he's grown-up to be a really nice guy. He recently graduated from Harvard University, his life was just beginning and I thought it was wrong to deny him the opportunity of a happy future. So I changed his name and his flight arrangements.'

'And who gave you the right to decide who should live and who should survive? The right to directly challenge a destiny sanctioned from above?'

There was no inquisition in the question; it was simply a statement of fact.

'Well, no one. But I thought we all had free will. You know, the right to make up our own minds.'

'You're confusing yourself with humans, Imogene. You don't have the right to determine whose lives should be extended, simply because you feel some sympathy for them. Now we have the job of clearing up your mess. Well this time we're passing the responsibility back to you.'

'You can't do that! You don't have the authority!'

'We do now. Permission's been granted to commission you with responsibility to ensure that this Tom Metzler, or Heaton as you've renamed him, doesn't create a paradox during his lifetime and…'

'How am I going to be able to supervise that?' she interrupted. 'I mean I need some help… he might live for years.'

'That's your problem, Imogene. You should have thought of that before you intervened. Now you'll be compelled to take human form, to discharge your responsibilities in the right and proper manner.

'And bear in mind that we'll be supervising you constantly, and should a time-paradox occur and we have to rearrange the historical consequences, you'll be held to account. I don't envy you.'

Oh shit! Now what had she done? It wasn't only that she would have to exist in New York - she hated the place - but, temporarily, she would have to adopt human form and spend every minute of every day ensuring her protégé did not commit any act that he could not have committed if he were dead. How the hell would she manage in human form? All that suffering, the anguish, the stress… dear God, how on earth would she survive?

But it seemed there was nothing she could do about it, the Powers that Be had determined the transaction and here she was now in human form.

An Angel's Kiss

CHAPTER FOUR

Tom emerged from what surely must have been a nightmare, his head throbbing with the dehydrating effect of the alcohol, still believing he was ensconced in London, expecting to check out of his hotel to catch the Pan Am flight to New York.

He looked around him and, with horrified incredulity, took in the familiar features of his pokey New York apartment. Glancing in the mirror, his face took on a look of horror; the reflection peering back at him had changed in subtle ways. He checked again to see if he was able to recognise himself. His face had thinned from its original rotund appearance; in its place was a visage he hardly recognised – it was almost as though he were meeting a stranger for the first time. His fair hair had changed colour; now dark and thick and desperately in need of combing; even his eyes were not recognisable, the blue replaced with deep brown. The smile that was always lurking at the corners of his mouth had also disappeared; in its place was a solemn gaze that might be interpreted as depressive. He shuddered at the reflection, staring at it as though it might simply vanish and he could be his old self again. This was the face he had seen in the passport; how could this be possible? He shook his head, frustrated, deprived of words to express his tumultuous feelings. One point did cross his mind; looking like this how would he be able to go to work? Then he realised that that was the reason the secretaries didn't recognise him yesterday; to them he was probably just a stranger.

What he did know was that he was without doubt still alive – the enigmatic alien, whoever she was, had accomplished that for him – but he wasn't happy with the way she had somehow altered his appearance. He sat on the bed, traumatized by his bizarre experience, and searched in the bedside cabinet for headache tablets.

He glanced towards the doormat to check if any post had arrived; he was expecting a letter from his parents. There was a note on the floor with his name on it, momentarily forgetting his pounding head he leapt up and grabbed it.

It was from someone called Imogene:

'I'll meet you at Starbucks on Sixty-Fourth Street in one hour. I'll explain everything to you then. Please don't be late. Imogene.'

Who the hell is Imogene? he asked himself, noticing that there was a time on the note that was only a few minutes old. She must have pushed it through the letterbox while he was checking to see if he was alive. Could it be the woman from London? The stranger who had changed his travel arrangements? If so, he had to see her.

Dashing out into the cold morning air, Tom looked down, dismayed to find he hadn't thought to shower or change as he left his apartment. His clothes, chosen in London, looked crumpled and out of place amongst the light covering of snow on the sidewalks. On the way to the coffee shop, he picked up a newspaper and saw the headlines: Pan Am explosion over Lockerbie: No survivors: Bomb believed to be the cause.

Shocked to the core, he was again hit with the stark realisation that he had somehow cheated his fate. Perhaps Imogene was the key; if she was the beautiful stranger she was the only link he had with his previous existence and he couldn't wait to see her again.

Entering the nearly deserted Starbucks, Tom spotted the woman immediately. Sitting alone and floodlit in a shaft of early morning sunshine she was dressed warmly. A cashmere coat was untidily thrown over the back of her seat and as she crossed her long legs he noticed she wore knee length black leather boots. She seemed different from the woman he had met in the museum; beautiful without a doubt, but less ethereal and more human than he remembered. Her hair seemed to be silkier, as though she had just blow-dried it, but her eyes had that same penetrating look as she met his eyes. He sat down heavily beside her and, without breaking her gaze, passed her the newspaper.

'Are you having coffee?' she asked in a sympathetic tone, brushing aside a lock of hair that had fallen over her eyes. Mesmerised by such a feminine mannerism he lost his concentration for a moment, 'What? Oh yeah. Sure.' He collected the mug of coffee and returned to the table.

'So, since you know who I am,' he said dryly, 'why don't you introduce yourself?'

She held out a slender hand.

'Imogene. My name's Imogene. We met in London yesterday.' Her hand was warm to the touch and it sent an electric current along Tom's arm.

'You changed my travel arrangements, you changed my name, you changed my looks – are you going to tell me why? I mean, I should be dead, shouldn't I?' Tom flushed with emotion as he stumbled over the words.

'Coffee first, and then we can take a walk. Perhaps we can take a cab to Central Park? I've heard it's quite lovely there, especially in the winter snow. I promise I'll explain everything to you eventually.' Imogene smiled gently but firmly, ignoring Tom's impassioned questions. Leaning across the table, she placed her left index finger on his lips, which had the effect of silencing Tom. It was almost as if he couldn't speak, and he realised that this amazingly beautiful young woman was having a devastating affect on him. Still silent, he followed her out of the coffee bar and climbed into a passing cab, allowing her to instruct and then pay the driver – or at least he wasn't asked to pay so he assumed she must have done so. She led him into the park and they walked companionably to the lake, where she sat on a bench looking out over the icy water, patting the space beside her and motioning him to join her. He wasn't at all surprised to discover it was completely dry, as if the snow had passed it by. He also felt unseasonably warm, as if the weather had slipped past them as well. A delicate smell of roses, emanating from Imogene, drifted around him as though he were immersed in a summer garden.

'Beautiful day isn't it?' she remarked, as she slipped out of her topcoat.

'Can we forget the weather and concentrate on your explanation?' Tom snapped out of his reverie, determined to get the answers he wanted.

She smiled. 'Of course. Where would you like me to start?'

'You don't need me to remind you... Er...'

'Imogene. My name's Imogene. Can you remember that?'

'Please tell me what happened to me. And who are you... What role did you play in this nightmare... And why?' the questions fell in a tangle from his mouth.

'Just relax, Tom. Let me start at the beginning. I want you to listen carefully and please don't say anything until I've finished. You can ask all the questions you wish to then.

'First off, I'm what you call an 'angel', one of those spiritual beings whose job it is to look after humans during the course of their lifetime...' Seeing Tom's look of pure astonishment, Imogene held out a hand to prevent him from interrupting, 'I told you not to say anything until I'd finished telling the story.' She seemed unconcerned at Tom's face, now drained of any colour, almost as though she had experienced it all before. 'Now, where was I? Oh yes, I was telling you I was an angel... or rather I am still an angel... And when I realised you were about travel on the Pan Am 747 to New York I decided I should save your life by altering your return flight arrangements. I knew there was a bomb on board so, as you said earlier, you should really be dead.

'Now, I knew at the time that I would be in trouble for this, I mean, it simply isn't allowed, but you were so young and attractive and full of vitality and so looking forward to the future that I disobeyed the rules and allowed you to live out your life with a different persona.'

'So why are you telling me now?' he interrupted.

'You're doing it again, aren't you? I haven't finished yet.' She glared at him for a moment before continuing. 'Anyhow, I was summoned to appear in front of The Tribunal to account for my misfeasance. My explanation was not accepted and I was informed that because I may well have triggered off a new tangent of history and created what could well become a time-paradox, I'll have to supervise you throughout the remainder of your life, in the guise of a human being, to ensure you don't make any decisions that could cause a time disruption. Do you understand what I'm saying?'

Tom sat, numb, with his mouth open, quite unable to take in what she had been saying. Had it not been for the dramatic alterations to his travel plans he would have said she was deranged and left the bench immediately.

But it had happened.

Urging his brain to accept the impossible, he considered quickly. If this Imogene was, as she claimed to be, an angel then what she said had to be true. One thing he did know was an absolute; he definitely should be dead, blown up in that air crash. His mind continued in turmoil with thoughts racing round his head, searching for some other more rational explanation.

'I can tell you're a bit surprised,' she said, an amused look on her beautiful face.

'Surprised? Fucking hell, of course I'm surprised! One minute I'm rescued from certain death and the next I'm told my Guardian Angel's broken the rules to save me and has to adopt human form and supervise me for the rest of my life! Of course I'm surprised! Wouldn't you be? No, you don't have to answer that. Can I ask you though, please, is this some kind of a wind-up?'

She looked at him steadfastly. 'No. It isn't a wind-up – I wish it were. Then I wouldn't be stuck with you. This isn't easy for me, you know. One minute I was happily saving your life and the next I have to listen to your moans.' She waved her arms over her body. 'Look at me – I'm dressed like a young woman and I haven't a clue how to behave like one. The least you could do is to stop whingeing and help me out with this problem.'

Tom ignored her protests. 'So am I right in thinking that you saved my life just because I'm good looking?'

'Don't be absurd,' she snapped. 'I've watched over you since the day you were born. I've looked after you from kindergarten, through school, all the way to Harvard and beyond. Always I've tried to influence you, but I was never able to make decisions for you. For instance, it always occurred to me that you were never meant to be a lawyer - you should have been a journalist, which is what you always wanted to be.

'So I felt sorry for you. The fact you're good looking is incidental to saving your life. And now look at me, stuck with you!'

Tom put his head in his hands, as if he were seeking some relief from this disaster. He didn't really know what to say or what might happen to him from here on. He only knew he was completely bewildered and simply couldn't comprehend how all of this could possibly have happened.

'So what do I do now?' he asked eventually, letting out a heavy sigh.

'Oh for Christ's sake get real, can't you? How the fuck do I know what you should do? I haven't been given any instructions – except that I have to watch over you very carefully to ensure you don't commit yourself to something that could alter the course of history or, equally, you fail to do something that could have exactly the same consequences.'

'I can't believe that an angel swears! Are you sure it's "allowed"?' It was Tom's turn to glare at her.

Imogene grinned wickedly. 'I rather like it,' she said. 'It's at least one of the better parts of being human.' She pointed a finger at him. 'And don't you dare criticise me – I've had to surrender my divinity for you. You might at least show some gratitude.'

Tom's mouth fell open yet again. Ignoring the question of gratitude, he ploughed on with questions, 'Just how do you propose to supervise me? I mean will you have to observe me every minute of every day? I think you'll have a job to do that – what'll you do when I'm working, for instance? You won't know what I'm planning till it's too late!'

'You're right of course. But I've already dealt with your position at Freedman's – as far as they're concerned you died in that air crash. A letter of condolence from the airline has been sent to your parents and a memorial service, for you and the others from New York who died in the crash, is to be held at St. Patrick's in the near future. So, you've ceased to exist. I'm already in the process of reorganising your living accommodation.'

'Hey! Hang about,' he snapped. 'I'm not going to pack in my job just because you say so! And I'm damned if I'm prepared to change my address. Why should I just because you're afraid of some paradox… or whatever that is?'

She sighed as if her patience was overstretched. 'These are not matters for you to decide. It's now been taken out of your hands. How could you possibly go back to your job when Freedman's have been informed you're dead? Your landlord's also aware that you're deceased and no doubt new tenants will be interviewed tomorrow.'

He rose from the seat and spluttered with indignation at this outrage.

'Now you're the one being absurd. Are you telling me you've made me disappear?' He clicked his fingers to emphasise his point, 'Just like that?'

She pointed to his pocket. 'Don't you have one of those mobile phones?'

He nodded and pulled the bulky transmitter from the inside of his jacket pocket.

'So, give your old firm a ring. Ask to speak to someone… What about your old boss, Art Neston?'

Tom shook his head, but responded. He dialled the number - and when he got through he gave his name and asked to speak to Art. There was a puzzled silence before he said: 'Could I speak with Tom Metzler, please. This is a friend of his? But I… What? Sorry… He was on the Pan Am plane crash… Oh… I'm so sorry… They've hung up on me,' he said, taking his seat again. 'She sounded terribly upset.'

He put his head in hands again, muttering, 'What the hell's happening to me? What have you done?' He spread his arms out, almost in a gesture of submission. 'I've lost my job, I've lost my apartment and now you've changed my name and my appearance. I don't even recognise myself.'

Imogene placed her hand on his shoulder. 'I realise this must be hard for you, Tom, but your presence at the law firm hardly caused a ripple in the fabric of creation. They'll miss you, temporarily, but eventually your absence will become a distant memory.

'But as I keep reminding you, this isn't easy for either of us, you know. A little while ago I was an angel in Paradise and now look at me'. She gestured again towards her own body. 'I have to submit to this burden of a physical being; now I feel pain and hunger and thirst – something I've never experienced before. I might conceivably become ill; I have a weakness of the flesh that is tempting for me… although I must admit that that is a peculiar sensation that could well give me pleasure, but it is nevertheless something exceptional in my experience.

'So we both have to suffer; you with your loss of occupation, me with the burdens of humanity. But can't you at least acknowledge, Tom Metzler - or should I call you Tom Heaton? That at least you're alive when you should have been dead?'

'I wish I were fucking dead,' he said, his head still buried in his hands. 'Why didn't you leave things alone? Now I have nothing – I'm not even sure whether I still exist in the outside world. What am I going to do for a living? How will I pay for anything?'

'Jesus!' Imogene pointed her finger upwards. 'Forgive me, it's just that this guy infuriates me. Will you try to stop moaning? I've arranged an interview for you at the New York Times on Monday. They'll already have received your C.V., which qualifies you admirably for the position as an assistant reporter – so you don't have to worry, you'll be accepted for the job. Your name's already changed – you're now officially Tom Heaton. I believe he was one of your old school mates. All of your papers are in order, including your passport. Oh, and by the way, I'll be working for you as your trainee.'

'What?' He gazed up at her nonplussed. 'I don't understand…'

'You don't have to yet, don't worry it'll all become clear eventually. Now, shall we go and inspect your new apartment?'

He shrugged as if this was of no concern to him. 'Is this some other miracle you've arranged? Where am I living now, Fifth Avenue?'

Imogene smiled and the skies around Tom lit up like a beacon, it was though she had become the North Star that he was destined to follow. Suddenly he didn't mind and for an instance he felt happy and free, and a great peace came over him. She was with him and she was worth a hundred jobs at Freedman's. He wondered whether or not she realised he was totally smitten with her.

'I've taken an apartment – a two-bedroom place in Greenwich Village – quite expensive, so I'm told, but we don't have to worry about that.'

She took his hand and led him away from the park and into what seemed to be a waiting taxi that sped them on their way to the Village.

In the taxi he said to her, 'Just how long is this… this partnership to last? I mean, is it short-term, like a few days or weeks, or am I now allowed to live to my full life expectancy?'

'It's a good question and one I don't have the answer to. Perhaps for the time being we should simply concentrate on reorganising your life so I can maintain my watching brief over you. Here we are.'

They stopped outside of one of the old terraced brownstone houses in the centre of the Village quite close to the Holland Tunnel; Tom also noticed that this time no one paid the fare, neither were they asked for one.

The apartment was in a block he vaguely recognised, a wealthy friend of his parents had lived nearby years ago. An elevator took them to the second floor and Imogene, who held a set of keys, let them into a spacious apartment. Swiftly, Tom calculated it must cost about a year's salary just to pay for the monthly rental. Unable to help himself, he looked around, captivated, it really was stunning. The entrance hall was thickly carpeted leading to a spacious living room, beautifully decorated and furnished with cream leather sofas, glass tables and soft rugs. Plush cream silk curtains framed the lovely views over the Village visible through the tall sash windows. In one corner, on a low level unit, was a television and a Bang and Olufsen video recorder, above it, on recessed shelves, was a Hi-Fi and speakers. Tom could barely contain his excitement and walked across the room to check out the top-of-the-range equipment, all of it subtly lit. Dragging his eyes away from the stereo, he realised that there were several objets d'art placed on occasional tables that looked like expensive antiques. Even the pictures on the walls were either original works of art or extremely good prints. Set off from the lounge was a modern kitchen that appeared to Tom as though it had never been used before. The coffee maker and stainless steel cooking utensils gleamed on polished wooden worktops, and Tom could see the dishwasher and huge fridge freezer. In the middle of the kitchen, under a light, was a central island edged with bar stools.

Imogene took hold of his hand again. 'Come. Let me show you the bedrooms.'

'I take it we have one each?' he enquired facetiously.

She laughed. 'Of course, but as far as the outside world's concerned you and I are an item. You are fortunate to have a girlfriend who's wealthy and allows you to share this apartment with her.'

'But you said you were only my assistant. How could you possibly be so wealthy?'

'Inherited wealth – from my grandmother. So, do you think you can adapt to that arrangement? About our being an item that is?'

'I guess – but it depends on where it might lead.'

'It could lead to you having an extended life.'

'I wasn't referring to that.'

'I know exactly what you were referring to. And the answer is no; that can't happen. The only human traits I can indulge in are the ones necessary for my survival in this body. I'm afraid sex isn't seen as a necessity.'

'Why? Would it interfere with your, what did you call it, divinity?'

Imogene smiled and said nothing.

'So what happens if I do meet someone and fall for her? Will that be permitted?'

'I don't see why not. But one thing you must bear in mind is that you can never have children. That's the kind of time-paradox the Tribunal's afraid of. So the safest thing would be for you to have an irreversible vasectomy, that way you can never be tempted. I'll set it up.'

'What?' Tom exploded, 'I'm definitely not having one of those… those things. I'll just have to use contraceptives!'

She sighed again; this whole human thing was getting intolerable. 'Your views don't come into this, Tom. You don't have any choice. There's a doctor I know at New York Central. He'll do it this afternoon.'

'What,' he gasped. 'In other words, if I'm supposed to be dead how can it be possible for me to have children? So you're going to make sure it never happens!'

'Now you're coming to terms with it. Do you like the bedrooms?'

'They're very nice,' he said miserably, accepting the change of subject. 'Which one's yours?'

'The one with all the women's clothes in the closets! You'll find some clothes for you in this bedroom – you won't have to buy anything for quite a while.'

'You seem to have thought of everything - I don't even have to give notice on my old apartment or collect my things!' Tom was surprising himself with how angry he was beginning to feel.

'Let me just ask you this. Are you going to follow me in the streets? Will you cook and wash for me? Will you clean the apartment? Will you take me to and from work? In other words, am I going to be imprisoned with you for the rest of my life, but starved of sex?'

An expression of sadness came over Imogene. She struggled to cope with his allegations until finally she said, 'It would be dreadful if you thought of me as your jailer. At first, until such time as you do accept the time-paradox, you will need to be monitored carefully, virtually around the clock. But eventually you'll get used to the rules of your existence and your major decisions will be less traumatic than they are now. In the long run, you'll be given free-reign. At least that's what I'm planning will happen. I'd hate you to think you're my prisoner... why not think of me as your protector instead?'

'You've ignored my question about sexual deprivation,' he muttered moodily.

'No I haven't. I've already told you what sex means for me... It would defile the very essence of spiritual immortality...'

'Perhaps you should taste the fruit,' Tom replied slyly.

'What's that supposed to mean?'

'You know... The apple on the tree... The forbidden fruit?'

'Oh – that! There was no apple. There was no tree.'

'What? How about Adam and Eve and the serpent?'

She sighed heavily. 'Tom, believe me when I tell you there was no serpent and no Garden of Eden either. God created this mythological story to ensure humanity inherited a code of moral conduct to live their lives by.'

'Bloody hell! You'll be telling me next…'

'And no,' Imogene said, interrupting him, 'you're wrong… I don't regret saving your life. The question of regrets is a human trait and not something I'm familiar with – at least, not yet.' She shrugged. 'I suppose if we stay together long enough I may well become adjusted to this body I now inhabit.' She spread her arms around her shoulders. 'Right now, it feels quite bizarre; I'm having difficulty dealing with all of the sensations that are presenting themselves.' She brushed the hair away from her eyes, in the now familiar gesture.

'Yeah. That may well be,' said Tom, 'but the sensations I'm dealing with are pretty bloody frightening. I'm not even sure I'll be able to cope …'

'Trust me. You will, given time. So, Tom Heaton, shall we go and try some of the local cuisine – I'm feeling quite hungry.'

Imogene took him to Dino's, an Italian Restaurant close to their apartment. Walking in behind her, Tom was astonished by the warm welcome Imogene received; it was as though she ate there regularly. She smiled her thanks as they were quickly led to a round table by the window, where the effusive head waiter poured them both a glass of cold Soave and handed them a menu. Within minutes the chef came out of the kitchen to take their order and Tom watched, incredulous, as Imogene chatted to him about the food before greedily ordering pasta, pizza and a veal steak; surely she didn't intend to eat it all herself? Sneaking another look at her slim body, he felt his temper rising, convinced she had taken it upon herself to choose for him too. He was therefore dumbfounded when she loudly closed her menu asking, 'What are you having?'

'I'm not hungry,' he muttered, aware it was a childish response.

'Oh come on, you must have something.' She cajoled and without another word she ordered him Spaghetti Bolognese.

After lunch, which again Tom couldn't remember if she had paid for, Imogene decided she wanted to go sightseeing. Chatting companionably, they headed North and traipsed pretty much the length of Broadway, looking at all the shows - she was quite interested in seeing West Side Story - and the cinemas; he remembered that he still hadn't see Rain Man. Heaving a sigh of relief as Imogene cut short a shopping spree in Macy's, his happiness was short-lived as Imogene announced they would be ice skating next at the Rockefeller Centre.

'Have you tried it before?' Tom asked her nervously.

'Of course not,' she said, fitting a pair of skates. 'It should be natural for me, don't you think?'

And to his utter surprise, it was. She skated around the Rockefeller Centre rink like a ballerina performing Swan Lake. Tom, whose skating skills were basic to say the least, could only stand and watch as she twirled and pirouetted in time to the music blaring over the sound system. Others on the ice gave way, hypnotised by her performance. Exhilarated and flushed from the cold, Imogene executed one more perfect figure of eight before gracefully coming to a stop by his side and gently taking his hand, announcing that it was time for dinner.

Tom groaned at the prospect of eating; he hadn't touched the spaghetti at lunch and he didn't feel like food now. The trauma of the last few days had seriously affected his appetite, but Imogene appeared completely at ease.

'There's a French Restaurant on West 45th Street,' she suggested. 'I'm sure we'll get in there. Come on, Tom.'

'I'd ask how you can afford to live like this - but you never seem to pay for anything, taxis, expensive restaurants, apartments even...' Tom mused. 'How the hell do you manage that?'

She smiled. *'Tom. I might well have to inherit this earthly body but part of my celestial being is still with me.'*

'So, when you need something — a taxi, or a meal or anything at all, it's for free?'

'No. Not necessarily. You see Tom, the world's mostly inhabited by people who are led by the heart - and when I meet these people they're very eager to accommodate my needs. Does that answer your question?'

'I guess, But it's still beyond me — as are you.'

'You'll get me in the end,' she replied with a knowing grin.

'If you say so,' Tom countered dubiously. 'But even so, do we really need another banquet? Couldn't you just have a sandwich?'

'Oh, come on. You'll enjoy it,' she teased as she took his arm and led him enthusiastically back in the direction of mid-town.

Once ensconced in the restaurant, Tom ordered a bowl of onion soup while Imogene dissected the menu, eating like she had never eaten before today. Mind you, he thought, that's probably the case!

'Very nice day,' she commented as they made their way home. 'I think tomorrow we should take one of those cruises — I'd like to see Manhattan from the East River. I've always hated New York but now I'm seeing it through entirely different eyes.'

Finding sleep elusive, Tom discovered a half bottle of whisky in one of the nightstand drawers but despite drinking it all, it still took ages before he drifted off into a dreamless sleep.

CHAPTER FIVE

The next day, Sunday, Imogene was up bright and early and was already dressed when Tom emerged from his bedroom. Standing in the living room, she was wearing a tracksuit and trainers and looked as though she was planning a ten-mile run.

'Have you seen the time?' she demanded.

'What? It's Sunday. I always have a lie-in on a Sunday.' He gazed at her in admiration. Her clear scrubbed skin showed no traces of makeup, but she smelled as if she had bathed in sweet-scented roses; the same aroma he had noticed in the park.

'Not today you don't. We have a cruise boat to catch.'

'What about breakfast?' he groaned, dragging his eyes away from her. 'I need a cup of coffee – I can't start the day without one.'

'Well don't expect me to make it for you – you'll find everything you need in the kitchen!' She huffed before turning on the television to watch the morning news. It was all about the Pan-Am crash over Lockerbie.

'Fuck you!' Tom yelled from the kitchen, putting on the kettle. 'I'm not a tourist guide!'

Despite his grumbling and bad humour they still managed to catch the morning cruise. Again he didn't notice any money changing hands, but now he simply shrugged as if this were a common incident. It had stopped snowing, but there was a cold wind blowing across the East River; Tom bought a coffee from the onboard café and decided to seek shelter under the covered area, huddled on one of the loungers.

Two hours later she woke Tom from his snooze: he had missed the Statue of Liberty, Ellis Island, the Empire State Building and a comprehensively narrated description of these unfolding attractions by an on-board guide. Secretly glad to have escaped the tour, he declined her offer of sandwiches still feeling decidedly sick every time he thought of the future. It was almost two days now since he had last eaten a decent meal. On the other hand, declaring that she was starving, Imogene wolfed down two bacon sandwiches and endless cups of coffee. She had enjoyed her morning enormously, having seen all the sights she had missed during her last trip to the big city.

'Lunch,' she stated after disembarking.

'Oh, no,' Tom said incredulously, 'today you can eat on your own – I'm going back to the apartment for a rest.'

'What, you mean a rest from me?'

'If you like. I'm fucked if I'm doing any more sightseeing today, or any other day. I have had enough of wandering around pretending everything's normal. It isn't! You go ahead and get your lunch, but ever since you informed me about my future, or lack of it, I can't eat because I feel sick. Now, is that clear enough for you?'

She took hold of his arm. 'Listen to me. You have to eat. I don't care if you have to force it down, but you must eat something. I know, how about a hamburger and fries? I'd quite like to try a Big Mac!'

Still protesting, he allowed her to lead him by the arm, crossing three blocks before coming to a McDonalds. He didn't say a word so she ordered for both of them, thrusting a burger, fries and coke into his unwilling hands and instructing him to eat.

'Right,' she said, after watching him grudgingly munch his way through the lukewarm food, 'this afternoon I'm going to visit the Metropolitan Museum of Art. Now, you can either come with me, as I suggest, or you can go back to the apartment with whatever's worrying you and drown your sorrows in drink. The choice is yours!'

'Whatever it is that I'm worrying about?' he snapped. 'I can't believe you said that. You know damn well what I'm worrying about – you, and the whole pantomime you've laid out in front of me. Or are you suggesting I should somehow instantly adjust to this screwy scenario?'

'I'm not suggesting you do so "instantly", but you're going to have to sooner or later otherwise your life won't be worth living – and don't whinge that "life isn't worth living now" because we've been through that. Now, are you coming with me or not?'

'I suppose I'd better,' he conceded.

So they spent the afternoon in the Museum of Art admiring the exhibitions; on a couple of occasions Imogene pointed to a famous artist and commented, pointing her finger upwards, that she had met him, although he had given up painting now. In fact Tom quite enjoyed the visit; it was a museum he had wanted to immerse himself in but had never found the time before now. It was already dark by the time they left, and, as if to pre-empt her, Tom said, 'Is it time for dinner?'

She laughed and replied, 'Not just yet. First we're going to have a drink and then we'll have dinner at the Heartland Brewery – it's on West 43rd Street –'

'I know where it is – what I want to know is how the hell do you know where it is?'

She gave him one of her sweetest smiles. 'Oh, I know where everything is in this town. And the food there's good, and if you like you can take me dancing.'

It was one of the best nights that Tom had had in a long time. After almost a year in New York he had yet to visit any of the places he had been to today with Imogene, and it was fascinating.

They had cocktails first at Dance Manhattan before moving on to the Heartlands Brewery where he placed his arms around her and couldn't remember anything of the dancing. Their bodies seemed to melt in an embrace as the music serenaded them; she was so unlike anyone else he had ever met and he knew that he loved her.

Back at the apartment she kissed him on the cheek, thanking him for a lovely evening, before quietly going to her bedroom leaving a despondent Tom almost destitute in his isolation. In bed he gave in to his feelings of wretchedness and allowed the tears to stream from his eyes, quite unable to control his emotions. He found himself sobbing at the predicament facing him. Alive, yes, but without an existence, without a friend in the world, without a family to turn to in his hour of need.

At one stage Imogene crawled into his bed, took him in her arms and comforted him, stroking his cheek, breathing the scent of roses on him, and whispering soothing words that he couldn't decipher. He could feel her breasts as they pressed against him and the inside of her thigh caressing his buttock, but there was nothing sensual about it; Tom allowed the tears to flow, feeling safe in her embrace, until he dozed off to sleep.

CHAPTER SIX

On Monday morning Tom stood trembling outside the New York Times' Eighth Avenue offices; not just because of the cold, although it was still icy, but also because of the challenge ahead. Never, since his early childhood dreams of becoming a journalist, had he entertained the idea that one day he would be working at the most prestigious newspaper in the city. Sighing, he knew that this was yet another example of his current lack of ability to ignore or disobey any of Imogene's directives.

His mind was virtually catatonic, following, not simply last week's dramatic events, but also the instantaneous arrangement that Imogene had set up for his vasectomy. It was bizarre, he thought, the doctor at the hospital had been expecting them, as though Imogene had known him from birth.

'Now, I'm going to give you a local anaesthetic and then the procedure. It will only take a few moments,' he had told Tom, correctly as it turned out. Minutes later, Tom had been deprived of the ability to father children.

He left the hospital with a glum look on his face. He couldn't shake the feeling that in a matter of days his whole life had simply ceased to exist; he had gone from a career orientated lawyer with a glittering future and the prospect of eventually meeting someone special to start a family with, to nothing. He had a past, no present, and as far as controlling his own life was concerned, no future. The vasectomy had proved without a doubt that he was no longer master of his own destiny. Imogene greeted him with a smile on her lips and even in his misery Tom couldn't help but notice she had a set of perfect white teeth, as if she had spent most of her life at the orthodontist.

Even waking that morning with Imogene lying beside him had not dispersed the cloud of depression that surrounded him. He was far from sure that he wanted to continue in this state of despondency; part of him longed for the clock to be turned back so he could climb aboard that 747 none the wiser about the fate that awaited him.

Climbing out of bed, still wishing he were dead, he wondering what future awaited him. He looked down at the beautiful girl who had stolen his heart and for a moment he felt that they had shared something together. But then it passed and he was left contemplating the pity he aroused in her, rather than the love he felt so deeply for her.

Imogene broke into his thoughts by tugging gently on his sleeve, bringing him back to the present, outside the offices of the New York Times. Smiling, she took hold of his hand and gave him a reassuring squeeze. He smiled shakily down at her as she increased her pressure, just her touch was helping.

'You don't have to worry, you know. You'll soon realise everything's been arranged.'

'So you keep telling me, and I do believe you. The problem is I have no idea how a reporter works. I'm not even sure I want to do it. What'll I say if they ask me questions? I mean I have no experience – say they send me out on an assignment? What the hell will I do then?'

'I'll be with you. Let me deal with that problem. Come on, we're going to be late.'

He was welcomed with open arms by the sub-editor, a youngish man with a mop of tousled hair that seemed to be permanently out of place. Greeting them both, he leaned forward to give Imogene a kiss on the cheek, as if he had known her all his life.

'Good to meet you, Tom. I'm Andy Clarke – I'm really glad we'll be working together. Imogene's told me all about you, and we have your details, so all I want to know is when you can start?'

'This is the New York Times, right?' Tom enquired politely.

'Sure is. It doesn't scare you, does it? You know we always welcome new talent, and you come highly recommended by our young friend here – that's all the endorsement we need. So, are you with us, Tom?'

'Yes. Yes, of course. When can I start?'

'Well, as you'll be working with Imogene, she can take you along now to your office... Well, office isn't the right word... It will be just a working space, but I'm sure you'll be happy there. Personnel will give you the details regarding terms and conditions later. Welcome to the New York Times, my friend!'

With a final wave, Andy Clarke disappeared into his office as though this was all pre-agreed.

'How did you do that?'

'It wasn't difficult. I'm now an old friend of Andy and his family and I've worked here since leaving college – or so he believes. I planted the idea of you joining me last Friday, but he's convinced it was his idea.'

'Have you any more tricks up your sleeve?'

'Only that you'll need quite a bit of guidance from me, but you don't have to worry, I'll be holding your hand all the way.'

So now he was sharing his office space with her, or was she just sharing hers with him?

As he sat at his desk a youngish man came in. He looked a couple of years older than Tom; slim and good-looking with dark hair and hazel eyes that held a perpetually curious stare. He stared at Tom as if he were some kind of an alien, before taking the seat next to his desk.

'Hi. My name's Scott Hardy. I'm with the crime desk. So, where did you appear from? I didn't realise we were advertising a vacancy.'

Tom half smiled at the puzzled reporter. 'Tom. Tom M... Heaton,' he corrected himself, remembering just in time that his name had changed. 'I was recommended for the job.'

'Nicely evaded - but you haven't answered my question. Where have you come from? I mean was it the Chicago Tribune, or the Miami Herald? It has to be one of the important papers to get a job here – I should know, it took me forever! And here you are, miraculously manifesting out of nowhere and landing a job we never even advertised. So tell me about it.'

Tom shrugged, somewhat stuck for words. Scott Hardy was about to interrogate him again when Imogene walked in.

'Are you normally so hostile?' she enquired politely. She must have given him one of her looks because Hardy's aggression seemed to evaporate instantly and a benign expression appeared on his face.

'Yeah... Sorry I asked,' he apologised. 'I was just puzzled by the appearance of a newcomer... I mean; I think I'm correct that we haven't advertised... but then...'

Seeming embarrassed, his sentence trailed off and he got up from the chair and drifted away.

'We're going to have problems with that one,' Imogene announced once the coast was clear, frowning slightly.

'I thought you handled him very well,' Tom said. 'Why should he cause trouble?'

'Because he's fundamentally evil. Such people are immune to my benign influence. In fact they resent it. Trust me, he'll be back.'

'Well, I've got more things to worry about than Scott Hardy,' Tom proclaimed. 'What is it I'm supposed to do now?'

Imogene passed over a sheaf of papers. 'Here. You can start with these. This is a list of recently deceased people – some of them were quite important. What you need to do is search through Who's Who, see which were the most important, research some of their achievements and then write their obituaries.'

'Is that all?'

She chuckled. 'It's a vital part of this newspaper, publishing the accomplishments of departed souls. You may find some of it enlightening.'

Shuffling through the names of potential candidates for the obituary column, Tom suddenly felt an overwhelming urge to ring his parents. Unsure of what he would say, but stirred by the list of recently dead people, all of whom must have families grieving for them, he grabbed the phone. Before he could change his mind his mother answered, 'Hello,' she said, tearfully, 'We don't want the press pestering us again. We've said all we needed to at the last interview so, please, leave us alone.' He could hear one last heavy stifled sob and then she replaced the receiver.

'You're wasting your time, you know,' Imogene said, breezing back into the office. 'Your parents believe you crashed on the Pan Am flight – you died along with all the other passengers. I might have been able to save your life but those who were close to you think you're dead. That's what I keep trying to tell you: there's no going back. Your old life has ended.'

'My family, my friends, even my college – everything's gone...' He shook his head in disbelief. 'I don't understand... Who am I now? How... How... Oh Jesus, Imogene, what have you done to me?'

'Christ! Do you never stop moaning?' Imogene's voice rang out harshly in the tiny shared space. 'I've saved your fucking life. Doesn't that mean anything to you? I thought you'd be grateful.'

'Grateful?' he said, a tear forming at the corner of his eyes. 'When you're telling me I no longer exist, that I'm simply a figment of your imagination. How the hell can I be grateful for that?'

She took hold of his hand once more and squeezed it sympathetically. 'You can function more or less as any other human can, except you have to be careful about...'

'Yeah, I know,' he interrupted angrily, 'the fucking time paradox! Which means I have to be watched pretty well every minute of every day until you're satisfied I've matured into my new existence. Why the hell didn't you just leave me to die?'

'You'll learn, trust me. And will you please stop whinging about leaving you to die. It's pointless anyway – you're here and there's nothing I or anyone can do to alter that. Now get on with those obituaries before you miss the copy deadline.'

Just before 4.30 pm, having carefully avoided him all day, Tom was dismayed when Scott Hardy poked his head round the door and said, 'I haven't forgotten your arrival, you know. I've been making enquiries and no one's even heard of you before today. So, do you want to enlighten me? Or shall I keep investigating?'

'What's it got to do with you?' Tom snapped. 'Haven't you got anything better to do than stick your nose in other people's affairs?'

Hardy came in and cosily sat on the edge of Tom's desk, his mistrustful eyes glittering with spite. 'As a rule, yes, I've plenty of better things to do. However, in your case there does appear to be a complete shortage of information. Such as, which newspaper you came to us from. Oh, and the small matter of how you applied for a job that wasn't advertised. How did you convince Andy Clarke to hire you?'

Tom glared at him, and told the story he had agreed over lunch with Imogene. 'I was recommended for the job by Imogene, my partner. I was a reporter for a small newspaper in Delaware but because we wanted to be together Imogene arranged this job. And for your information, I didn't have to convince Andy Clarke about anything – he was already persuaded before I was interviewed.' At least this bit was more or less correct, Tom mused, since Imogene had dazzled him into giving him the job.

Hardy was about to press the issue but stopped as Imogene reappeared. 'Still sticking your nose in, are you Mr. Hardy?'

'I'm curious, that's all.'

'Then why don't you go and discuss it with Andy Clarke - he's the one who does the hiring and firing? Not me or Tom here.'

Without a word Hardy shuffled out of the office.

'You were right about him causing trouble,' Tom said. 'The only question now is what can we do about it?'

'At present, nothing. Not a damn thing. But I can tell you, he'll dig and dig till he comes up with something close to the truth. And if that should happen…'

'What?' he interrupted. 'You mean we'll have to get the hell outta here?'

She shrugged. 'If you like or… We'll have to leave it at that for the moment. Come on, we have work to do.'

Before leaving for the night two hours later, Imogene decided to take up the incident directly with Andy Clarke, pointing out that Scott Hardy had been aggressively unwelcoming to Tom. Andy didn't require much convincing; unlike Hardy, he was already mesmerised by Imogene's persuasive influence. Dragging a reluctant Hardy into his office minutes later, he surprised the crime reporter by demanding that he desist from snooping into Tom's sudden appearance. 'What?' Scott yelled, incensed at this odd request from the most aggressive editor in New York. 'Just give me one good reason why I shouldn't check out his history! At the moment he's like the Invisible Man. Outside of today, he just doesn't exist! Don't you find that all a bit odd?'

'Here's a good reason,' the normally genial Andy hissed. 'If I hear you've been in his face again, you're fired!'

Hardy swallowed down his temper and resisted the temptation to shout back. Biting his lip he spoke quietly, 'Understood, boss.'

Shutting the door on his way, out he felt a cold rage fill him; Tom had made a bitter enemy.

CHAPTER SEVEN

*'How dare that jumped-up fucker threaten me!' Hardy snarled to himself.
'If Clarke thinks he's gonna fuck me up now after all I've been through
he can fucking well think again!'*

*Six years of conniving and conspiring had gained Hardy his coveted
post as a senior reporter with the Times - as well as a rapacious and
vicious worldview and a gunshot wound to the side of his chest. So he was
not going to stand for anyone, even his Editor in Chief, telling him that if
he so much as looked at Thomas Heaton's appointment again he would be
summarily dismissed. In truth it was absolutely bizarre. There was no
logic in the threat and he doubted Clarke would carry it out.*

*Hardy's fury only grew as he passed down the corridors of lined with
journalists. In all, there must have been at least eighty reporters in the
cubby holes and not a single one, other than himself, had challenged this
Heaton's appointment. To make matters worse, even the deputy editor was
mesmerised by her powers.*

It's like the little witch has cast some kinda spell on
everyone around her! he raged to himself. Every last one of
'em - except me…

*For all his internal bravado, Hardy was badly shaken. Why was
Clarke so protective of Heaton that he'd fire Hardy just for checking him
out? What the hell was all the secrecy about? Surely his had been perfectly
natural questions to ask: where had this guy come from? What was his
background in journalism? Where had he worked before? And more
importantly why had he been given a job — him and his so-called mistress
— when no job had been advertised?*

*He sat down at his desk, brimming over with rage. One or two of
his subordinates came up to him for advice but he waved them away; his
patience had boiled over and he was in no mood for anyone.*

*'Fuck off, Susan,' he snapped at the senior of his assistants. 'Can't
you see I'm busy?'*

She crept away, embarrassed at his behaviour; she also felt ashamed as if she had done something wrong. Hardy had been known to swear before but not with such violence. Susan was a thirty-five year old tubby blonde, tentatively hanging on to the last vestiges of youth. She was quite pretty in a way, although the odd line was starting to creep in on her face. She couldn't believe what she had heard and tears began welling in her eyes. How could he treat her like this?

Hardy ignored her and went over Heaton's recruitment with the same kind of magnifying glass that had been used on his own appointment. Nothing could explain why or how the man had been recruited. He was not even sure exactly why he resented this Heaton guy so fiercely. Maybe it was that seething resentment of the smug preppie types with their college degrees and rich mommies and daddies to give them the whole world on a plate… But then again, it was not as if, his own credentials were above suspicion, or as if he had earned his position through talent and hard work. He recalled the day when he was appointed to the Chicago Tribune as a Runner. In other words he started by delivering messages and running errands. It was Father Murphy who had gotten him the job. He was sixteen at the time and no doubt heading for incarceration but he had great aspirations for the future. He had looked down the line of journalists; he was the youngest on the paper and he had realised that it might be years before a promotion was available, especially given his less than wholesome background, which was common knowledge. But he knew, given his foresight, that before he reached the age of twenty, he would progress to become a fully-fledged journalist.

So he waited. He ran errands for the seniors. He delivered messages for the seniors. He sucked up to whoever might give him a chance at promotion. And little by little he was afforded the chance to involve himself in editorial activities at the Tribune.

When he was eighteen, he saw his chance to progress. In his sociopathic mind he understood that there was no point in trying to leapfrog his mentor; that would have been really stupid. So he planned instead to remove the next in seniority above him.

Since his dissolute father had been heavily and fatally involved in dealing hard drugs, Hardy was more than conversant with the machinations and protocols of the underground narcotics trade - in fact he had not exactly kept his own nose clean! So it was fairly easy to arrange for one of his old gang to plant enough cocaine under the passenger seat of the journalist's car to support a charge of dealing the stuff. Tipping off the cops to ensure Bill Griffins' arrest was even simpler.

The plant went without a hitch - and the hapless journalist's arrest caused a sensation at the paper. Bill Griffins had never been known even to take drugs, much less deal in them. Nevertheless, given the circumstances, he was retired from the Tribune. Bill tried to insist that this was a set-up but he had no evidence to defend himself. The fifty-five year old man was tried, convicted, and was awaiting sentence when he hanged himself in his garage.

It was an enormous tragedy both for his family and everyone at the paper. Hardy eagerly awaited developments, convinced that the latest turn of events couldn't have worked out better for his career. And he was right. The next day, after a number of management meetings, his mentor was promoted to Assistant Editor of the legal team. And he took Hardy with him as his assistant.

Here he was, eighteen years of age and already on the ladder to success. Had he been asked if he had any regrets about Griffins' death, he would merely have shrugged and confirmed that that had been his destiny.

Years went by and Hardy appeared to have progressed as far as he was able at the paper. He was now twenty-two, approaching twenty-three, and his mentor, John Allardice, did not appear to have any ambitions to move upwards. So Hardy reckoned that either he did something dramatic or else he would be stuck as a junior reporter until Allardice died. And that gave him a thought. What if Allardice were to 'pass-on', as the obituaries so delicately put it? Surely he was the prime candidate to replace the senior journalist.

He gave it some thought as to how it should be done and when; and also who he would pick from the old drug gang to carry out the execution. Scott knew from his conversations with Allardice that at weekends he was in the habit of walking his dog through the nearby park. Hardy reconnoitred the area. Running alongside the park's perimeter was a main road that crossed the path that John Allardice walked with the dog.

It was also the way he had to go on his way home. All that was needed was a car to wait for him to cross at the lights then hit him with terminal velocity. In an instant, Allardice would be no more and Hardy would be promoted. He recruited one of his old drug gang to carry out the act; one who owed him an enormous favour. He explained what was needed and then coerced him into accepting the role. First he would have to steal a car, the night before, which wouldn't be too difficult, then dress himself in a hooded top so he wouldn't be recognised and then wait for his opportunity at the side of the park. Hardy also gave him a photo of John Allardice so he would recognise him.

'Piece of cake,' he said to Nick, the guy in question.

'What happens if the cops come along?'

'So, you won't do it. We'll wait a week till the coast's clear. OK?'

'Yeah. Right. I'll do it. Then we'll be clear. Yeah?'

'Absolutely, Nick. You won't owe me a thing.'

It was three weeks later before the incident happened. It was a clear day; no traffic in the area and Nick was waiting for Allardice to cross, which he did when the lights turned to green. He gunned the accelerator to the floor and the car must have been doing sixty when it smashed into Allardice's legs. The impact hurled him some thirty feet in the air, the dog with him, and he hit the rear end of the car as it hurtled away.

Nick was trembling. He had never done anything like this before. After three or four hundred yards he opened the car door and vomited on the ground. He looked back but there was no need to check on the man; he was clearly dead, and so was the dog. Shakily, he jumped from the vehicle and fled through the park, thinking that when they found the car they would soon realise it was stolen - and he was untraceable. What he wasn't aware of was that he had left the photo of John Allardice on the car seat.

It was some little time later that Hardy was given the details at the paper. According to the police, the picture of Allardice they had found in the car suggested that this had been no accident. Yet there appeared to be no motive; why would anyone want to kill off a respectable middle-aged gentleman? He had no record of convictions, not even traffic offences. And he had led such a quiet life, especially sedentary after the death two years ago of his wife. It was a puzzle, even at the paper. Senior management meetings were held after the funeral to discuss what should happen within the paper. Hardy held his breath. Murder to him - and that was now what the police were describing it as - was merely a step function to achieve his ambitions. Scott acknowledged that he had no conscience, that was something ordinary people suffered from.

A couple of days after the funeral, he was called into the Editor's office. This is it, he told himself, struggling to control his nerves.

'Mister Hardy,' Andy said to him, 'have you ever thought of moving to New York?'

'New York!' He was aghast. What the hell was this all about? 'Why would I want to do that, Ed? I'm quite happy here.'

'Simply because I've been offered the job of Editor in Chief - at the Times, no less… And I believe that if you work there then I can keep a… a parental eye on you.'

Hardy was nonplussed. 'I'm sorry, Andy but you're confusing me. What is this business about keeping…'

'Keeping an eye on you? Well, the police have told me that they've so far, caught the driver of the car; evidently he left a trail of DNA on the floor, and he does have previous convictions. Up to now, he hasn't named

anyone else involved with him, but if you consider the evidence - that is the
photo of John Allardice in the runaway's car - you might well come to the
conclusion that whoever was involved with the driver had something to gain
from his death...'

'And that someone might be me?'

'It does spring to mind. However, rather than wait for a confession, which we understand might well be his word against yours, I've decided to offer you a job with the New York Times. As Editor in Chief at least I can stop any other attacks you might be planning here in Chicago. You got that, Mister Hardy?'

'I can see the logic, Andy, except you've already decided that I'm
guilty of killing off John Allardice.' He shrugged. 'Whatever conclusions
you've arrived at they can only be circumstantial; no court in the world
would convict me over a man with form. So what you're proposing isn't
exactly a fair proposition – now is it?'

'Probably not, Hardy. But surely you can't blame me for wanting to keep you where I can see what you're up to. Anyway, the job in New York isn't something to be sneezed at; the salary's considerable higher than at the Tribune, you'll have more freedom than you have here - and you get an apartment with the job. So, what do you say?'

'And if I refuse?'

'Then I'll turn the full fury of the law on to you. As you say, you might not be convicted of John's murder in the end - but the cops are sure gonna give you a going over and convicted or not, I doubt very much if you'll ever get another job in journalism. So think about it, Hardy, will you? I have another three weeks here on the Tribune and I'd like an answer before then. Clear enough?'

Hardy nodded and left the office.

Three weeks later he joined the New York Times.

Back then, Clarke's suspicions had done Hardy no harm. On the contrary, they had actually secured his job at the Times! He had no need to worry about Clarke and his pathetic threats, he decided. He swore he would not be deterred from his enquiries. He would check every available source, every contact he had in the journalistic world, to see if there were any trace of Heaton's background. And if that truly offended Andy Clarke, he would meet that head on and challenge the bastard.

This matter was far from over.

CHAPTER EIGHT

As the weeks passed Tom's new career in journalism flourished. Guided by Imogene's ever-watchful eyes, Tom left the obituaries behind and became Court Reporter on the crime desk, dealing with minor misdemeanours. There was one drawback to this; he now had to work in the same team as Scott Hardy. However, even this didn't put him off. It seemed that Clarke's snarling response had worked – Hardy ceased questioning Tom about his life, and merely ignored him now. Tom relaxed, he was more than happy to be ignored, but Imogene knew they had made an enemy and was constantly waiting for Hardy's next move.

Tom and Imogene usually had lunch together at one of the coffee shops close to the paper, and at nights they invariably dined out. When they did eat at the apartment - Tom still refused to call it home - it was Tom who did the cooking. He once jokingly commented that if they had married she would have made a lousy housewife, as she never cooked or tidied up.

After challenging his old-fashioned view of marriage, Imogene stopped, suddenly serious, 'I would hate you to start thinking that one day we might get married,' she stated flatly.

'You're serious, aren't you?' Tom said, looking earnestly at her deadpan face, 'I mean am I so unattractive?'

'No, of course not, you're lovely, but you know perfectly well what I mean,' she said carefully, watching his face to make sure that he understood. 'I mean it,' she said, noticing the slight look of hope crossing his features. 'This friendship we share is as good as it's going to get. Marriage is not an option.'

He left it at that, consoling himself that at least she found him attractive, hoping that in time she might have a change of heart.

One morning, about a month after they started living together, Imogene awakened him; she was standing by his bed with tears in her eyes.

'What's the matter?' he asked, shaken as he had never seen her cry before.

'I'm… I'm bleeding,' she sobbed.

'Where?' he asked, and then as realisation dawned on him, he pointed to her crotch and said more gently, 'Do you mean down there?'

She nodded. 'Am I ill?'

Tom tried to disguise his grin. 'No, you're menstruating. It's something all women do – once a month.'

'Why?' Imogene looked horrified.

'Well… because women… well, they have eggs, inside their fallopian tubes… That's how they become pregnant.' He sighed. 'Don't you know anything about the human body, Imogene?'

'Not very much, no,' she shook her head sadly, 'and no one warned me about the bleeding,' she said. 'So what do I do?'

'You need some towels or tampons. If you like I can get them from the pharmacy; there'll be instructions in the box to show you what to do.'

'Thank you, Tom. I thought I was ill.'

Even as Tom was explaining the functions of the human female, Imogene was examining the conflict raging within her about her dual role as an angel and as a human. The two were simply incompatible. Being an angel was a natural phenomenon; what she really meant was that it was natural because it was the nature of her existence. On the other hand, having to embrace her new humanity in parallel with her heavenly perceptions was a collision between the two entities, each battling each other; neither convinced one or the other might win.

It made Imogene very sad and mostly lonely, even in Tom's presence. She even found herself challenging the Tribunal's decision. What right did they have to condemn her to a life on this earth as a human? And what would have happened as she refused? A small part of her was tempted to challenge the directive but on reflection that was the human part; the part with which they had endowed her.

The face in the mirror each morning confirmed that she was indeed human; that didn't mean she accepted it. Nor did she accept all the frailties of humanity. The hunger... The thirst... The pain, as and when it arose... These monthly periods that she still couldn't understand.. And, more than anything, the desire for sexual encounters, all of which were related to Tom and his relentless overtures. It was the closeness of him that destroyed her equilibrium, destroyed the balance she was trying to introduce into her life; in fact, the truth was, it destroyed all her desperate attempts to gain control over her everyday living.

She sighed and tried to obliterate the depression hanging over her. She splashed the eau de cologne from the bathroom cabinet over most of the visible parts of her body, hoping this might cheer her up; she even put lipstick around her mouth; wasn't this what human women did every morning? So Jennie, her friend at The Times, had told her. It didn't make any difference. In essence she was Imogene, the denounced angel, fallen from heaven. She sat for a moment on the toilet, another of those human habits she despised, and allowed a tear to fall on her cheeks.

Out loud she asked herself, 'Is this all I have to look forward to for the rest of Thomas's life?'

She sobbed, for a while, wondering whether she should go to work. Her heart was no more in that routine than it was in the penalty of living.

'What have I done that's so terrible it deserves this punishment?' she sighed.

Just then a quiet, reassuring voice whispered in her ear, 'Come to St. Patrick's my child and I will give you peace.'

'

An Angel's Kiss

CHAPTER NINE

Eventually the winter gave way to spring. Tom quite enjoyed their Sunday walks through Central Park, especially when the flowers and the trees burst into blossom. They would sit on a bench overlooking the lake watching the passers-by. Once he tried to hold her hand but she was having none of it – she simply shifted to the other end of the bench.

He still took her dancing, except now his manner was almost formal as if he were afraid to touch her.

'Why are you so distant?' she asked him.

'Because you intimidate me,' he answered, trying to be honest. 'If I get too close to you I'm aware that you'll resist me, as you did in the park when I tried to hold your hand. So now I feel more comfortable keeping some distance between us. Does that answer your question?'

She nodded, neither agreeing nor disagreeing, listening instead to that quietly insistent voice in her head: Come to St Patricks.

When it rained, especially at the weekend, they would go to one of the museums. Tom was beginning to find them all a bit boring, but Imogene still delighted in all the new experiences.

Soon they were sweltering in the heat of summer in the city. On Broadway, the smell of petrol fumes and tarmac melting on the sidewalks blended with the shouts from street vendors frantically trying to sell souvenirs to tourists. In Central Park, office workers desperate to grab a few rays picnicked before returning, relieved, to the cool of the air conditioning. Tom took Imogene to see West Side Story three times - she really was into musicals - and he was happy to see the pleasure the shows gave her. At the weekend they escaped to the beach at Long Island and it took his breath away to see Imogene in a sexy bikini, although he knew that he could never show her how he really felt.

One magical weekend they flew up to Niagara Falls and stayed in a hotel on the Canadian side, although she insisted on two rooms as usual. To Tom it was ironic to spend so much time with his 'girlfriend' only to encounter such sexual indifference.

Summer dragged on relentlessly, four months of perennial heat, and throughout all of this time Tom felt as though he had to exercise an unusual degree of self-restraint. He longed to hold her, let her know how he really felt, to touch her hair as it shone in the sunlight, to take her hand as if they were lovers, but knew that if he did she would reject him.

Although his relationship with Imogene remained frustrating, his career began to really take off. After almost twelve months at the paper, he graduated to join the Crime Reporting Team, as an assistant. The only downside to this was that he now worked directly under Scott Hardy.

There were one or two instances when random events drew him closer to the edge of committing the proverbial 'Time-Warp' error but every time Imogene pulled him back from the edge.

Stark realisation dawned on him when he attempted to pull a young boy from a fire that it wasn't just things about his own life that he couldn't change. Distraught as Imogene held him back from helping, he knew it would have been quite easy to rescue the boy; his clothes were on fire but his life could have been saved. He was grief stricken as Imogene reminded him that as he no longer existed it wasn't credible that he could have saved the child. The experience was almost unbearably traumatic and left Tom flooded with immense sadness.

On the next occasion an armed robbery took place in a 7/11 store when Tom, who had been at the rear of the store, tried to intervene. Again, it was Imogene who had to restrain him, regardless of the fact that the store owner died. It was a shocking reminder of just how limited his future actions were; and indeed, just how insignificant he himself had become.

This exacerbated the deep melancholy in his life. Sure he had an enjoyable job at the New York Times; he lived a life of comparative luxury but the meaning to his existence was circumscribed by whatever dictates Imogene sanctioned. To be constantly with her should have been a joy, but however much he tried to show his love for her she remained distant. It was as though human physical feelings just didn't enter her consciousness; she might occupy human form but in essence she was completely spiritual.

Sometimes, in his frustration, he considered the hookers lingering on the sidewalks, catching his eye with their over-painted faces and high stiletto heels. Occasionally returning a smile and catching a glimpse of bra strap or a stocking top he felt tempted. However, bought love and affection was not what he really wanted, so he always turned away ruefully shaking his head, ignoring their jibes. From time to time, in his lonely bed, he thought of masturbating, but with Imogene so close this became impossible. So his life took on an underlying feeling of hopelessness; the sense of wishing he had died in the 747 crash still hadn't left him and more and more he was debating whether he should take his own life.

Once, he took the lift to the roof of the Empire State Building – it was almost dusk and virtually deserted; Imogene believed he was finishing up at the courtroom. It crossed his mind that here was the perfect opportunity to end it all - until he realised that in jumping from the building he could land on a pedestrian below and cause the time paradox he was constantly warned about. Miserably, he rejected the idea and took the lift back to the ground floor.

Time passed and little or nothing changed. Except that his work became perfunctory, his behaviour less and less spontaneous. Persistently, he continued to try to telephone his parents, which was pointless because they had changed the number and become ex-directory.

Unbeknown to Tom as he contemplated suicide, taking her unruffled demeanour at face value, Imogene was far from serene. She was still worrying away at the conflict raging within her about her dual role as an angel and as a human - and all the time she heard that quiet voice whispering in the back of her mind that there was a place where she could find peace. She was beginning to question whether her divinity could withstand the almost daily pressures that her partner imposed on her, however unintentionally. It was the sheer closeness of him that most deeply disturbed her equilibrium. Finally, instead of merely hearing it, Imogene actually listened to that voice in her head: Come to St Patricks. Come to St. Patrick's, my child, and I will give you peace.'

What have I got to lose? she told herself one afternoon at the Times office and, filled with fresh resolve, she cut off a phone call in mid-sentence, dropped the sandwich she was munching and strode purposefully out of warren of cubby holes without a word to any of her colleagues - none of whom seemed to notice her leaving.

Stepping out of the New York Times Building's foyer into Eighth Avenue, Imogene turned unthinkingly into Times Square's hubbub, past Radio City Music Hall and, as if on autopilot, hurried past the Rockefeller Centre until the towering Neo-Gothic splendour of the Basilica of St Patrick's Cathedral loomed up before her.

Tucked away at the Saint John Baptist de la Salle altar, Imogene was lost in prayer, for who knows how long. One minute the sun had been streaming through the Papal Bull stained glass windows and then the next, or so it seemed, darkness had fallen. Still her contemplative trance and her search for guidance continued until finally, as robotically as she had entered, she crossed herself, hurried out to hail a cab. She hardly knew where she was heading - only that the same gently insistent voice had returned, now urging her to an address in the Bronx.

Travelling north in a cab, the driver apparently unconcerned by her lack of instructions, she was somehow able to offer precise directions - left here, right at Yankee Stadium, left at this bar or right at that set of lights... And when eventually the cab pulled over outside a tiny monastery tucked away in a backstreet, she suddenly knew exactly who she had to ask for: Friar Mancini, the voice urged. She pressed the age-old doorbell and waited for what seemed like an eternity but was actually a good five minutes, before an envelope-sized hatch opened in the door and a gentle - but this time very earthly - voice asked what she wanted.

'I've been sent to speak with... Friar Mancini,' Imogene breathed.

'The Abbot... Why?'

'It's personal. I believe if you ask him he might be expecting me. Tell him Imogene is here and I need to speak with him.'

Without a word, the owner of the voice slammed shut the flap and she was left to wait for what seemed like another eternity.

Finally, the heavy door opened and a finger pointed for her to follow an expressionless monk. She was led through a series of seemingly endless corridors, until the monk stopped at an oak door where he knocked, seemingly hesitantly.

Abbot Mancini, by comparison with his dour brother monk, was a middle-aged and jovial man, balding with an almost permanent twinkle in his eyes. Imogene wasn't sure whether he was growing a beard or if his stubble was simply because of laziness.

He held Imogene by the shoulders as if he were intent on embracing her.

'Imogene!' he exclaimed cheerfully as if greeting a long lost friend. 'I've been expecting you. Come in, please.'

He led her into a rather spacious office and showed her to a chair opposite his own. Abbot Mancini must be the Friar, she concluded,

'Are you aware why I am here,' she asked. 'I mean, do you know who I am?'

'More or less,' he said. 'I was warned that an angel would be visiting me some time today, and I was told some of the circumstances. But I would like you to fill me in on the details if you don't mind. Can I call you Imogene? Or do I call you Sister?' He asked.

'No. I'm not a sister – my earthly name is Imogene. You may call me that.'

'And please, call me Augusto. Now, where do you want to begin?'

So Imogene recited the history of the Pan Am 747 and her decision to save Tom from certain death. She followed that up by describing the conflict she was now enduring and how her body was at serious risk of giving in to the temptations she was constantly exposed to. She told Augusto that she believed she was in love with Tom and consequently was fighting to protect her divinity.

'I yearn for him, my body longs to unite with his. I have prayed for guidance, Augusto – endlessly. But it wasn't until today I received word that I was to come and see you.'

'Have you spoken to the young man about your feelings? Told him how you are sorely tempted?'

Imogene looked at him with indignation. 'No. Of course I haven't. He would never leave me alone if I did that.'

'So, is there nothing you can share with him about your feelings? Perhaps he might understand.'

'I doubt that, Augusto. Every time he sees me he's intent on undressing me.' She shook her head. 'I really don't know what to do. I have tried and tried my utmost to explain my dilemma to him; he doesn't seem to understand that if I were to … I would corrupt my spirituality.'

Augusto gazed at her, a puzzled expression on his face. 'Does he understand what you mean by corruption?'

'I'm not sure. The problem with you humans, present company excluded, is that you tend to believe that sex is a normal part of the human condition'

'And isn't it?'

'No.' she said defiantly. 'It is a gift from God. It sensitises the relationship between a man and woman to avoid the animalistic expression of copulation.'

'Jesus, Imogene!' Augusto said dramatically. 'Aren't you overstating the inherent desire of people to propagate? I'm not altogether sure that God has anything to do with it other than to create the condition.'

'Yes. But you are overlooking the fact that procreation's an indelible part of God's fabric – it is fundamental to His own existence.' She hesitated, then added, 'I'm sorry… I shouldn't have said that… it's beyond my remit.'

The friar gazed at her, this time sympathetically. 'Now you're losing me; that's something only you'd have knowledge of. Obviously, I have no special insight into the way God works his mysterious ways. However, it seems to me the prime function of our existence in this world is to procreate. Isn't what Jesus said an absolute: "Go ye out into the world and multiply"?'

Imogene snorted but didn't respond.

Augusto continued, 'I can only try to help you with temptations of the flesh, my dear, especially as those of us here in the monastery have led a life of abstinence. But the real assistance I can deliver is to offer you a sanctuary away from the ordeal of living – a retreat where you may find peace, where you may rest your weary head and allow God to infiltrate you.

'It is not for me to say whether or not The Tribunal's right to force you to inhabit an earthly body – they're a much higher body than I could ever hope to attain.

It is true though, and I have to say this, that what you did, in saving the life of your catechumen, was improper and usurped a celestial dictate. But, despite that, I believe you'll find relief in this monastery; and that's what I am offering you now. Will you accept?'

Imogene looked at him, tears in her eyes. 'Yes, please, Augusto.'

He rose from his chair.

'Good. Now, let me show you your bedroom.'

With that he led her from the room, down some corridors, until he entered a small but comfortable bedroom with an en suite bathroom.

'This is the room we usually allocate to the Bishop when he arrives – but don't worry, he isn't due yet for another six months.'

'It's very nice,' said Imogene. 'I really do appreciate you helping me. How can I ever thank you?'

'Just by being here. We're blessed that an angel should share our humble abode with us, partake of our food and join with us when we celebrate the name of the Lord.'

He handed her a key. 'Please, this is the key that will allow you to visit us whenever you choose. You need not call; simply let yourself in, your room will always be made up for you.'

She kissed him on the cheek and allowed him to lead her to the door.

'God be with you always, Imogene,' he said as she departed.

CHAPTER TEN

As the anniversary of his death approached Tom's spirits declined even further. Miserable and depressed, he was surprised when Imogene threw another bombshell at him.

'I think we should visit your parents,' she announced one morning, as they sat together eating breakfast at the kitchen table.

'What?' he exclaimed, amazement jolting him from his now customary moroseness.

'You heard. I said we should visit your mother, I think it will help you adjust to your new life. They're having a memorial service for you next week at the local church; it's one year since the crash - and I think you should go.'

Tom was so astounded he dropped his toast on the floor.

'But they think I'm dead!' he exploded, 'I mean, what will they say when they discover I'm still alive? You told me they think I died in the crash, and now you're suggesting I should visit them! Have you gone mad?' He shook his head incredulously.

She sighed, letting him know that he exasperated her. 'Don't be ridiculous! I am not suggesting you meet them! I just want you to witness the memorial service; watch it from some concealed part of the church. I just want you to see your mother – I think it will help you.'

'Oh really, and what about my father? Will it help him too?' Tom retorted angrily.

Imogene shrugged as she poured another cup of coffee. 'I don't believe you have an affinity with your father. Besides you never really liked him; he was the one who coerced you into law rather than doing what you wanted to. I just feel that you are so depressed that seeing your mother again will lift your spirits.

So, I'll make arrangements for us to travel this weekend to Pennsylvania – we're both free for a long weekend.'

'Do I get any say in the matter? I might not agree.' He scowled at her realising this was yet another decision taken out of his hands.

'Yes, of course you do. All you have to do is say yes!'

Imogene left the table, making it clear that as far as she was concerned that was the end of the discussion. On the Friday morning, both dressed warmly for the winter conditions, they travelled across the river to Newark and caught the morning flight for the short journey to Philadelphia. It was a crisp mid-winter's day with gathering clouds hinting at the first winter's snowfall, beautiful and fresh, but Tom was unable to appreciate the weak winter sunshine and clear air.

From Philadelphia they hired a car, joined the Delaware Expressway, and crossed the Delaware River to drive the thirty miles to his parent's home on the banks of the Brandywine River, a short distance from downtown Wilmington. Imogene admired the scenery as they drew closer and closer. Tom, studiously ignoring her, noted without surprise that she seemed to know the route, as though she had been that way before.

Tom's parents lived in a secluded area, five miles from the city centre, and only a short distance away from the church. Tom couldn't help feeling excited as they drove down a tree-lined avenue that led to the Brandywine River bordering the house; it bought back so many memories. His father's favourite hobby, since a heart condition had forced him to retire early two years ago, was fly-fishing for trout and the river bank had been the last place that Tom had enjoyed a rare meaningful discussion with him. A difficult man, not given to sharing his feelings with his wife or son, Tom had never enjoyed the close father son bond that he desperately sought. Approval was the most he had ever received from Jerry Metzler, and then only when he had reluctantly agreed to make law his career.

In sharp contrast to the cold relationship he shared with his father, his mother, Mary, had always been the delight of Tom's life. Warm and loving she had always given her son the security and support that he needed. She was a few years younger than his father and had a wonderful zest for life that twenty-five years of marriage to a dour, cold man had still not extinguished. It was this brightness and the ability to see the best in everyone that had initially attracted Jerry to her. Although she wasn't Jewish, he had willingly abandoned his religion, and ignoring his disapproving orthodox family married her.

The last time Tom had seen his mother was at the Thanksgiving festivities. Tom was always impressed by how young she looked with her long dark hair and slim athletic figure. He knew that she would have been absolutely devastated when she was told that he had died in the air crash and he wondered how it had affected her. No doubt she would have thrown herself into her work at the Du Pont Hospital for children where she worked as a paediatrician.

As they approached the entrance to the chapel Imogene stopped the car. 'Wait here', she said.

'Why? This is my memorial service. Surely I can't be recognised? I don't even look like Tom Metzler anymore.'

She got out of the car. 'Generally, you're right. However, we need to find a suitable hiding place; your mother may well recognise you.'

'How can she possibly do that? She isn't psychic!' Tom looked confused.

Imogene laid a hand on his arm, gripping it tightly. 'Will you please stop arguing with me,' she asked. 'I'm doing this for your benefit, please believe me. Your mother might not be psychic, but she does have an unusually sensitive insight into people.'

Tom followed her to the church, staying by the entrance in the darkness of the porch, where he could hear the pastor delivering a eulogy. He had thought he would feel terribly sad attending his own memorial service, but was astonished to find he was actually quite intrigued. He peered inside the chapel, quickly ducking back into the shadows, amazed to see so many people present. He hadn't realised so many people knew him or knew of him. Perhaps it was because he had 'died' in such tragic circumstances.

He recognised his parents, sitting silently at the front close to the altar; his father ram rod straight and his mother leaning into him slightly, seeking comfort. The familiar sight of them gave his heart a jolt and he felt a sob inadvertently rise in his throat.

'We can sit at the back,' Imogene whispered to him. 'I don't think anyone will realise who you are.'

Tom choked back tears and followed her inside. He watched his mother's head fall forward in grief as the pastor spoke of the special qualities of her son, and seeing her bowed head he shared his mother's anguish. Desperately wishing that he could run forward and comfort her, he whispered to Imogene, 'I have to leave. This is a mistake.' His voice was cracked with emotion, 'You never told me it would have this effect.'

She followed him out of the church. 'I didn't realise, I'm sorry. Look, why don't we wait in the car and you can see your mother when she comes out?'

'What? So I can watch her suffering, thinking her son is dead?' he wiped his hands across his face in anguish. 'I'll be sitting there, knowing I have caused all this, and not be able to do a thing about it! It is wrong, so wrong. I never should have listened to you.'

'That isn't fair,' she protested. 'What your parents are going through is the process of grieving for a dead son – and the truth is you are a dead son. You can never reclaim the life you once had; you can never go back, pretend all of this never happened. It has happened, and OK, you might blame me and part of you is right, but do you really want to be dead?'

'At least I wouldn't have to witness this! Watch all those people, especially my parents, grieving – sharing all this sadness. Can we leave now … please?'

'No.' Imogene said firmly. 'I want you to see your mother. I want you to go up to her when she comes out of the church and give her your sympathy. Shake her by the hand and express your condolences. Tell her you're an old friend of Tom's; you could say you were at Harvard with him.'

'Are you crazy?' he interrupted, fury turning his face red. 'Or are you completely insensitive? She's my mother for God's sake! You expect me to offer my condolences for… for being dead …' He turned away so she wouldn't see his tears; he felt more alone and isolated than ever before.

'She won't recognise you, Tom, but believe me when I say that it will help the two of you. All I'm asking you to do is trust me.'

'You know since this whole thing happened, I've endured a lonely and desolate life. I've lost just about everything I ever loved. It's almost as if God's abandoned me; and now I have to listen to you trying to convince me I should celebrate my survival! You know, I can't think of a single reason why I should.'

Imogene let out a sigh and placed a 'Guardian Angel' hand on his shoulder. 'You may not be happy with your life at present, but I promise you, when this entire trauma settles down you can proclaim your existence, almost as if it were an act of God.'

He scowled at her. 'You think so? What, after almost twelve months? Well, I can't see any point in continuing this discussion,' he turned away, 'you obviously have your own thoughts and they happen to conflict with mine.'

She smiled knowingly. 'I realise you don't believe what I'm saying, but one day you will wake up in the morning and find there is still joy in your life. Now, here is your mother. Are you going to do as I suggest?'

'If you say so,' he said sulkily, as his mother exited the chapel. Mentally pulling himself together, he went across to her, waiting until there was a gap in the well-wishers, before he stood in front of her. Grief had etched deep lines into her face and he could see that she had been crying. Her sadness seemed to emanate like a dark cloud around her.

'I'm… I'm so very sorry about your loss, Mrs Metzler,' he managed to stammer, trying to keep the pain from his voice and the tears from his eyes. 'We all miss Tom.'

His mother, smartly dressed in a dark blue suit, gazed at him with curiosity. 'Do I know you?' she enquired, puzzled. 'You seem familiar… but I can't place you?'

Imogene was right, he thought. My own mother doesn't recognise me.

'No, I don't think so,' he said. 'I knew your son from Harvard; we were good friends.'

Mrs Metzler stared at him for another second, before opening her arms and enveloping him in a warm hug. As he surrendered to her embrace, breathing in her familiar scent and wishing he could stay there forever, she reached up and whispered in his ear: 'Thank you for coming, it means so much to me.'

'I'm sorry we couldn't have met earlier, in happier times.'

His mother glanced over to the car, exchanging a meaningful look with Imogene. 'Tell her I understand,' she said, 'and please let me know where to get hold of you, I'd like to contact you later. That's if you don't mind?'

'No… no. I'll be happy to talk to you.' Tom stammered. His mother smiled and her face lit up; transforming her back to the sparkling, beautiful woman she had been before her tragic loss. 'Good,' she said, still holding his hand tightly.

He hastily scribbled his address and phone number onto a piece of paper that she produced from her navy clutch bag, and walked back, puzzled, to the car.

'What did she say?' Imogene asked him.

'It was really odd. She said to tell you she understands, whatever that means. Oh, and she asked me for my contact details. Can you explain?'

'I looked into her soul, and she understood.'

'What? She knows you're an angel?'

'I'll tell you later. But I'm glad it went OK.'

As they drove away Imogene placed a hand gently on his arm, 'Feeling better?'

'No. Not really. I can't believe I just did that to my own mother; did you see the state she was in? How could you have ever thought that it would make things better? It was just cruel.'

'She understands, believe me. And it will help you – if not today then soon' She looked across at him, a pained expression on her face. 'Why is it that whatever I do you still moan? You know I said earlier that one of these days you'd wake up with joy in your heart?'

Tom nodded without much conviction.

'Well, I'm beginning to wonder! Perhaps the Tom I'm seeing now is the real one. Have you always been this miserable?'

'Imogene!' Tom exploded, 'I've just met my mother who thinks I'm dead and, thanks to you, she now has a thought placed in her head that I might still be alive! How on earth can you expect me to be joyful?' He placed a hand on her forearm. 'I'm sorry if you think I'm constantly moaning, but today, of all days, I'm grieving.' He let out a sob. 'You couldn't possibly have an insight into what I am suffering! So why don't we leave it at that? I'll endure my grief on my own and you can think whatever you like about me.'

There was silence for a while, apart from the purr of the engine. Suddenly Tom pulled over onto the hard shoulder. He sat there, saying nothing, until Imogene gently touched his face. He turned towards her and then, despite her resistance, took her hands in his.

'I don't blame you for thinking I'm a wimp, I just find it so hard to cope with what's happened. What I would like you to know is that in the past I was a man of courage and the will to take on the world. I thought I knew where I was going and what the future held for me.' He sighed heavily. 'Now, I appear to be nothing. The only thing I do know in this new uncertain life is that I love you with all of my heart and soul. I would do anything for you, even though you don't seem to care. Whether as friends or lovers I am committed to you forever.' He shrugged. 'I just wanted you to know. No. Please don't say anything. It was something I just had to say to you.'

The rest of the journey was continued in silence.

CHAPTER ELEVEN

The memorial service broke up with the customary platitudes; even the vicar gave Mary a kiss on the cheek.

'I'm so sorry for your loss, my dear. If there's anything I can do all you have to do is ask.'

Mary shook her head. 'That's very kind of you, vicar, but I've managed throughout the past year, with the help of my husband, so I'm sure we'll be alright. Thank you so much for the service – it was heart-warming.'

After the final goodbyes, with her head still spinning from the encounter with Imogene and her son's mystery friend, she climbed into the car with her husband.

'That went very well,' Jerry commented. His original name was Jacob but he had changed it to the Christian version when he married Mary.

Mary merely nodded, she was so caught up in the vision she had received. Her insight told her she had received a communication from an angel, someone who was on this earth to inform her that her son Tom had not died in the Lockerbie disaster but was here, now, shaking her hand and telling her he had been a friend of her son. It was surreal. Bizarre might be a better description; yet she knew it to be true. However it had happened or why she had no idea. Perhaps the angel had somehow intervened and prevented Tom from boarding the aircraft? But then why had his features changed so dramatically? Had it not been for the angel's intervention she would never have recognised her son.

She realised now that that was the reason the angel had attended the memorial service, to let her know that her son was not dead. But then where had he been for the last year? Why hadn't he been in touch before? Her head was still spinning from the information and she knew she would have to visit him at the earliest opportunity in New York for an explanation.

In the meantime she still had the children to take care of at the Hospital. Mary had always had an affinity with children; that was why she had become a paediatric consultant. Sometimes she found it heartbreaking to see their suffering and she exerted herself, working long hours into the night, trying to save them. Now, she thought, perhaps that was why the angel had chosen her; because she had given up most of her life to cherish and protect children.

'Are you alright?' Jerry asked her on the way back to the Du Pont Hospital. 'Only you seem to be distracted. Was it the service? Has that affected you?'

She shook her head. 'No. The service was strangely uplifting. I was just thinking about Tom, wondering where he might be now.'

'Oh Christ, Mary, we're not going to get into all that religious crap again are we?' Relinquishing his own faith had made Jerry intolerant of others, and he now described himself as an atheist. 'I mean, if we are, please keep it to yourself, I don't want any part of it.'

'So you've told me, many times. Look, you asked me a question and I'm merely answering you as truthfully as I know how. So, let's just leave it at that shall we?'

After the memorial service Tom's life settled back into a routine, albeit even more boring than before. He continued to share the apartment with Imogene, went out for the occasional meal with her to the local restaurants and even managed to prepare for Christmas, although Imogene couldn't understand why he bothered. However, despite their emotional closeness he never got any closer to her physically.

When he had been promoted to the crime reporters' desk she had too, so they still worked together. There was little drama in his working life and he was surprised that his dream job failed to stimulate him in the same way law had. Although he was often commissioned to attend court hearings and had sat through the trials of some of the most nefarious characters, including rapists and murderers, in New York he continued to work largely on autopilot. It was interesting but it was hardly Pulitzer Prize material.

Scott Hardy had also been promoted and was now the senior crime reporter with the Times. His predecessor had been tragically killed in a car accident; the driver hadn't stopped even though, by all accounts, he was responsible. There were rumours that somehow Hardy was involved in the fatal accident, although he maintained a cynical watch over Tom and continued to pester him for information about his background. Nor was he overgenerous in trusting Tom with any of the serious investigations that crime reporters become renowned for; under Hardy it was highly unlikely he would qualify for a Watergate-style assignment.

One day Scott began interrogating him while briefing him in his private office. 'I'd like you to tell me how it is that you managed to persuade the Sub-Editor that you're some kind of super reporter?' he demanded. 'So far, having researched all of the newspapers in Delaware and the surrounding district, I've seen nothing to confirm your submissions about your prior experience. In fact, Tom Heaton, none of them has even heard of you!'

Tom sighed, but said nothing. Christ! It was twelve months ago and he still wouldn't let it go.

'You're not seriously insisting that you qualified for this position with the Times because of your girlfriend, are you?' Scott went on.

Tom shrugged. He had run out of things to say. The only thing left was to tell the truth.

'It's quite simple really, Scott. The truth is I was booked to travel on the Lockerbie 747. I should have died along with all the others. But Imogene, who's my Guardian Angel, decided I was too young to die so she rescued me by arranging an alternative flight from London. Only at the time I didn't realise what was happening – or what was going to happen. She only informed me the day after the crash.

'And, as I was prematurely deceased, she had to arrange an alternative career and lifestyle for me – so, she picked the New York Times, coerced the Sub-Editor into giving me the job, and here I am. Working alongside you.'

'Well, if you're going to be fucking sarcastic about it ...'

'Oh, but I'm not,' he interrupted. 'I realise you must find it hard to believe but that's the truth.'

'Oh yeah?' Scott exclaimed. 'So what did you do before... before you died?'

'I was a lawyer, with Freedman's. But I could hardly go back to them, could I? Not after they were informed I was on the Pan Am air crash. Anyhow, Imogene decided I was more suited to a career in journalism. So she arranged it.'

Scott shook his head, his eyes rolled back in astonishment. 'Is that the best you can do, Heaton? I don't know about journalism, you should take up a career in fantasy writing. Fuck me, I've heard everything now.' He leant across the desk. 'Why don't you tell me the truth? Just tell me what paper you worked on in the provinces.'

'What, so you can check up on me? Tom said grinning.

'Why not? Is it some sort of secret? I want to know who I'm working with, that's all. I need to know what qualifications you have. Today I mean, not in some Alice in Wonderland fantasy. Did you graduate with a degree in journalism? If so where? Come on Tom, talk to me. Think of this as your confession time.'

'Look, everything you need to know you were told by the Sub-Editor after he hired me. There are no secrets… if you don't believe I was saved from the Lockerbie disaster then you'll just have to go out and search for your own truth. You're good at that, aren't you? I mean, you're the senior reporter at the crime desk; it shouldn't be too difficult for you to manufacture some evidence.'

'So you're sticking to your story. Is that it?'

'There's no other story to tell. Not if you insist on the truth.'

'Yeah. Well I might take you up on that offer – go out and find out the truth.'

'Really? Good, then you'll be able to confirm my story. Then you can apologise to me and Imogene.'

Tom failed to mention this discussion to Imogene. If he had, she might have been able to prevent the disasters that followed.

Christmas Eve came but the only celebration Imogene was interested in was Midnight Mass. Reluctantly Tom went to St. Patrick's with her, and discovered it was indeed a celebration. The Bishop held the mass. There was a choir of – he almost described them as angels, they certainly sounded like them. Partway through the Mass, he refrained from taking communion until Imogene took him by the hand and led him to the altar.

'Join me,' she whispered.

By then he had no choice but to hold out his hand and take the wafer from the Bishop and then place it in his mouth.

It really was a joyous occasion and on the way out Imogene handed him a small gift.

'What's this for?' he asked.

'Isn't this what you humans do at this time of the year? It's a Christmas present.'

'Yes… but I haven't bought you anything. I didn't think you'd want a present from me.' Tom stuttered, embarrassed by her uncharacteristic gesture.

She giggled, like a child, 'It's OK, Tom, you've been taking me out all over town, I didn't expect anything from you.' She pointed to the parcel. 'Open it. You may not even like it.'

He gasped in surprise; it was crucifix, a gold crucifix with a chain, which he could wear around his neck.

'It's so beautiful,' he said, putting it on. 'I never expected you to give me anything and I'm… well, I'm so delighted.'

'Now, when you get these physical temptations you keep talking about, you can pray to the Virgin Mary, God's mother, to help you resist.'

They both chuckled as they left the church and headed for home.

The following day Imogene had a further surprise for him when he finally surfaced from his bed. The kitchen was well lit, the oven was on, and the smell of cooking filled his nostrils. An opened bottle of wine, together with place settings, was on the table.

'What's this,' he managed to stammer, rubbing his eyes.

'This, my dear partner, is Christmas lunch. No doubt not as good as your mother used to make but nevertheless the complete package.'

'Did you make it yourself?'

She laughed. 'Of course not, silly!' She pointed towards the cooker. 'I had it all delivered early this morning. I'm sure it should've cost a lot of money but….'

'Yeah, I know. It was given to you as a present,' he interrupted cryptically.

They both laughed and it was a relaxed and enjoyable Christmas day that they shared. The surprise factor made it even more special; Tom hadn't dared think about what they should do to celebrate the festivities. Sure that this Christmas was going to be miserable and bleak, he was filled with peace as he reflected that it had turned out to be one of the most memorable occasions of his life.

CHAPTER TWELVE

For once, Hardy was true to his word. Determined to either prove or disprove Tom's wild story - and to use either outcome to his own advantage - he took a few days' annual holiday and caught a late evening flight to London Heathrow. He had arranged beforehand a meeting with Oliver Hanson, one of the senior journalists at the Times' London office whom he had met in the paper's New York office before Hanson's departure for England's less sunny climes. They had kept in contact from time to time, usually in the course of a story.

Never having been to London before, Hardy first caught the underground from Heathrow to Green Park and then a taxi to Buckingham Gate where he was welcomed by a very well-fed Oliver. Rounding out at the middle and accumulating several chins, he must have weighed-in at around two-hundred-and-eighty pounds by Hardy's reckoning. But he was cheerful and his smile made Hardy feel at home. They shook hands and Oliver asked him if he had slept on the plane.

'Some. Enough,' he replied abruptly.

'Come, Scott, let me show you around the building.'

It was on three storeys with a lift accessing all floors but mostly the building was inhabited by young girls sitting dourly at computer screens typing God knew what. Oliver led Scott into his office – it was more of a cubbyhole that Hardy occupied in New York.

'What are they doing?' Hardy asked.

'They're transmitting all of the daily inserts direct to the mailing room at Headquarters. Something important might come of them, especially if they link up to another story your lot might be chasing. It was clear that Oliver's unit didn't specialise in any particular stories – they just inherited the earth.

'You mean the New York Times?'

'Of course. So, Scott, it's a pleasure to welcome you to our establishment, but tell me, why are you here? I mean, did the Times send you, or is this a kind of holiday visit?'

Hardy smiled. Oliver was much nearer to the mark than he imagined.

'In a way you're partly right; I'm not here on official business although what I'm after could well make international headlines.'

'Really. You intrigue me. How can I help? I assume you do need my help … yes?'

'Well, I can't explain just yet but I'm looking into passenger manifests. In particular the Pan Am manifest for the Lockerbie disaster.'

'The manifest? Not asking much are you! That manifest was published ad-nauseum for weeks after the crash – I should think pretty well everyone knows who was on the flight, their names, their occupations, where they lived and so on… What on earth do you need it for now? And why come all the way here to get hold of something that's readily available in New York? Unless, of course, as you say, this is just a vacation.'

Hardy shook his head.

'I'm not making myself clear. Let me start again. What I'm trying to get hold of is the original manifest that Pan Am had in their possession just before and just after boarding.'

Oliver shook his great head. Hardy watched a couple of his excess chins wobble with the motion.

'Now you're confusing me, Scott. I'm not even sure these details will be available after all this time, but why the hell would you want them? And, tell me again, why would this turn into international headlines?'

'As I said, Oliver, I can't explain at the moment. Let's just say I'm looking for a missing passenger. One who was on the manifest before boarding but not after that.'

'You mean a passenger just disappeared? Surely the airline would have known that? Any missing passenger's automatically tannoyed and the flight won't take-off till he or she's found. What the hell's all this about, Scott?'

'I said...'

Oliver interrupted by saying, 'Then you'd better start explaining if you want my help. Especially this stuff about missing manifests from a sabotaged aircraft.'

'OK. There's a guy working at the Times who seemingly was appointed when no vacancy was advertised. He knows little or nothing about journalism, but he has a partner working with him, a young woman called Imogene. One night, after Heaton – that's his name – had way too much to drink, I questioned him again about his background in journalism. Then he finally told me the truth. He said he was due to fly on the Pan Am aircraft that crashed, but that Imogene, rescued him.'

'Rescued him? I see.'

'No you don't see, Oliver. Imogene, so Hardy told me was his Guardian Angel; and her penalty for having rescued him was to be forced to take human form - and then to oversee him for the rest of his life.'

'Jesus, Scott. Is this some kind of a joke? Or are you in any way being serious? Surely, you don't expect anyone to believe this, do you?'

There was a heavy sigh. Hardy had expected this. That was why he had been reluctant to tell Oliver the truth.

'Look, you can believe me or not. Right now there's no way I can prove this to you - that's why I didn't want to tell you the truth; I knew fucking well you wouldn't believe me.'

'OK... OK... let's assume for the moment you're telling me the truth; one of the ways to prove it, as opposed to asking this... Imogene... to back up your story ... is to have a look at the manifest you wanna see so badly.'

'And if that does prove it?'

'You may well have the makings of a serious international headliner!'

'Yeah - and one that you might well steal from me?'

"Hardly. All we'll have is your word for it - that and a manifest showing a missing passenger - if you're right. So let's see... Eileen!' he shouted to one of the girls at her computer. 'Gotta minute?'

'Oliver? What can I do for you?'

Eileen was evidently one of the senior girls. She was middle aged with a face that might once have been pretty; now it was simply plain with a frown on her forehead as though that was what had deleted her attractiveness. Her auburn hair, sweeping down across her face, disguised some of the frown.

'The Lockerbie crash... Do we have a record of the manifest from Pam Am?'

'I would think so. Do you want the original or just a copy?'

'If you can find it, I'd like the original.'

'Give me a few minutes, Oliver.' There was a gleam in her eye as she said this, telling Hardy that she was one of the girls that Oliver had had his gigantic leg over. Rather him than me! he thought.

'Have a coffee, Scott. You look as if you need one.'

'Thanks. So, what if we don't find anything?'

'I doubt we will find anything. The only manifests we're able to access are the ones released by Pan Am at the time of the crash.'

'So what the hell are we doing chasing these up?'

'Because if the real missing manifests aren't there, we have journalists' entitlement to question Pan Am.'

'You mean before they go into chapter eleven?'

'That still won't help them; if they refuse, we'll just ask the administrator.'

Shortly after, Eileen brought in the manifest.

'Not much here,' she said. She looked at Scott. 'You could've got this in New York.'

'Thanks, Eileen,' Oliver said, taking the sheets off her. 'Now. Where are we? Here we go – look, Scott, two hundred and fifty-seven passengers before boarding and two hundred and fifty-seven died in the crash; that was before the eleven people on the ground. So, there you have it. No sign of any missing passenger. So, where does that take us?'

'Fucked if I know, buddy. But I'm certain Heaton was telling me the truth; this woman Imogene is definitely an angel.'

'Hmmph. Is she indeed? The only thing left for us to do now is to wander over to the Pan Am offices and ask the manager for the actual manifest.'

'You think he'll give it to us? Just like that?'

'I doubt it. Look, Scott, why don't you book into a hotel, wander around London for a while, see some of the sights – you haven't visited London before, have you?'

Hardy nodded reluctantly.

'Can you recommend a hotel.'

'Sure. Why don't you check into Brown's, it's near the end of Lower Bond Street. It's an excellent hotel; I'll see you back here at say, around five- o'clock? Is that OK?'

'Sure. Good luck with the manifest.'

'I'll do my best.'

When he had left, Eileen turned to Oliver and said, 'He's a strange one. He's come all this way to look at a manifest that he could easily have seen in New York. Or do you think there's more to it?'

Oliver let out a long breath.

'Tell me, Eileen, what did you think of him?'

'Truth? I think he's more than weird. There's something murky about him; almost as though he can read our darkest thoughts.'

'That probably sums him up better than I could. But I don't think we should cross him – agreed?'

'Sure. I wouldn't like to get on the wrong side of him.'

After booking in at Brown's, Scott threaded his way through Saville Row and then on to Lower Regent Street where most of the upmarket shops were. He went into the Cashmere shop and bought a roll-neck sweater that cost him an arm and a leg. After that he wandered down to Piccadilly and admired the statue of Pegasus perched in the centre; he watched as a number of tourists took photos of the mythical icon. He didn't really know where he was going but a sign led him to Trafalgar Square. It was an impressive place with a giant statue of Nelson dominating the square.

By now he was getting tired, more so since he was still suffering from jet lag. So he flagged a taxi and asked to be shown the sights of the city. It was a truly remarkable journey; down the Mall and on to Buckingham Palace; thereafter along Bird Cage Walk, where the Queen's carriage drove her on her way to Parliament; then past the Houses of Parliament themselves and along the Thames and finally ending up at Harrods where he disembarked. The total cost, in Sterling, was close to thirty pounds, including the tip, which Hardy thought was well worth it. He then walked into Harrods for a look around and was amazed, not so much at the vast range of goods they sold, but at the prices of everything.

Someday pretty soon now, he thought grimly, I'll be able to afford to shop here.

He had a late lunch at a nearby coffee shop – in London they were called sandwich shops. He strolled over lunch, trying to delay the time before he was due to meet up again with Oliver.

Precisely on the hour, he walked into the offices of the Times' London address and met up with Oliver, who took him into one of the meeting rooms.

'So,' Hardy said, 'what've you got to show me?'

'Well, this is all very strange.'

'Tell me.'

'I have here the manifests before and after boarding. But there's something very odd about them.'

'Odd? How d'you mean?'

'Look. Here's the prior-to-boarding manifest and it shows the two-hundred and fifty seven passengers...'

'Does it show a Thomas Metzler?'

Oliver checked thoroughly and said, 'Yes, it does. Here, Thomas Metzler. Is that the guy you were looking for?'

Hardy nodded with restraint. This was certainly not what he was looking for.

'Is that it?' he asked.

'No. Not really.' He handed over a further manifest. 'That is, supposedly, the after-boarding manifest. As you can see it's all distorted. There is no way you can tell who actually was on board... I suspect that since all two-hundred or so passengers died, the airline reconstructed the whole thing for the world's media with all of the original names on it. Does that make sense?'

'Yes,' Hardy said, his unable to contain his excitement, 'this is exactly what I was looking for. You see, there may well have been the same number on the aircraft as on the pre-departure list, but what we don't know is if Metzler was on board. Most of the bodies were unrecognizable, so he could have been changed at the last minute. Or else,' he said sombrely, 'he wasn't on board.'

'You mean someone else took his place?'

'I don't know what I mean, Oliver,' He threw the manifest on the desk, 'except that this goes a long way towards proving my theory. Metzler wasn't on board that aircraft; either he was replaced by some unknown stranger, or else they flew with only three-hundred and fifty-six passengers.'

'But you'll never be able to prove that though, will you?'

'Probably not. But that's only a part of the puzzle I'm trying to fit together. But thank you anyway, Oliver. You've been a great help.'

'I take it you'd like me to keep quiet about this? Am I right?'

Hardy smiled. 'You guess right.' he said. 'And I owe you one.'

Hardy caught a late flight from Heathrow after cancelling his booking at Brown's. It was a shame, he thought; it might be nice to have stayed there and sampled the London nightlife, but he was busy and he had things to catch up on in New York.'

CHAPTER THIRTEEN

Tom finally met his mother during heavy snow at the end of February when she was visiting New York for a medical conference. They had already exchanged telephone calls without revealing much in the way of information. As far as Tom was concerned his mother thought he was a friend of her son's from Harvard. To be honest, it was enough for him just to hear her voice.

He met her as she arrived at Penn Station, and was taken aback when she gave him the warmest of hugs. He could feel the sensation emanate through the thick winter coat she was wearing. Even the blizzard didn't seem to put her off.

During their taxi ride to the hotel, through the snow drifts, they sat in companionable silence, Tom feeling quietly happy when his mother locked her arm in his. He still wasn't too sure why she wanted to see him and Imogene refused to reveal what had happened at the memorial service; other than to say that she had looked into the older woman's soul.

'Why aren't we going to your apartment, Tom?' Mary finally asked.

'Because Imogene has some guests there and it would be inconvenient.'

'But I thought she was an angel? At least that's what she told me, and I believed her. Why would an angel need to have meetings?'

Tom viewed her with astonishment.

'Mrs Metzler, how do you know she's an angel? I mean, as far as I know, you haven't exchanged a word with her yet.'

'Because she told me, not with words, who she really was – and who you are. In that single instant when our eyes met it was as though she was able to transmit her thoughts. So you don't have to be surprised. All Imogene did was to confirm a feeling I'd had for some time, mother's intuition if you like, that you weren't dead.'

'But you seem so calm about it! I'd have thought you'd be dumbfounded.'

'I know, it's weird, isn't it? But have you actually looked into her eyes, Tom? Seen how much love and compassion they communicate?'

Tom was still in shock.

'So you know about the Lockerbie disaster and how she changed flights for me?'

'Well, not exactly. All I know is that Imogene's responsible for you being here. I'm not sure exactly why she did it, all I do know is that you're still alive ...' she put her hand to her heart, suddenly too overcome to finish her sentence. 'Oh Tom,' she finally managed, struggling with the emotion in her voice, 'you can't believe how happy this makes me.'

'So, is it all right if I call you Mum?'

'No. I know it's hard, but I don't think it would be appropriate. Why don't you call me Mary? Let's keep pretending that you're, or rather were, a friend of Tom's at Harvard. That way no one needs to know.'

'What about Dad? Does he know?'

'No. You know that your father's an atheist; he wouldn't listen to me let alone believe me if I started telling him about angels, in fact we both know it would just make him angry. He'd probably think I needed sectioning.'

Tom didn't say anything, remembering that before meeting Imogene he too was an atheist, or at least an agnostic, neither believing in Heaven nor Hell. It was one of the few things that he had in common with his father. Now, confronted with the indisputable evidence of Imogene's existence he had been forced to think again.

Tom smiled; an image of his father's face if his mother did try and tell him popped into his head, and he nearly laughed out loud in amusement.

'OK, Mary. Shall we have dinner?'

'That would be nice. I'm not due at the conference until tomorrow, so let me have a shower and we'll meet up later and dine in the hotel. Is that all right with you?'

'Sure. I've got some work to do at the office, so why don't I join you in the lobby at around five-thirty for a drink first?'

The hotel restaurant wasn't too busy when they entered later that evening, so Tom chose a table in a quiet corner where they could talk uninterrupted.

'Well,' his mother said as soon as they were seated, 'I don't really know where to begin, it's all so bizarre. I mean...' She stopped, looking up into his eyes, confused about where to take the conversation next. 'I just have so much I want to say,' she shrugged.

'Let me go first, Mom... Sorry, Mary. But let's order first - we've plenty of time.'

Tom waited until the first course arrived, noticing that his mother was barely picking at her prawn salad.

'Aren't you hungry?' he asked.

'No, not really,' she pushed her fork into the mountain of iceberg lettuce and speared a prawn without looking. 'To be honest, since I saw Imogene I've found it hard to concentrate on anything much. I just can't seem to get my head around... well, around you being here.' Mary dropped any pretence of eating and pushed her plate to one side. 'It was in all the papers that you had died, along with all the others on the plane and those poor people on the ground. Can you imagine the terror they must have gone through? I just don't understand how you weren't on the plane.'

'I'd like to think I can understand how scared they must have been, but I know I can't. Something so awful is just unimaginable; bodies being blown apart in mid-air, torn to bits.' He shook his head in disbelief. 'It scares me even more when I'm reminded, like now, that I was supposed to be one of the victims.'

'So what happened?'

Slowly he took his mother through the events of that day, starting with his visit to the Natural History Museum and the strange girl, then his encounter with Imogene at the hotel bar and ending, as he explained, that she had handed him some travel papers for a return flight the following morning instead of on the Pan Am 747 flight in the evening. Mary looked more and more amazed as Tom continued.

'She also handed me a passport in the name of Tom Heaton; frankly, the photo looked nothing like me, I mean the real me.'

'But didn't you check to see if you were still booked on the 747 flight?' Mary interjected.

'Yes, of course I did! My name was still on their passenger list, or at least that was what they told me. I know it sounds strange, but I just knew she was trying to warn me about something, so I did as she said and caught the early morning TWA flight from London. When I arrived back at the office no one took any notice of me; it was as if I didn't exist. Then I heard about the explosion and I realised what had happened, but I promise you, Mary, I didn't know about it in advance.'

'So what did you do?'

'Do? I ran. I ran from the office all the way to my apartment and drank half a bottle of whisky. I knew something... something ethereal had happened but I had no idea what or why. I mean it wasn't as if I was someone famous, someone who might change the world. The... well, the next morning I woke up with the worst hangover and saw a note on the mat. It was from Imogene asking me to meet her in Starbucks.'

'What did she have to say? I mean, was she able to explain why... don't misunderstand me Tom, I'm so glad – so relieved – you're still alive, but surely she gave some explanation?'

'Oh, she did. Apparently I was a mistake, her mistake. She got herself into big trouble with the "Powers that Be" in the process. They, whoever "they" are, - I'm sure she called them The Celestial Tribunal - made her into human form and have insisted that she watches over me as long as I'm alive in case I cause a time paradox, as she calls it. Basically she has to make sure I don't do something that I couldn't have done if I were dead - as I should be. Otherwise I'd change the course of history and Imogene would be held to account.'

He shook his head in confusion.

'You have no idea how frustrating it is to be monitored nearly every minute of the day! It's also bizarre. I mean I'm glad to be alive but who wants to be under the shadow of an angel – especially an angel who's committed an indictable offence?'

'But what I don't understand is why you're now working at the New York Times,' Mary commented, seeming to accept his explanation without question. 'You had such a good job at Freedman's, with such important career prospects. Your father was so proud. How did you manage to get this job? You don't know anything about journalism.' She sighed and leant back in her seat, oblivious of the waiter removing her untouched food.

Tom took his time before replying.

'I got the job because all of my previous existence was extinguished at the moment of my death. I'm not talking about my qualifications or my experience. It's just that everyone thought I was dead, like you and dad, so in reality I ceased to exist, especially at Freedman's. I rang them a couple of times and they thought it was a sick wind-up; as far as they were concerned I'd died in the air crash. They even threatened to call the police if I didn't stop.

'So Imogene arranged the job for me. She knew I always wanted to be a journalist so she manipulated whoever it was to make it happen. You know how it is with angels – especially after your exchange with her at the memorial service. My apartment was cancelled, as you'd expect, and now I share a beautiful two-bedroom apartment with Imogene in Greenwich Village. Something I couldn't possibly afford but, well, she just arranges things. She never has any money, she simply arranges things.'

'Are you sharing her bed then?' his mother asked quizzically.

He shrugged, expressing his disappointment.

'I wish I could. But she won't allow it. She says that although she inhabits an earthly body, intrinsically she's still an angel.' He shrugged again. 'But she's so beautiful, I think I fell in love with her from the moment I met her.'

Mary nodded sympathetically.

'I know what you mean. She is very beautiful. It must be really difficult for you, feeling the way you do and having to live under the same roof. Can't you leave? Get yourself a place on your own? You must be earning good money now at The Times?'

Tom didn't reply for a moment, as if the idea had suddenly been put to him. Then he said, 'I guess I've been hoping that she might come round – you know, she might begin to feel the same way as I do. But I don't believe that's going to happen, not now after more than a year's gone by. I think you're right. Perhaps I'll start to look around.'

'Would you like me to advance you the money? I can afford it you know.'

'No. Thanks…' he was still having the utmost difficulty in addressing her by her Christian name, 'Mary. I doubt they'll allow me to own a flat as my resurrected self; remember, I'm not supposed to be here. Whatever I.D. documents I have are either forged or else they were transcribed in heaven.'

'Why don't you move down to Wilmington? At least we can be closer there and we could meet regularly. No one needs to know who you really are.'

'It's a nice offer, but I doubt Imogene would accept it for a second. She was insistent we meet but she wants us to maintain a respectable distance. Anyway, we can still see each other when you come to New York; it's only two and a half hours on the train.'

They continued to talk for hours about angels and the meaning of life after death. It had always been his mother's conviction there was a Heaven and Hell, or at least a Heaven. Her belief that angels were part of the natural order of things enabled her to trust everything that Imogene had said - unlike his father, who had graduated from an agnostic into a committed atheist, refusing to acknowledge that there were other opinions besides his own. If his mother brought up the subject of religion he either buried his head in the newspaper or disappeared into his study.

Tom told his mother that it was at his father's insistence that he had studied law, so his change of direction into journalism, despite the circumstances, was rather welcome. At least now he could sample the life he might have had. They arranged to meet the following afternoon, after his mother's conference was over.

Later, lying on his bed, he couldn't help thinking about Imogene, how beautiful she was, how much she captivated him and how much he loved her. He had agreed with his mother that he should look for another apartment, but in reality the thought of being without his 'angel' brought on a crushing wave of depression. He couldn't really live with her and neither could he survive without her.

CHAPTER FOURTEEN

Early evening the next day, Tom met up with his mother and took her to St. Patrick's Cathedral on 5th Avenue before she caught her train. It was somewhere she always felt at home when she visited New York. There was a service taking place at one of the small altars and Mary went to observe it while Tom read some of the literature at the back of the church.

'Were you aware that Imogene's here?' his mother asked, pointing towards a small group at the side altar.

'No, I had no idea. Perhaps she's come to say goodbye to you.'

'But how would she know where we are?'

Tom grinned mischievously. 'I don't think there's anything she doesn't know. Let's go and ask her, shall we?'

Just then Imogene came across and kissed Mary on the cheek. Mary rubbed her cheek as though the exchange was engagingly spiritual.

'Hello, Mary. I've come to ask if the two of you might join me in a prayer of thanksgiving at the Saint John Baptist altar… It might help me a little and I'm certain it will help both of you.'

They nodded their agreement and followed Imogene down the long central aisle towards a little chapel, where they knelt together at the altar in supplication and listened to her plea for forgiveness and support. She also said a few words about Tom and his mother and prayed that God would watch over them and give them His blessing.

'Thank you,' she whispered, squeezing their hands, as they left the altar. 'Now it's time to say goodbye.'

She leaned forward again and kissed Mary on the cheek. 'I hope you've enjoyed being in New York and spending time with your son.' She glanced over to Tom. 'You certainly appear to have cheered him up.'

'Will I be able to see him again?' His mother asked.

'I don't see why not. Providing you give us some notice and you have sufficient cover at home.' She then hugged Mary and stroked her face lovingly. 'You've been very brave – and don't worry, I'll look after him.'

A little while later, feeling spiritually uplifted, Mary caught her train from Penn Station. It suddenly dawned on her that her emotions were probably due to Imogene's appearance in her life, together with the comfort she felt at the sight of her son. She knew she would never be able to tell anyone but that did not lessen her relief - or her enjoyment of her secret.

CHAPTER FIFTEEN

Unknown to Mary, as she went to catch the train home from Penn Station, she was being followed, as she had been since meeting up with Tom the previous evening. The culprit, Scott Hardy, had followed Tom from the moment he went unannounced from the office. Scott knew that there was no staff briefing, so he had to be going on a personal errand. His journalistic instincts and his curiosity about the young reporter prompted him to follow him to Penn Station where Tom met this middle-aged woman. He watched, hidden, as they embraced each other.

Must be a relative, Scott thought, slightly disappointed. But he followed them anyway, right up to the hotel on Fifth Avenue where the woman appeared to be staying. He waited until they went into the elevator, and then checked the register for her name.

Mrs Mary Metzler, he read, from Delaware. Jesus! Wasn't that the name that Heaton had given him when he related his story about the angel? He was puzzled. This didn't exactly substantiate Heaton's story but it did lend it credence.

The register didn't list her hometown but he figured it must be close to Philadelphia in Pennsylvania. Knowing that part of the country reasonably well, he felt safe assuming that it was likely that she lived in Wilmington.

'She's here for the medical convention,' said Brent the receptionist, who knew Scott very well from the Times. 'Two days, I believe. It's something to do with children.'

'So what's her relationship to the young man she is with?' he enquired.

'Don't know, tell the truth. Want me to find out, Scott?' he asked.

'Yeah,' he said, slipping a fifty into the other man's waiting hand. 'See if you can do it so she doesn't know. I don't want the man finding out someone's checking into him. There'll be another fifty when you give me the information. Ring me at the office later.'

'Will do.'

It was the following day when the receptionist rang him with the news. Mary Metzler was a paediatrician operating out of the Du Pont Hospital in Wilmington; the receptionist had been correct in guessing that she was here in New York to attend a Medical Convention for Genetic Child Ailments.

'So what's the attachment to the young guy?' Scott asked.

'Well, it's strange really. The Metzlers lost their son in the Lockerbie disaster – when was that, just over a year ago? I've checked, Scott, and there doesn't seem to be any connection between the two. At least not one that I can discover.'

'Is he a nephew maybe? Or maybe related through his mother? Or maybe she had another son?'

'No. No other children. Tom was the only child.'

'Tom?'

'Yeah. Tom Metzler. Christ, he was only twenty-two when he died.'

'Curious. But thanks anyway, Brent, I'll need to check into it.'

This was something that definitely had to be looked into.

Scott puzzled about it over the following couple of days. It wasn't until the receptionist phoned to let him know that Mrs Metzler was due to check out that he decided to follow her.

Before he left he asked Brent what had happened the evening before.

'Well, they had dinner here in the hotel, stayed for a couple of drinks, she gave him a big - and I mean a big - hug and then they went their separate ways.'

'Did anyone hear what they were talking about?'

'No. But the maître de said they were whispering – kinda secretively.'

'Yeah. Right. Now you're making it sound like a conspiracy.' He sighed. Obviously nothing important had happened.

Upgrading his ticket to first class, Scott joined his quarry in the same compartment and hastily placed his laptop on his knee. Now he could be sure to see where she got off, even though he was convinced that it would be Wilmington. He settled himself down for the journey, noticing that the weather was getting worse. No doubt by the time they reached their destination it would be snowing heavily.

'Why have you summoned me here today?'

'Because, Imogene, we need an explanation of your behaviour.'

'Behaviour? I don't know what you mean.'

'Oh, we think you do. You recently arranged for your protégé to attend his own memorial service in Wilmington. There you introduced him, albeit by some cabalistic method, to his mother. What do you suppose gave you the right to do that?'

'Well… Tom had become depressed… He was verging on the suicidal. I felt that if I brought him and his mother together it would help him. And probably help her too. And it worked. Now he seems to be much more settled – more relaxed about his situation. So I don't know how you can blame me for that. I mean I was helping him, isn't that what I'm supposed to be doing?'

We thought you'd claim that, Imogene. Well let us explain what it is you've achieved, shall we?

First off, you were instructed to oversee this young gentleman by removing his previous existence from any earthly contacts. Prior to the meeting with his mother you were treading a fine line but at least you were achieving your objective. Depressed he might well have been but you should have reminded him that he had no right even to be alive...'

But that's what I did... repeatedly. But it didn't impress him... in fact he kept saying he wished I'd let him die on that aircraft. I was sure he was going to take his own life...'

Then that's what you should have allowed to happen. We realise you're inhabiting an earthly body but that's no excuse for your humanitarian behaviour. You have to remain detached, focused only on your primary concern and that is to avoid, at all costs, the time paradox, something you're doing little or nothing to avoid at the moment.'

'So you're saying I should have encouraged him to commit suicide?'

'If needs be, yes.'

If you'll pardon me, Chairman, but that doesn't make sense. I went to all that trouble to rescue him from that air crash and now you're proposing that what I should be doing is urging him to take his own life. Is that correct?'

No. We're not asking you to do anything... However, if the young man wishes to terminate his existence then you must allow it to happen.'

Well, I don't agree with that. Look, I realise that you're all frustrated by my actions but I've cooperated with your directives. I inhabit this wretched body, but at the same time avoid any of the temptations that come with it, and I also try not to create a situation that might lead to the time paradox. So, would you mind telling me, please, how does introducing him to his mother cause a paradox to manifest itself?'

Because, having introduced him to his mother, both in Wilmington and recently here in New York, you've allowed an intruder to impose himself on the scene. Someone who, given the slightest prompting, will energise himself to uncover what he now suspects is some kind of conspiracy.'

'An intruder? I don't understand. Who d'you mean?'

'One of your colleagues at the New York Times – a Scott Hardy. Your boss I believe.'

'Oh shit!' She let out the expletive. 'How did he get involved? The last I heard the News Editor had discouraged him. What's prompted his interest again in Tom?'

'Because your protégé has revealed to him the simple truth about the air crash – how he was supposed to have travelled on the Pan Am flight and how you rescued him because you are an angel... You can guess the rest.'

'But... but Tom didn't say anything to me about this. What on earth was he playing at?'

'We believe he revealed the truth thinking it would persuade Hardy not to investigate any further. But, as we've now seen, the opposite has occurred. The information has inspired him to delve further. He has, albeit indirectly, uncovered some truths about Mrs Metzler: where she comes from, why she was in New York... Now, he's seeking to unravel any secrets she might be withholding...'

'And how can he possibly do that?'

'Because, right now, he's following her on the train from Penn Station. He hopes she'll lead him to her home and from there he'll be able to progress his enquiries further and uncover the relationship between Mrs Metzler and her son. And believe us, Imogene, he's a resourceful investigator and he won't stop till he confirms what he already suspects.'

'We have to stop him.'

No. Not us. You will have to stop him. Otherwise this whole charade will unfold before us and what might happen after that could be a disaster. And a further warning to you...'

'Not another one!' she interrupted. 'What is it this time?'

'You must maintain a cautionary watch over your emotional responses. In substance you're anthropological but your essence is divine; you're still a spiritual being.'

'Are you suggesting I'm becoming human? With human emotions?'

'We're merely asking that you're watchful – should you feel any temptations arise in your being then we'd urge you to place yourself before God at the altar. He will counsel you. Further, you must consider Augusto a spiritual template; he'll guide you through your human confusions.

At a certain time, if things progress as we fear they might, you'll be offered a safe haven where you'll find sanctuary.'

'I don't know what you're talking about.'

'You're not expected to at present - but you will eventually. For the time being, please deal with this interference.'

'I will deal with it,' she said, sighing with the weariness of it all. She left the Tribunal shaking her head and wondering what she had allowed to transpire.

⟞══⟝

'Excuse me, sir. We've reached our destination.'

'What? Sorry… What did you say?' Scott rubbed the sleep from his eyes and then scanned the deserted carriage. 'Where… Where are we?' he stammered. 'What d'you mean our destination? Where the hell is this place?'

'Washington DC, Sir. We tried to wake you back in Philadelphia – and then again in Baltimore. But we couldn't rouse you.'

'But I wanted to get off at…' he rubbed his eyes again.

'Yes, Sir. Where did you want to disembark?'

'I… I don't remember. I do know I didn't want to come as far as Washington. Oh shit! What time is it?'

'It's 19.30 hours, Eastern Seaboard time. I'm sorry but we can't leave you here overnight. The cleaners are waiting to service this carriage.' The attendant stretched out a hand and pointed to the doorway. 'Please, sir, if you don't mind? Oh, and that'll be a further 182 dollars.'

Scott was confused as he left the train. He couldn't remember falling asleep; neither could he recall what his ultimate destination had been.

'What the hell was I doing on that fucking train?' he asked aloud. 'And why was I going to Washington?'

He checked his diary but there was no entry. The only indication was a reference to Tom Heaton. But that was all. No clue as to why he should have been on a train. Perhaps I was following someone? he thought. Someone whose name for some reason I can't remember, and then I fell asleep.

It still didn't make any sense. How could he be following someone and then forget who it was? He shook his head, and then realised that he would still have to make his way back to New York. On impulse, he summoned a cab and instructed the driver to take him to Dulles Airport. No doubt he would have to catch the red-eye; he only hoped his memory would reassert itself in due course.

CHAPTER SIXTEEN

Life for Tom resumed its monotonous and often repetitious routine. Some of the time he enjoyed his work, some of the time he enjoyed being with Imogene, especially when they were alone and he was able to talk. But despite any fulfilment he might experience, there was still something missing from his life. Both he and Imogene were aware of the problem; it was suspended between the two of them like a silent but invisible threat.

Dramatic events unfolded around the world, some of which caused excitement at the New York Times. In 1989 the Berlin Wall came down, along with the fall of Communism, and in 1990 Margaret Thatcher witnessed her own downfall in the UK. Neither of these developments roused Tom from his lethargy; he carried on with a sense of frustration all but consuming him.

That was until he met Molly.

One Tuesday morning, Scott Hardy's news desk got a tip off from one of their stringers about a fatal street stabbing, close to the Bronx. As Scott was busy following another lead he grudgingly sent Tom down to interview witnesses, hoping for an exclusive on the story. His first impression was that this was a particularly vicious mugging. Hastily scrawling his copy, Tom was astounded to be pushed aside by a very attractive female demanding that the witness Tom had just spent ten minutes chatting up give her an interview for CNN Television. He was so taken aback by the intrusion he allowed her to dominate the proceedings. It transpired from her questioning that the incident was not a street mugging but a deliberate premeditated murder. Tom followed her in open mouthed awe as she proceeded to question other witnesses, including two detectives, until eventually she was able to determine that this was a drug related revenge attack. No doubt the officers involved would incur the wrath of their superiors for releasing vital information in an unscripted television interview. Pleased with herself, Tom watched as she smirked happily, impressed with her own powers of persuasion.

That was how he first met Molly; a five foot four pocket-battleship, dressed sombrely in a dark blue suit, with subtly tinted red hair; her pale grey eyes, which had an interrogative quality about them, seeming to draw Tom into their depths, encouraging him to wish he could know her better.

She hardly spoke to him throughout the interviews but after she finished she handed him a business card, flashing him a mischievously enchanting smile, and asking him to call her sometime.

It was a defining moment in his life. He said nothing to Imogene and called Molly two days later to arrange to meet for lunch.

'Hi. I'm Molly, Molly Sinclair,' she said with a smile. 'It took you long enough to call me.'

'Sorry,' he was so nervous he almost stammered. 'I was quite busy filing the story you gave me. I'm Tom, by the way, Tom Heaton. You probably don't know it but I work at the New York Times. A Crime reporter.'

'Really? I guess you're new at the job? I know most of the people at the Times but we haven't met before, have we?'

He laughed. 'No, I would have remembered.' Grimacing to find himself coming out with such a trite comment he continued, 'I'm not that new, but think I was so hypnotised by your reporting skills that I almost forgot what I was there for! Tell me, Molly, are you always that assertive, or was that a special day?'

'If you're working for CNN, in a man's world, you have to be direct.' She challenged him, and then glancing flirtatiously from under long eyelashes she continued 'Anyway, it is all part of my perspicacity.'

'Aaah, you are telling me you have the ability to assess situations shrewdly and draw sound conclusions. I bet you don't use words like that when you're interviewing! Or are you trying to impress me?' Tom was surprised to find himself flirting back.

She shrugged, suddenly serious again. 'I doubt you need to be impressed. It's just that you looked like you were struggling and I knew there was a story that you were missing, and of course I had a deadline. What you didn't know at the time was that the victim was known to us on the Crime Desk – we knew he was involved in drugs so it was likely that this was a revenge attack.'

'Why didn't you tell me at the time? And here was me believing you were some kind of an investigative genius …'

She didn't say anything as they both ordered a Caesar salad and a bottle of Perrier water.

'As you mentioned, Molly, we've never met before,' he started to break the silence a few moments later. 'I mean I've seen you on television, but I'm surprised we haven't bumped into each other before now, especially in the courtrooms.'

Molly chuckled as she dug into her salad. 'I doubt you would have met me – that was my first live interview. Before that I was merely a runner, someone who follows the 'Lead' and takes orders. Sure, I've been in front of the cameras before, but only as an assistant.'

'So how come you were given the opportunity?' Tom leant forward showing interest.

'Because Steve Simpson was on sick-leave, he's the Crime Anchorman, so I jumped at the chance to go down there.'

'And now? Have you moved up a rung?'

She shook her head. 'I don't know yet. I'm hoping the interview two days ago will raise my profile and help me up the career ladder. Like I said, it's hard to get on in a man's environment.'

'I thought we were out of the dark old days and things had got better! Surely it should be the best person for the job!' Tom was astounded; he had always thought CNN a progressive company with a rigorous commitment to equal opportunities. 'Anyway, you gave a damn good account of yourself; I think they'd be crazy not to promote you.'

She reached across and touched his hand. 'You're very sweet, Tom Heaton. So tell me, how long have you worked at the New York Times?'

Tom kept his hand under hers. He wasn't sure whether or not she was winding him up or if this was a serious approach. Fleetingly he thought of Imogene and what she might say. Pushing this thought to the back of his mind he smiled back at Molly.

'I've … I've been there for just over a year. Started, a bit like you, as an assistant and then graduated finally to the Crime Desk.'

'And do you enjoy it? I mean, what did you do before the Times?'

He hesitated for a moment. He had never been good at lying. 'I worked at a provincial newspaper, and yes, I do enjoy it.'

'Good to meet a man happy in his work, which paper was that?'

'Oh, you wouldn't know it. It was a small town paper in Delaware. I got the opportunity to come to New York through a friend of mine and, rather like you,

I thought it might help me up the ladder.'

'I know Delaware quite well, Tom.'

He nodded but maintained his silence, afraid that he might give himself away.

Molly got up from the table. 'We'll have to do this again. Do you have a card?' she asked.

'I'd like to,' he said, giving her one of his business cards. 'Perhaps we could go out to dinner next time?'

'We'll see. I have to go now – I'll call you. Bye Tom.'

CHAPTER SEVENTEEN

After she left he sat at the table for a while puzzling at the encounter and wondering if she would call. Molly was certainly enigmatic; one minute she was outgoing, bubbling and vivacious, the next she was coldly assertive, all business like, as if she were late for a meeting. He shook his head, paid the bill, and walked back to the office. At the very least she had done him a favour with the story; what he had thought was a mugging gone wrong had turned out to be a revenge killing making front page news, with his name as the by-line.

He heard nothing from Molly for a few days, not that he was disturbed, after all, he kept telling himself, they had only met for a quick lunch. Imogene had left him alone recently. As far as the office was concerned she was still his assistant, sometimes accompanying him on assignment, but by and large she left him to follow up whatever story he was working on. They still gave the outside world the impression that they were a couple, but in private they were lifetimes apart. Imogene was outwardly considerate; she was kind and sometimes compassionate. But she refused to be drawn into a discussion about sex, which almost obsessively, was occupying his thoughts. She made it clear time and time again that although she inhabited an earthly body, doing many of the things that humans do, she would not share her body with him or anyone else in the world. Inherently, she was, and would always be, an angel.

Frankly, he was becoming a little sick of hearing about it, but he was still deeply in love with her. In his mind she was a virtual goddess, but there remained a widening gap between them after her proclamations. So he found himself wondering about Molly, wishing that she would ring, if only to create a diversion from his lustful thoughts.

Finally, four days after their lunch together she did ring him, inviting him to dinner that evening at a plush Italian restaurant by Columbus Circle, close to the CNN Time Warner buildings. This time he had to tell Imogene. She frowned on hearing the news.

'How did you meet her?' she asked suspiciously.

He told her the truth. 'We met when I was interviewing witnesses to a street stabbing. Molly works for CNN.'

She frowned again. 'Why would CNN be interested in a street stabbing?'

'Because the victim was known to them – he was evidently into drugs and this was some kind of a revenge killing.'

'I see,' she said, unconvincingly. 'And you hit it off straight away – at least enough for her to invite you to dinner.'

'We had lunch together the other day.' He muttered feeling embarrassed.

Her lips tightened. 'And you thought I might not be interested? Didn't it occur to you that I should be involved in your assignations?'

'It isn't an assignation - it's a date with an attractive redhead! Since when do I have to ask your permission before going out? I am over twenty one you know!' Tom's sense that he should have told her made him even more defensive than usual. 'I haven't been in a relationship for over twelve months and am fed up with living like a monk! Anyway, why should you care? It's not like I can get her pregnant or anything, is it?'

'I'm not suggesting you might make her pregnant, Tom.' Imogene frowned as she tried to explain to him without making him even angrier. 'It is just that I do need to know everything about her… What's her family like… Has she been married before… What are her intentions…'

'Intentions??' Tom interrupted incredulously. 'Intentions? What planet are you on? We've only met a couple of times!'

Imogene motioned for him to be quiet. 'Look, if I don't know these things, how can I decide whether she is a threat or not?' She had in mind Scott Hardy and the secret he had divulged; sure that Hardy would not rest from investigating Tom now he was fortified with some dangerous ammunition.

'What do you mean a threat? She is just a nice girl who happens to be showing a bit of interest in me; can't you just leave it at that?'

Imogene sighed; Tom really was testing her patience. 'I have to assess whatever risks you might be drawn into. I mean, we don't know anything about her. Do we?'

He frowned at this imposition. 'Listen, why do we need to know anything? What if this is just a date with the only objective to spend a night together? Real women have desires too, you know, and I'm not entirely unattractive.'

Imogene blushed; obviously he had embarrassed her. For a moment it crossed his mind that she might be jealous.

'Yes, I know,' she continued to explain, 'but when someone, a complete stranger, makes you a target, I have to be suspicious. And if this does translate into something more permanent then I will still need to be involved.'

He grinned at her obvious discomfort. 'What are you suggesting, Imogene, a threesome?'

'Don't be so flippant,' she snapped. 'I'm being perfectly serious. If this relationship persuades you to do something we will both regret then it becomes my responsibility to stop you. So I would appreciate it if you kept me in the picture.'

Tom sighed. He couldn't even have a simple relationship without her interfering.

'Yeah. OK.' He promised, trying to sooth her suspicions, 'But only if it develops into something more meaningful.'

The row left a further element of friction between them and had Imogene been anything like human then Tom would have said she was sulking. She was certainly worried - that was for sure.

CHAPTER EIGHTEEN

Dinner with Molly that night was very enjoyable. He had deliberately dressed casually in loose-fitting trousers and a black shirt, with his now favourite pair of loafers. Molly looked as if she had just come from the office in a pin striped suit, only a lace blouse softening the severe cut of her wide legged trousers and double breasted jacket. It had been a long time since Tom had dated a young woman, particularly one as attractive as Molly. She was vivacious, almost on a high, and Tom hoped that her euphoria wasn't chemically manufactured. He was afraid to ask in case it offended her, but if his misgivings were correct then he would be duty bound to report it to Imogene.

'You're lovely,' she said enigmatically, gazing at him.

'So are you,' he confirmed. 'I didn't realise you'd be so relaxing to be with.'

'Yes. We make a good couple, don't we?' Molly stopped short, seemingly horrified by what she had said. 'Oh, don't let me frighten you off!'

He felt his cheeks colouring. 'No I won't. It still surprises me that you find me attractive.'

Her eyes twinkled. 'What, are you joking with me, Tom? You're gorgeous!'

He grinned and placed his hand over hers. 'Well, you're rather gorgeous too, you know.'

'You're so sweet.' She said squeezing his hand in return. 'Shall we go home to my apartment?'

She said it so disarmingly that Tom choked back his gasp. She must have read his mind! He had been sitting there with an increasing erection while Molly rubbed her leg across his calf. Hurriedly, he paid the check, and as they left the restaurant he felt her hand in his as she leaned over and gave him a kiss.

She only lived a few minute's walk away, and he did wonder if the whole evening had been calculated. Shrugging off his doubts he told himself he didn't care. He was so frustrated after all this time, longing for the touch of a woman, that he would have disregarded any warnings that Imogene might have given him.

Molly's living accommodation was spacious but impersonal. It was almost, he thought, as though she spent little or no time there. A large lounge was filled with numerous settees, covered with a scattering of cushions, around an open fireplace that looked as though it had never been lit. One corner of the room was entirely given over to a state-of- the-art television system and when he looked closely there appeared to be some kind of computer attached to it. The only significant feature of the room was the array of telephone systems, each with its own automatic answering service. But other than these utilities there was no sign of residence whatsoever. They didn't pause in the living room, nor did she ask him if he would like a drink. The only concession to his presence in the flat was for Molly to slip off his coat and hang it on a nearby hallstand. Then, in front of him, she stepped out of her suit and released her bra, then, gripping his hand tightly, she led him into the bedroom where she wrapped her arms around him, smothering him with kisses, her tongue deep inside his throat.

As they lay naked on the bed she asked him, 'Have you come prepared?'

'No. No,' he gasped. 'We don't need it – I've had a vasectomy.'

'A vasectomy? Why? You haven't got a brood of children somewhere, have you?'

'No. It's only temporary. I can have it reversed whenever I need to.' It was becoming second nature to him to lie.

Then he was lost. Well and truly lost; instantly transformed from the almost dutiful eunuch to a ferocious animal, allowing her soft flesh to devour him. He literally couldn't get enough of her. It was as if he were drowning in the pleasure her body gave him; one minute he was on top of Molly, the next she mounted him and rode him hard.

They continued virtually through the night, thrusting and withdrawing with repetitive enjoyment for both of them. He remembered dozing a little before climbing back on her again, his erection directing his body with almost mindless will, trying to relieve himself of the months and months of deprivation.

'My God!' she said at last, breathlessly. 'When did you last have sex?'

'I can't remember it seems so long ago.'

'Did I ask before, do you have children?'

'No. No children.'

'But I thought you had a partner. At least that's the gossip about you around town.'

'You mean Imogene? The girl I share with. What do they say about her?'

She leant forward towards him, exposing her breast and causing Tom to feel aroused again. 'That you and her are an item. I mean you work together and you live together. And I assume you share a bed, so how comes no sex and why the vasectomy? How old are you, Tom? Twenty-four? Twenty-five? If you haven't got any kids then you're very young to take such drastic action - unless of course you actually hate them.'

Tom turned away, unable to respond. After a while he said, 'No. I don't hate them. It's just that… well, if you really want to know they'd be in danger of inheriting a fatal disease from me.'

This was the story he had agreed with Imogene in the event that something like tonight should ever happen.

'Jesus! Does that mean that you have it? Is it terminal?'

He smiled. 'No. I'm a carrier, which means that I can pass it on. Shall we change the subject, Molly? It isn't something I really like to talk about.'

'Sure. I'm sorry – it must be awful for you.' She climbed out of bed. 'I had better get ready for work.'

'Yeah. Me too. Will I see you again?' he asked, suddenly nervous.

She paused, naked, on the way to the bathroom. 'Would you like to?' she asked, pouting her lips.

Tom grinned. 'I think you know I would.' He strode across the floor and gave her a kiss. 'I'll ring you.'

'Sure. But I think you should get dressed first!'

CHAPTER NINETEEN

Imogene was waiting for him in the office when he arrived, a serious expression on her face.

'So, what happened?'

'What is it you want, Imogene? A graphic description of the night's events?'

'You know exactly what I mean, there's no need to be sarcastic. I was worried about you – I still am.'

'Yeah, sorry.' Tom had the grace to hang his head. 'Well there was nothing at all to be worried about. I had a great time with Molly. We got on really well.'

'Very well, by the look of you!' she retorted sharply.

He grinned. 'Well, since you mention it, yes we did. I had almost forgotten what sex was like.'

'Are you going to see her again?' she said ignoring the jibe.

He frowned. 'What is this, Imogene? An interrogation?'

She looked startled at his response. 'I'm concerned, that's all,' she pleaded.

Tom gave her a wicked smile. 'You're not jealous, are you?'

She raised her head disdainfully. 'Don't be ridiculous. It's like I said before, if you're going to make something of this with her then I need to know exactly who she is.' Her hand went up in the air. 'Of course I know that she works at CNN, you told me. But we don't know anything about her. Has she been married? Does she have any children? Does she already have a boyfriend? What about her parents? You know the kind of things I'm interested in, Tom.'

'Yes, but why? Why would you think she might be a potential danger for me? For fuck's sake, I've only just met her and, apart from being incredibly sexy, she seems to be a really nice person.' He shrugged. 'You aren't making any sense, Imogene.'

'Not to you, I'm not. But how do you know this isn't just a - what do you call it? A set up?'

He chuckled at her definition. 'Now you're the one being ridiculous. A set up by whom? And why? What on earth can she find out about me that we haven't already rehearsed thousands of times?'

'What about Scott Hardy? Isn't this the type of thing he's likely to engage in?'

'I haven't heard anything from Scott Hardy since I told him …'

'Told him what, Tom?' she interrupted.

He cast his eyes away from her. 'Well, since I told him the truth… you know, about the Lockerbie disaster… about how you were an angel and how you saved me…'

She looked at him in purported horror, as if this were the first she had heard of it. 'I don't believe this. Why did you reveal that to him? What the fuck did you think you were doing?'

'Oh come on,' he stated flatly. 'He reacted just as I thought he would. He said I was being sarcastic and fantasizing and that seemed to be the end of it. As I've said we haven't heard anything from him since then.'

She frowned, almost as though she was collecting her thoughts. Then she said with an edge to her voice, 'You might not have heard anything, but I have. Did you know that he tried to follow your mother home to Delaware on the train? What do you think that was all about, Tom?'

Tom's eyes shot open at the news. 'Oh Christ! Do you think I triggered that off?'

'Well something did and it certainly wasn't anything I said. I had to stop him.'

He looked apologetic. 'How did you do that?'

'I sent him off to sleep. He didn't wake up until the train arrived at Washington DC. But I know he still suspects something. Maybe he believes that Mary really is your mother, although I doubt that.'

'Well, I don't believe it.' He spread his arms around his face and his body. 'Look at me. No one would know I was the same person as Tom Metzler. Are you sure you're not imagining this and that really you are jealous of Molly? That's what this is all about, isn't it?' He grinned at her as if he'd caught her out. For a second he thought she might be going to hit him.

'Can you get it through your thick head that this isn't anything to do with jealousy,' she flashed at him. 'I've told you before, that's a human trait and not something I share. Let me remind you, Tom Metz...' she hesitated, a puzzled look on her face as if she couldn't understand why she had almost committed the cardinal sin. Then eventually she said, 'I'm sorry. That was foolish of me ...'

'Another human trait.' he cut in.

'Look,' she said, somewhat apologetically, 'we both realise that we're in a difficult situation and if you accuse me of jealousy it's precisely because of what we do share. You're supposed to be my boyfriend and our masquerade could disintegrate, leaving us both exposed. Particularly if you start spreading the word about me being an angel'

He snapped back at her. 'So, in truth, you don't want me to go out with other women? Is that it? You prefer that I continue my life as a sexless eunuch? Is that really what you want?'

Then something happened that Tom thought he would never see; tears formed in her eyes and trickled down her face. He didn't say anything but went over to her and held her in his arms. 'I love you, Imogene, very much. I couldn't do anything to hurt you. But please, don't make me live my life without love.'

'What can I give you? What is it you want?'

'I daren't tell you – not without offending you.'

'I… I can't do it,' she said sobbing. 'I love you Tom, more than you'll ever know. But you have to understand how hard it is for me at times to cling on to being an angel. My body's becoming more and more sensitive and more and more vulnerable to the temptations of the flesh. If I listen to these sirens they'll destroy me. You have to help me!'

She returned his embrace leaning her head on his shoulders. Tom wanted to kiss her, but at the last minute she drew away. Instead, he kissed her on her forehead and held her even tighter. She had just told him that she truly loved him. It surprised him, but in a way it was the most natural thing she had ever uttered,

'I will try to understand,' he said, genuinely.

'You must be discreet,' she said, wiping away her tears. 'And please, will you try not to describe your sexual details to me? I'll still have to check up on Molly if only to protect us.'

'I promise, Imogene, I will try to help you,' he said.

'I need to go to the Bronx,' Imogene said, as if she were talking to herself.

'Pardon?'

'To the monastery. I really think I need a refuge; somewhere away from all of this.'

Tom shook his head. It was one of those mysterious statements she made from time to time. He didn't argue with it.

CHAPTER TWENTY

'So how did it go?' Scott asked Molly. They were lounging about on the sofa in the apartment they had shared for the last twelve months. It had been Scott's idea to coax Molly into seducing Tom and he was anxious to discover how it had gone. Molly threw her head back and laughed, holding out her glass to indicate she would like Scott to top it up. 'Exactly as planned, darling,' she said swallowing a little white wine. 'I have to say though, that he fucks like the proverbial rabbit. He genuinely believes that I picked him up because he is so ... so enchanting! It was like feeding candy to a greedy child. He's also convinced the apartment we spent the night in is my home. I just hope he never finds out it belongs to CNN.'

He nodded his head. 'Good. So where do we go from here?'

'Don't be so eager, Scott. This relationship has to develop. We are treading dangerous ground here – that is if you're right and whatever he told you produces fruit.'

'Look, Molly, something in what he says already is fruitful. I checked on the Lockerbie disaster and there was a guy on board called Tom ...'

'Tom who?' she cut in. 'My Tom?'

Scott shook his head. 'I don't know – at least not for certain. It was someone called Metzler, which is the same name as the woman who your Tom met in New York. I also checked and the dead guy did work at Freedman's the lawyers, as he told me.'

She frowned. 'So, why are you confusing Heaton with some guy who died in the crash? I don't see the connection between them.'

'You're forgetting his story; that a Guardian Angel saved him from the crash. Surely, if that were true then he would have to change his name, wouldn't he?'

Molly screwed up her eyes as though she were having difficulty concentrating. 'Yeah, assuming that what he told you was the truth.'

'I've thought of that already. But why would Mary Metzler want to contact him in New York if there wasn't some kind of a relationship between them?'

She shook her head. 'I dunno. I thought that's what we're trying to work out – well that and the substance of his story. Isn't that why I'm sleeping with him?' She questioned him with a piercing look.

'Yes, of course, but it isn't the only strange thing to happen is it? I followed Mrs Metzler on the train from Penn Station, heading towards Delaware, when the next thing I know I'm woken up in Washington D.C. with no idea how I got there!'

'You fell asleep,' Molly interrupted cynically, pouring another glass and keeping the bottle of wine next to her.

'I realise that,' he said, biting off the words. 'But when have you ever heard of an insomniac falling instantly asleep and having to be woken by a train attendant?' He glared at her for a moment. 'No. Something happened. Something that fits in with what this Tom character was telling me about a mysterious Guardian Angel. I know why I was on that train because I had Brent, from the hotel, on the phone yesterday asking me if I'd followed that woman all the way to Delaware.'

Molly retained the smile on her face but Scott was unsure whether it was humour or if she was getting pissed.

'It still sounds bizarre,' she commented. 'And you've got me behaving like an unpaid whore trying to reveal Tom's secrets.'

'No. You misunderstand me, Molly. His secret's already out. What we're looking for is incontrovertible proof – something that will underpin what he's been telling me.'

'You mean like his partner's an angel who saved him from the crash? Oh come on, Scott, isn't that stretching fiction too far? How would you ever be able to prove it?'

He continued to glare at her as though she was stretching his patience. 'Yeah? And what if the woman I followed really is his mother and she knows what actually took place on the night of the air crash? And what if we were able to get hold of DNA to prove he is the same person? And what if falling asleep on the train was because it was induced? What if this Imogene woman actually is an angel?'

'Of course, that would explain why you fell asleep – it was the angel who caused it.' She smirked at his repetitiveness.

'I'm not joking. Think of the fucking story we could both have! You break it in CNN as our front page headline comes out.'

Molly scowled as if she had heard enough. 'Wonderful, but I still don't see how following that woman could have benefited your theory. I mean what did you think she was going to tell you? 'Oh yes, since you have trailed me all the way to my home in Delaware I will now confess that the Tom Heaton I met up with in New York is actually my son. I suppose you know all about his Guardian Angel, don't you?'

Scott looked puzzled for a moment as if she had suddenly become deliberately obtuse.

'I wanted to discover where she lives,' he stated patiently. 'What she does with her time. How she's coping with a dead son. Find out about her work and her husband. Then I was going to engage her in conversation by letting her know who I am, that is, a senior crime reporter on the New York Times, already in the picture as far as her son is concerned, so I could test her reaction. I would slip in the Guardian Angel business when it became appropriate.

'We have to bear in mind, Molly, that the Pan Am plane was blown up by a bomb – I'm not suggesting that Metzler had anything to do with it but if we were somehow to prove that he didn't travel on that aircraft then… well, you can imagine the enquiry that would follow. So I want to alert Mrs. Metzler that she could become the target of an FBI investigation, see if that persuades her to let slip some information. Does that explain why I was following her?'

Molly gazed at him askance. 'Fuck me! You want to prove he wasn't on that aircraft? When all the papers reported he was and we have had memorial services for him and all the other victims? That's some quantum leap don't you think? And how are you going to achieve that? You can hardly do a head count.'

'I know. But there has to be some way of checking if Metzler actually boarded the flight.'

Molly shrugged. She had heard all of this before. 'Yeah. Well the best of luck to you. But what if you're wrong? What if you're simply clutching at straws and you've turned me into an unpaid prostitute?'

'You're not going to tell me you didn't enjoy it?' he said nastily.

She sniggered at him, much the worse now for drink. 'Yeah. Well fuck you Scott. This isn't about enjoying it – this is more to do with whether or nor not I trust your judgements. And frankly I'm beginning to wonder if you aren't pissing up a rope!"

He raised his hands in an apologetic gesture. 'OK. I'm really sorry about that. I didn't want to offend you. Look, why not go along with me for the time being, see what happens over the next couple of weeks. I need to investigate Heaton's background; check out where he did live before joining the paper. All I've managed to achieve so far is to discover that he definitely didn't work on any of the Delaware newspapers. I might find someone who can look into him and then we can decide what our plans will be in the future. OK?'

She raised her shoulders as though she had no choice but to concur. 'All right. I'll meet up with him again and I'll follow your instructions – But don't expect any short-term miracles.'

CHAPTER TWENTY-ONE

Imogene let herself into the monastery through the locked gate, passing no one on her way. Augusto had promised that if temptation overwhelmed her she could stay here at the monastery and kneel at the altar of her God. Once again she sent a silent prayer of thanks up to the powers that be for directing her to him.

Walking silently, she remembered the corridors that led to her room and as she passed the door of the Abbot's office she felt a wave of relief that this too appeared empty. She was not altogether sure that she wanted an interview until she had sorted out her own tangled and confused feelings.

Tom had been absolutely correct when he accused her of jealousy; she had been mortified to feel the sickening angst of envy when she thought about him with another woman. It was all she could do to refrain from throwing herself into his arms and succumbing to the sweet pleasures she imagined with him. Placing her overnight bag in her room, she wiped the tears from her eyes, covered her head and headed towards the chapel. The place was deserted as she knelt at the altar and raised her face towards the crucifix.

'My dear Lord ...' she began, when suddenly a figure appeared alongside her. It was Augusto.

'We'll pray together, Imogene,' he said. 'That is if you don't mind?'

She nodded and gripped his hand before clasping her hands together in a prayer. They were at the altar for almost an hour before she genuflected and rose to her feet, feeling much more relaxed. The Holy Spirit was with her.

Augusto led her to his room and ordered coffee.

'Will you stay for a few days?' he asked, concerned at the troubled expression on her tear stained face.

Pressing her lips together as her emotions threatened to overwhelm her again, she nodded her head. 'Yes, please, Augusto. I need some peace.'

'Do you want to talk about your problems?'

'Not just yet, Abbot, maybe later.'

Silently they drank their coffee and afterwards she went to her room to lie down and try to empty her mind. She couldn't understand where these feelings had originated from; it was as if a powerful human urge was beginning to consume her, dominating her divinity. The prayer today had helped, and yet, her desires hadn't simply disappeared. Her nipples were hard as she felt them and she noticed that there was wetness between her legs. She closed her eyes and moaned: 'Dear Lord, what is happening to me? Please, make it go away.'

Fortuitously, God appeared to have heard her, because she drifted off to sleep. But the longing hadn't vanished as she fought the temptation to melt into the arms of Tom. It was Augusto who woke her.

'You were having a troubled sleep, my dear,' he said softly. He pulled up a chair and sat at the side of the bed.

'Why don't you talk to me, Imogene? Perhaps I can help.'

She let out a long sigh. 'I have prayed, Augusto, but I'm not sure that my God can help me. Or that He even wants to.'

'Are you having desires of the flesh?' asked Augusto. 'Or are you simply confusing this with love?'

'I don't know – you're asking me questions I don't have the answers for. In my spiritual life I held the love of all beings. Now, in human form, I'm unable to differentiate between the love of one man and the ineffable qualities of all humans.

All I do know is that they won't go away. They're with me most of the time and I don't know what to do.'

'And who is this one person in particular?'

'It's the man I saved from the air crash. We now live together, in separate bedrooms of course, but he keeps … well, not tormenting me… but engaging me with his sexual desires. He tells me he loves me, and I believe him, but for him the essence of love is the consummation of two bodies, and I am forbidden to engage in copulation.' She placed her head in her hands. 'I don't know what to do, Abbot.' She glanced at her body, tears in her eyes. 'I hate this human form. It wasn't my idea, but I'm stuck with it, and I don't really know how to deal with my feelings.'

'You feel you want to surrender to him?'

'Yes.' Imogene spoke quietly, so he could only just hear her heartfelt words. 'Especially now he appears to have a girlfriend.'

Augusto gazed at her intently. 'Then perhaps you're giving in to one of the most natural human feelings; jealousy. Do you feel jealous?' he asked.

'I don't know; possibly. I'm just so confused.' She shook her head. 'No. It's true. I am jealous – at least I think that's what these feelings are. Now he has a girlfriend who is giving him what he needs, while I have to accept a dual role of the human form inside a spiritual being.

'You don't know what it's like to be trapped like this! The Tribunal didn't give me any advice or warn me of how it would affect me or what I could do to deal with it when it did occur.'

She placed her face again in her hands and sobbed. 'This punishment's making me so distressed, Abbot. I wish I could make it go away.'

'Could you not move away from this man? Live somewhere on your own?' Augusto suggested carefully.

'Not yet,' she sobbed. 'At least I don't think so. I'm charged with monitoring his every movement to avoid a...'

'A time paradox?' he interrupted.

'Yes.'

'So tell me. What would happen if it did occur? Something he did that you couldn't foresee. What would the Tribunal do?'

'I would have to deal with the consequences since, however inadvertently, I would have caused it.'

Augusto took hold of her hand. 'And what would be the consequences, Imogene?'

'I don't know. It would depend on the circumstances. It's possible I may be cast-out. All I do know is it would fall to me to deal with.'

He squeezed her hand, sympathy pouring from him. 'Why don't you take the risk? Leave him for a few days, let events take their course, see what happens. In the meantime stay with us and pray. We'll all try to help you. God will not allow the endorsement of your distress.'

Imogene was silent for a while. Then she said, 'Thank you, Augusto. You're very kind and I might take up your offer. I know it will help to be immersed in a spiritual environment.'

'Will you tell him what you've decided?'

She nodded.

'Good. Now, let us eat with the brethren.'

CHAPTER TWENTY-TWO

Tom was in sexual seventh heaven during the following weeks. He and Molly were dining out two or three times a week at different restaurants, but eating became perfunctory as they were so anxious to rush back to bed.

Time after time he ravished her until he became convinced she had an inexhaustible supply of carnal energy. They devoured each other, exploring each other's bodies with delight until they lay, exhausted, in twisted sheets damp with sweat.

They made love two or three nights each week, until one morning, as Tom was relaxing in her bed, yet again sexually satisfied, Molly threw a bombshell at him.

'I don't think we should go on seeing each other,' she suddenly announced.

'What?' was all he could say. 'I don't understand – what brought this on?'

Molly withdrew herself from his embrace and sat up in the bed. She looked at him levelly. 'Because I am becoming much too attached to you and as this relationship doesn't seem to be going anywhere, it is easier if we separate now. That way I won't get hurt – call it self protection if you like.'

'I... I don't understand,' Tom exclaimed, his voice filled with horror. 'What do you mean, Molly? I thought we were happy together – we have so much in common, we share so many nights together, and the sex is absolutely incredible. I thought you enjoyed being with me too? Where else do you think we should be going?'

'It's because you have to ask a stupid question like that that I'm leaving you. We obviously don't have as much in common as you thought.' Her voice rose an octave.

'But... but what else could we have in common?'

There was, again, an edge to her voice. 'You're doing it again, it's as though you've become completely insensitive! You only care about the sex. You don't seem to care a toss about me and my feelings.'

'But I do. I'm... I'm very fond of you. I thought you knew that?'

'Really?' sarcasm tinged the sadness in her voice. 'What about your girlfriend, Imogene? You continue to live with her, what's that supposed to mean? You keep company with the local fuck; occasionally share a meal together and then afterwards run back to your true love.'

'That isn't true,' he insisted.

'Isn't true?' she snarled. 'What the hell do you mean it isn't true? You're still sharing the apartment with her, aren't you?'

'Yes. But...'

She let out a long sigh. 'But what? Am I right or aren't I?'

'We don't have sex together.' He blurted out suddenly.

'What? Are you trying to tell me it's just a platonic relationship? Where you kiss each other goodnight on the cheek,' she asked in astonishment. 'I don't think so!'

'It's true. Imogene is a... well; she doesn't go in for carnal affairs.'

The laugh escaped her as she put a hand to her face. 'This is a joke – right? How can she not go in for... whatever you called it... "carnal affairs"? What is she, a closet lesbian?'

He gave a worried shake of his head, afraid he had let something slip. 'No, of course not; she's just got old-fashioned values. She says she wants to wait until we're married before we have sex.'

She looked at him realising he might just have revealed one of the secrets that Scott Hardy was searching for. 'Tom,' she said contemplatively. 'This is the 20th century. Don't you think the idea of saving yourself for marriage is a bit Stepford

Wives? No one remains a virgin anymore, men or women, not unless they are planning to join a monastery or become a nun!' Seeing a glint in his eyes, she carried on. 'Is that it? Is your precious Imogene planning a spiritual existence? Poor Tom, sex is right off the agenda then! Is there a divinity about her that she allows only you to share?'

Tom almost jumped out of the bed at this suggestion. He kept shaking his head as if that would protect him from the truth.

'Now you're being silly,' he muttered. 'You're trying to make out she's some kind of a Guardian Angel …'

'Is she, a Guardian Angel?' Molly cut across him. 'Because I've never heard of a woman who denies the man she loves sex 'because she's waiting to get married'. Have you? Before now, I mean? She looked across to see the impact her words were having on him and satisfied to see his face paling, she continued. 'Even if it were true, although to be honest I'm a bit cynical about religious hocus pocus, it isn't something I could openly disclose. I mean I'm hardly likely to boast about splitting up with my boyfriend because he has a Guardian Angel!

'Regardless of what she is or isn't I'm not prepared to carry on seeing you while you're still living with her. I don't care if you're fucking her or not, the fact is you go home to her, not me. Surely, you must understand that?'

Tom returned her gaze feeling somewhat shamefaced. He felt like he had betrayed Imogene's secret again, even though he knew that this time he had said nothing.

'No. I do understand, Molly. On the other hand, if you're religious it isn't that strange to wait for sex until marriage – I don't think that makes her a Guardian Angel. She made it clear how she felt when we first met, and after that the subject of sex never really came up.'

I bet it didn't, she thought, as Tom inadvertently revealed the truth about his 'partner'. Especially if she is who Scott believes her to be; it's highly unlikely that a Guardian Angel would agree to sex.

'I believe you,' she said mendaciously. 'However, my decision remains unchanged. We can't go on seeing each other, sharing the same bed, when you leave me and return home to Imogene.'

She got up from the bed, slipping on a robe to emphasis the fact that her luscious body was no longer available to him. 'Perhaps we'll see each other around; we might bump into each other during a news break or something.'

'Molly,' he gasped. 'You can't leave me like this. How will I manage without you?'

'Ask your partner to give up her virginity.' she said scathingly.

Tom pretended not to hear the heavy sarcasm in her voice. Eventually he said, 'Molly, I don't want to lose you. What if I move in here with you? You know, we live together?'

Trying to pretend that she hadn't been working towards this goal, Molly pretended to consider his suggestion for a moment.

'No,' she said emphatically. 'The last thing I want to do is to coerce you into doing something you don't actually want. Go home, Tom. Think clearly and if you decide you really want to be with me then ring and we'll discuss it.'

With that she disappeared into the bathroom leaving a disconsolate Tom alone to get dressed. He left the apartment after a few minutes feeling wretched. This was the second woman in his life who had dismissed him.

CHAPTER TWENTY-THREE

Half an hour later he arrived at work, but there was no sign of Imogene. Then he remembered that she was going to spend some time at the monastery. Unsure if this was a new spa centre, but suspecting she meant a real monastery, he realised he had no idea where it was. Trying to remember their conversation he vaguely recalled her saying that it was somewhere in Brooklyn.

To make the morning even worse, Hardy stuck his head inside the office space and noticed her absence.

'Where's your girlfriend today?' he asked, mockery heavy in his voice.

'She... she's not too well.' Tom stammered.

'Really?' Scott's eyebrow rose in clear disbelief. 'Well this is the third time this week that she's been missing. When do you think she'll emerge?'

'Dunno. I think it's some kind of flu.' Tom improvised unconvincingly, 'I'll let you know tomorrow.'

When he arrived back at the apartment Imogene was nowhere to be seen. There was a brief note on the kitchen table informing him that she was going to the monastery.

'Where the fuck is this monastery?' he asked himself. 'And when exactly will you be back?'

It then occurred to him that possibly she wouldn't be coming back. He had, after all, been spending most of his time fucking his brains out with Molly, and totally neglecting Imogene. Perhaps she was finally sick of him, disgusted by his lust. The thought of not seeing her again made him feel nauseous. He just couldn't contemplate life without her. Wrapped up in his own torment and the conviction that he had let her down, he didn't stop to consider that she might feel jealous of his affair.

'I will change,' he muttered aloud. 'Just come back to me and I promise you, Imogene, I will change.'

He decided there and then he would forget the idea of moving in with Molly. She was certainly a good fuck, but that was only because he had been deprived of sex for over a year. Perhaps Imogene would be back in the morning.

But she wasn't. Nor did she arrive at the office. Hardy stuck his head inside the office to ask him where she was.

'She's sick; I told you yesterday.'

'Oh yes, so you did,' he said with derision. 'Are you sure she hasn't left you?'

'What do you mean?'

'Well, it's just that you were seen the other night dining with Molly from CNN. I was told that the two of you were all over each other; in fact my source told me you should have booked a room! So tell me, Heaton, are you fucking Molly? Is that your secret? Perhaps Imogene has found out and left you?' He grinned maliciously. 'Can't say I'd blame her!'

'It has nothing to do with you,' Tom said, as firmly as he could. It was the only thing he could think of to say. Of course Imogene knew about his affair with Molly, but he knew she wouldn't relish the idea of it being broadcast around the office.

That is if she ever came back.

'So, I want to know if she's coming back – otherwise I need to make other arrangements.'

'She's coming back. OK?' Tom said with as much conviction as he could muster.

'Who are you trying to convince, Tom, me or you? We'll just see, shall we?'

Imogene wasn't at the apartment when he got back that night. It was Friday night and Tom had thought he'd take her out for dinner, despite the rain. He looked around at the empty apartment and thought how lonely it was without her. He shrugged and hugged his arms around himself as if he were freezing. Then he thought about ringing Molly, but stopped when he realised that she would be bound to ask if he had decided to move in with her.

He put on the coffee pot, sat down and thought about dinner. He had missed lunch worrying about Imogene and he was hungry. He also needed a drink; in fact lots of drinks.

Eventually he headed off to a bar he knew over on Sixty-Third Street; one he used to visit when he lived in the area. He ignored the rain, not even bothering to pull up the collar of his coat.

He ordered a hamburger, a beer and a large whisky. Eating the burger so quickly he hardly tasted it, he downed the beer and the whisky chaser almost as fast. He finally left the bar at close on two, so inebriated he couldn't remember where he lived. Finally, he fished in his pockets and found one of his business cards with the address printed on the back. Flagging down a taxi, he tumbled into the back and handed his business card to the driver. He couldn't recall getting into the apartment, much less slumping into bed, still fully clothed.

He woke at around eleven the next morning with a monumental headache. He stumbled into the bathroom, thought he would vomit, changed his mind, and stuck his head under the cold water tap.

'Jesus,' he muttered aloud. 'I must be fucking stupid.'

The smell of yesterday's clothes; stale beer, cigarettes and fried onions, made him retch again before staggering into the shower and standing dazed, as the cold water drenched him for five minutes. This cleared his head a little, although he was still a bit dizzy, as he put on an old pair of jeans and a sweatshirt and made his way, slowly, into the kitchen.

Imogene was sitting there with a cup of coffee.

'You look rough this morning,' Imogene said as she sat sipping her coffee.

Barely managing a grunt in reply he felt crushed by a wave of his old depression, back again with a vengeance.

'So? What happened to you?'

'Where have you been?' he asked, ignoring the question, his head still splitting from the hangover.

'To the monastery; I told you in the note.'

'You didn't say you'd be away for so long,' Tom could hear the whining note in his voice.

She grinned. 'Did you miss me?'

'I don't want to talk about it. Please, Imogene, just leave me alone will you.'

Her face a picture of concern, he saw to his amazement that she followed him out of the kitchen.

He turned at the door of his bedroom. 'Look, I have a tremendous hangover, my head is killing me and I don't want to talk. So back off and leave me alone; I'm off to bed.'

CHAPTER TWENTY-FOUR

Leaving him to sleep his bad temper off, Imogene went to Saint Patrick's Cathedral and spent two hours at the altar. Retreating for a couple of days to the monastery had helped her; at least it had until she saw Tom again when her heart began to pound again.

'Dear Lord, please help me', she prayed. 'I realise I have to be punished because of my transgressions and I understand why I have to inhabit this earthly body, but please, my Lord, do you have to inflict these temptations of the flesh? In my heart I am a divine spirit, so why do I have to suffer these urges? Please God, hear my prayers and relieve me of these temptations.'

She repeated the mantra for the best part of two hours, before going for a sandwich in a coffee shop. She didn't want to go home, afraid of what might happen if Tom stood too close, so she returned to the monastery desperately hoping for some relief from her lustful feelings.

She didn't return home until the following Monday morning.

Tom scowled at her as she changed for the office. 'Been back to the monastery, have you?'

She nodded, not really feeling like talking.

'Did you know that Scott Hardy was asking after you?' he said.

'Really? What did he want?'

'He thought you'd left the Times. I told him you were sick.'

She smiled half-heartedly. 'That was kind of you.'

'Do you want to talk?' he asked. 'I think I should tell you what happened with Molly.'

She sighed. 'Perhaps we can talk later, but this morning we have to cover the trial at Central Courts of Giuseppe Valero. The jury will be sworn in today and we have to be there.'

'I'm well aware of that,' he muttered.

Valero was a famed Mafia controller, only one rank below a Godfather, accused of being involved in a shootout in the Bronx back in the summer. It seemed Valero had got a little too big for his boots, threatening to break away and start his own outfit, and it was his own soldiers that had left him on the ground with a bullet hole in one shoulder and a shattered leg. It was barely conceivable that he was still alive; one of the soldiers had shot at him from the car, had missed and killed a pedestrian.

It was, Scott Hardy claimed, a Mafia setup. The problem for the Mafia was that they had missed the opportunity to kill him, and now they were concerned that Valero would break 'Omerta' - the vow of silence.

'Have you heard anything more from Scott?' she asked as they settled in the cab.

'No, nothing. But then, why should I?'

'I'm simply trying to make conversation. Now tell me what went on the other night, or is it a state secret?'

'She kicked me out,' he said sulkily.

'Why?' Imogene looked surprised. 'Did you have a row?'

'No. It was because of you.'

'Me?' She exclaimed with horror. 'Why did I have anything to do with it?'

Tom sighed. This wasn't the place to discuss a delicate matter like this but he could hardly change the subject now. 'She says that as long as you and I live together, we have no future together.'

She looked at him curiously. 'What does that mean exactly?'

He whispered below the noise of the traffic, 'she believes I am fucking you, and says I can't have two women.' He hastily checked that the cab driver wasn't listening before continuing, 'She wants me to either give you up and move in with her, or stop seeing her altogether.'

Imogene looked shocked. 'So what did you tell her? I mean have you told her anything about you and me?'

He shrugged. He was past caring at the present. 'I told her you weren't interested in sex.'

'We share a flat but we don't have sex? Is that what you told her, Tom?' Imogene looked aghast.

'What else could I say? That you were an angel and sex would betray your spiritual essence?'

'Don't make a joke of this, you bastard.' She snapped, and then lowered her voice as the cab driver half turned around. 'This is a serious issue. So what did she say after you told her that?'

Tom looked dejected. 'She said if that's true then you're either a lesbian, or a religious nut. She even suggested you might be a Guardian Angel!' He sighed. 'What could I tell her; the truth?'

'I hope you didn't admit the truth!' Imogene said flatly.

'I could hardly do that, could I? I sort of... well, I sort of left it up in the air. I did say you were religious and didn't believe in sex before marriage.'

'That's charming! So what are you going to do? I mean, is the relationship finished or is it a trap to ensnare you into living with her?'

'How the hell do I know? She seems genuine.'

'Humph. Well, she would be wouldn't she? Look, we'll discuss this later,' she said, as the cab pulled up in front of the Courts. Getting out into pouring rain, Tom cursed as he drenched his shoe in a puddle, but turning to warn Imogene he noticed that it didn't appear to affect her. In fact, she wasn't even slightly damp as they entered the main doors. It must be another of her magic tricks, he told himself.

CHAPTER TWENTY-FIVE

Tom sighed again as they entered the courtroom and joined the crowded press area, hoping that it would be Imogene that took notes of the jury selection.

The one question she hadn't asked him was what he was planning to do with Molly. She hadn't even pleaded the inevitable that it might bring about the catastrophe she dreaded. The problem was, whatever way he looked at it, he loved Imogene and would do anything, even drop Molly, if he had a bit of encouragement from her. He controlled another sigh as he sat beside her in the press box, nodding to one or two of his acquaintances, and wondering where the hell all this might end.

Imogene looked straight ahead, trying to ignore his presence.

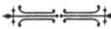

Scott Hardy collected Molly from the CNN offices to take her for lunch. They both sheltered under his umbrella.

'Are you sure this is wise?' she questioned him as they entered the restaurant.

'Don't worry. They're both down at the courts for a jury selection. No doubt they'll be tied up there all day. In fact, in my experience they're likely to be there for the best part of a week.'

They were escorted to a table and when the maître de had left Scott asked her, 'So how did it go?'

She looked at him questioningly. 'That's all you seem to ask me these days: "So how did it go?" How the hell do you think it went?'

'Sorry, he apologised. 'But I merely want to determine whether or not you were able to convince him."

She shook her head. 'I split with him. I told him we were finished and he should go back to his lover.'

'What?' he gasped in astonishment. 'How did that happen? I thought you were going to entice him into sharing an apartment with you. What went wrong?'

'I decided that if this affair is going to work then I have to give him the choice between Imogene and myself. So, I chucked him out on Friday morning with an ultimatum. That's where it stands at present.'

He leaned forward, as if to whisper in her ear. 'Christ, Molly, you're taking a chance, aren't you? What if he decides to stay with his, whoops, nearly said Guardian Angel, I mean Imogene?'

She picked up the menu as the waiter arrived, ignoring him for a second or two. 'The fish here is supposed to be amazing. I'll have the fresh salmon,' she said to the waiter. 'With a side salad, please. Oh, and,' she put a hand out to stop the waiter, 'Mineral water, thanks.'

'So are you going to tell me,' Scott asked when the waiter had disappeared. 'Or am I expected to guess what is going on inside your pretty head?'

'I'll tell you this Scott, Tom confirmed that he and Imogene aren't lovers. That, and a couple of other odd things he said, could support your theory that she's an angel.'

Scott frowned at this news; it was something he just couldn't get his head around. It was one thing to speculate that Imogene could be an angel, but to have some kind of confirmation disturbed him.

'Could you repeat that?' he suggested.

'You heard me. He didn't deny she's an angel, although I admit he didn't actually say she was, but he distinctly led me to believe that she has some essence of spirituality. Also, apart from no sex, he also told me that he's had a vasectomy – how weird is that? He tried to tell me it was something to do with a genetic disease that he could pass on to his children, but I didn't believe him.'

'Jesus,' he gasped. 'You've unearthed a gold mine.' He paused for a moment as the waiter cleared the table. Then he said, 'Why didn't you believe his medical story?'

'Oh come on, Scott. Does it matter what I believe? If it's something that runs in his family it's easy to check out – all you have to do is resurrect your journey to Delaware and check it out on the spot. Or, if it's that rare you'll probably find it in the medical journals.'

He pursed his lips thoughtfully. 'That isn't a bad idea. I'd like to find out why he's had a vasectomy so young – you know, when and where he had it done. I wonder if it's something to do with her being a Guardian Angel, and he's lying about the sex.'

'It would make sense,' Molly said. 'But if that's true then it's going to make it harder for him to decide which of the two of us he wants.' She sighed. They used to have an awful lot more to talk about in the old days than sex, or the lack of it in Imogene's case.

Scott interrupted her thoughts, 'Well, maybe you should've thought of that before you gave him the push. Now he might not come back to you.'

'Yeah, well, for what it's worth, I don't think they're having sex, and if you're right and she is a Guardian Angel then that would support my theory …'

At that moment the adjacent table filled up and Scott hastily asked when Tom was supposed to give his decision.

'Your guess is as good as mine; but if there's going to be some delay then perhaps you can put some pressure on him at work.'

He nodded thoughtfully, but said nothing.

CHAPTER TWENTY-SIX

When Imogene and Tom finally emerged from court for lunch, Tom was totally confused. All morning he had listened to the prosecution attorney, followed by the defence attorney, disagreeing on the choice of appropriate jurors. Of the thirty plus who had been called, so far only two had been selected; if the defence lawyers weren't careful they would run out of standard refusals. The way things were going it looked as if they would be there the remainder of the week.

'Do you want lunch in the cafeteria?' he asked Imogene in the hallway.

'No, I'd prefer to go somewhere where we aren't known – I don't want to encourage eavesdroppers.'

They wandered around outside until Imogene spotted a small café. At least the drizzle had stopped, Tom thought, as he hurried to keep up with her.

'This should be OK,' she said, almost dragging Tom inside the warm café, the smell of fresh coffee and cakes instantly surrounding them. They joined a small queue, before ordering at a counter that was piled high with tempting pastries and bowls of fruit. Ordering two cheese and ham baguettes, Tom noticed that she did actually pay the small Italian-looking man that served them, before leading him to sit at the table furthest away from the counter.

'So, have you decided?' She asked sharply, almost as though it were a cross-examination.

'I thought we were going to have a civilised discussion about this,' he replied, tightening his lips, feeling instantly defensive.

She leaned forward towards him. 'We are, providing you're going to tell me the truth.'

'What do you mean 'the truth'; I am telling you the truth.'

'No, you're not, Tom. The truth is that you've already decided what to do and now you're wondering how to break it to me without causing too much offence. Am I right?'

'Well, not entirely,' he accepted, vigorously shaking his head. 'I mean, I'm considering moving in with Molly, but I really haven't made up my mind.'

She paused whilst a youthful waiter, who from his startling resemblance was the café owner's son, served the baguettes and gave them each a red and white gingham paper napkin. Smiling dismissively at the hovering young man, Imogene began again, 'So, what you're actually saying is that you're the one with the freedom of choice. In other words I don't have a say in it?'

He visibly cringed at her statement, as though it was something that hadn't occurred to him. 'No, you're right, Imogene, and I'm sorry, I really didn't mean to offend you like that. Of course you have a choice – you can either kick me out or …'

'What, Tom? What's the alternative? Allow you to fuck me – that is the expression isn't it?' she spat contemptuously back at him.

'Jesus,' he almost hissed at her. 'Do you have to be so crude? I was hoping it would be making love if we got together, you know how I feel about you. You're supposed to be a … well, you know what I mean; you shouldn't use language like that!'

'Tom, it doesn't matter what you call it; sex, fucking, making love, shagging, copulating. I know that you still lust after me, I can see it in your eyes – I don't need to be able to read your thoughts to know what you want. But no matter how much my body craves the experience, nothing has changed between us. I would be a liar if I didn't admit that sometimes I long for your embrace, but I realise that it's just the human part of me. It doesn't mean anything,' she hesitated, 'it isn't the real me. The inner me; the spiritual me will always continue to resist that sensation.

'So, if you do decide to leave me, we'll have to work out how I can still check up on you – to make sure you aren't about to do something disastrous.'

Tom's mouth hung open in dismay. 'Is that all it means to you? How you may or may not continue your supervisory role?'

'What else should it mean?' she glared back at him, defiantly.

'Well, won't you miss me – just a little?' Tom's heart felt as though it was dragging along the stripped pine floorboards of the café. 'We have shared some … well, some really good times together, as well as some awful ones. Won't you regret that I'm no longer with you? Haven't you got used to us living our lives together, sharing each other's sadness and happiness? Won't you feel at least a bit sad when you wake up and realise I'm no longer there? Surely the human part of you must be reaching out to me, wishing you could love me, if only a little? Or have I really meant so little to you?'

A tear formed in the corner of her eye and she allowed it to trickle down her cheek. 'You can be so cruel, Tom. You must know how I feel and although I do love you, in a spiritual way, you must understand that I can't keep going around in these perennial circles. That's all we seem to talk about these days – whether I will or I won't respond to your desires.'

He almost snarled at her at this riposte. 'Well, if you love me so much why won't you at least try to give in to your human side? Allow us to love each other in the real sense; is it really so evil and bad?

Imogene got up from the table, tears now streaming down her cheeks. 'It seems that you're determined not to understand.'

He got up to follow her, but she physically pushed him away, murmuring. 'Please, Tom. Leave me alone,' and walked out of the café.

Waiting ten minutes before retracing his steps back to the courtroom, he was a bit surprised to see that there was no sign of Imogene. All he found were some scribbled notes on the jury selection that morning; seemingly left for his attention. He had to spend the remainder of the day trying to concentrate on the proceedings. From to time he was forced to ask some of his colleagues to fill him in on what was happening. They dutifully obliged, considering his request highly amusing.

'Have you pissed off your girlfriend?' one of them asked.

'Well, we did have a disagreement, and I'm trying to catch up with what's happening.'

When the court was finally adjourned he had to go back to the office to complete his storyline but there was no sign of Imogene, and no one had seen her all day. It was late evening before he had tidied his copy and filed it with the sub-editor. He then virtually fled from the office and caught a cab to the apartment.

Racing up the stairs, too eager to wait for the lift, he was distraught to see that Imogene was not home. Looking around for clues, his eye caught on a suitcase full of his own clothes, and his heart sank as he realised she had taken his decision out of his hands by throwing him out. Devastated he tried to think of where she might be; if he could find her perhaps he could talk her into taking him back? A little voice in the back of his head asked if this was what he really wanted. Trying to ignore it he slumped onto the sofa, images of Imogene filling his mind. The little voice gathered strength and finally Imogene's face was replaced with Molly's. Listen, said the voice, perhaps she has done you a favour by forcing your choice. She doesn't want you, but Molly does. She is waiting for you, warm and loving, and ready to fulfil your emotional and physical needs.

CHAPTER TWENTY-SEVEN

Almost succumbing to the temptation to leave and run to Molly, it suddenly dawned on him where Imogene might be. Grabbing his coat and dragging on winter boots, he set off into the freezing night air in the direction of Saint Patrick's. Thoughts spun around his head as he walked, his hands deep in his pockets, fists clenched with nervous tension. Even if she were there he wasn't altogether sure what he could say to her. He supposed he could apologise, but was unsure what he was apologising for. Certainly he was sorry to have unintentionally hurt her, but what did he really want from her; understanding, absolution? He sighed again and walked even faster, trying to be honest about his feelings, at least to himself. Did he really want her to release him with her blessing, so he could go to Molly and enjoy her earthly delights, but retain Imogene's ethereal love? Totally confused he accepted that there just wasn't an answer to this conflict of interest; although in his heart of hearts he knew that he loved Imogene more than life itself.

Arriving at the church, sweating with nerves and puffing from walking so quickly, he spotted Imogene worshipping in the St John the Baptist Chapel. She was alone and she looked so forlorn that he desperately wanted to go up to her and hold her in his arms. As he walked towards her she half-turned and a small smile turned the corners of her mouth up as she realised who it was. She rose from the altar bench and whispered to him, not in a pleading voice, but almost as an admission.

'Tom, I'm so sorry. I just can't do it. I've been praying here for most of the afternoon, seeking advice from my Archangel.

He has informed me that under no circumstances am I to embrace you in the way you wish.'

'You've packed a suitcase for me,' he said, wishing he could respond to her with something meaningful. 'I wish there was something I could say to change your mind. The only thing I can say is that my physical desires are merely a reflection of my love for you. Putting it into your words, I want to make communion with you.'

'I understand, but the answer is the same. Please, will you leave the apartment before I get home, and let know where you are.' With that she kissed him gently on the lips for the first time. Even though the kiss was swift and chaste the effect it had on him was colossal; he felt at once immense peace, total exhilaration and a headiness that left him breathless.

'Phew! Where did that come from, Imogene?'

She smiled, a little sadly. 'It was the Kiss of an Angel, but behind my smile is a veil of tears. Be strong, Tom, won't you, I will always think about you.'

'Will I see you in the office?' he asked, totally confused.

'I don't know. I doubt it. I think that it's time for you to be liberated from my supervision.'

It was Tom who left the church in tears, unsure whether or not he had made the right decision. He stopped, leaning against a mailbox in an effort to clear his head and stop the sidewalk from revolving around him. Pulling himself together, he hailed a cab and went back to the apartment, paying the driver double to wait whilst he cleared out the remainder of his belongings. Looking at the rooms he had been so happy and so miserable in he could hardly believe that it was truly over. Finally, leaving the key on the side where Imogene would see it, he slammed the door and walked away.

Unable to face Molly, he asked the cabbie to take him to the Holiday Inn off 39th Street. Lonely and disconsolate Tom followed the bus boy up to his room, tipped him, and then slumped on the bed. Too tired and depressed to even consider food, he fumbled in his bag for sleeping pills, took two, undressed, and before he could start to think about the series of events again was already falling asleep.

CHAPTER TWENTY-EIGHT

Waking at seven the following morning with a cracking headache, as though he had been drinking heavily, he dressed slowly still dazed from the night before. His mobile phone lay on the nightstand and he immediately thought about ringing Imogene. Already it was impossible to get her out of his mind; he missed her terribly, more so now that she had effectively abandoned him. It did cross his mind that she may think that he had abandoned her, but only for a second. The truth was, he told himself firmly, Imogene had forsaken him in his crisis. He then considered phoning Molly, actually ringing CNN and asking to speak to Molly Sinclair, before changing his mind and hanging up.

So he skipped breakfast and walked to the office as the drizzle of yesterday turned into a light snowfall. Only the hope that Imogene would be there kept him warm as he shivered his way through the snow.

She wasn't.

'Where's your partner this morning?' Scott Hardy asked in his usual aggressive manner.

'Dunno,' Tom mumbled, unable to meet his eyes.

'Well if you don't know, and you're her boyfriend, I can't think of anyone who might. Can you?'

'Look. I've told you, I don't know where she is, so please, just leave me alone!' Tom was in no mood to play stupid games with his despised boss.

'You mean she's done a runner?' Hardy choked, unable to conceal his pleasure. 'What bad news for you!'

'I think maybe she's resigned.' Tom replied, fatalistically.

'Oh really? It gets better and better! Have you got her resignation letter?'

Tom shook his head, dejected and only too well aware of Hardy's glee at his discomfort. 'No. I haven't seen her since yesterday.'

'So where was she this morning then? No breakfast for two? You must have seen her before you left the apartment? Or has she resigned from you too?' His voice was heavy with derision, as if he already knew what had happened.

'Mind your own fucking business!' Tom howled in anger and emotional pain.

'It is my fucking business, Tom' Scott snarled back at him. 'I'm the boss, in case either of you have forgotten. And she hasn't said anything to Andy Clarke? He is expecting her at an editorial meeting this morning; perhaps he wants to promote her. What shall I tell him?'

Tom sighed; he was feeling very emotional this morning and couldn't stand this type of hassle. 'I think you'll have to ask Imogene – I can't hand in her notice for her, now can I? Anyway, I'm due at the Courts shortly."

'No you're not. I've sent Mariella; the sub-editor was not terribly impressed with your copy last night. If you check this morning's paper you'll see he's made some significant changes.'

'Are you suggesting I can't handle this?'

Scott's lips turned back. 'I've always thought you were way out of your depth. Now the editorial team have come round to my view. The Valero trial could be one of the most important mafia trials in New York for many years and you were treating it like some Sunday tea party!'

The telephone ringing stopped him short. He picked it up. 'Hardy. Yeah. He's here, Andy. I'll send him along.'

'You're wanted,' he said to Tom. 'Andy Clarke wants to see you – now.'

The meeting with Andy Clarke was brief and to the point. Imogene had formally resigned and it was as if Andy had come to his senses. Andy had the feeling he had been dreaming and just woken up to discover he had a bogus reporter on his books, all because of her influence. He doubted he would ever be able to understand what had happened, the whole incident was a deep cauldron of mystery. All he knew was that he had to put things right. In many ways he was relieved that she had disappeared; it certainly made firing Tom easier. There was no notice to be served, no severance pay, simply a curt goodbye that culminated in the separation of everything Tom believed he had possessed. It was one of those defining moments in his resurgent life when, although he took offence at his summary dismissal, he couldn't argue with Andy's decision. He left the office feeling that he was an impostor that had just been exposed.

Standing for some moments in the snow-clad street with loneliness, sadness and desolation consuming him he felt vulnerable to the outside world. He didn't dare contact Molly, afraid that she would admonish him when he told her he had lost his job. Nor could he tell her how or why it had happened. Andy Clarke had given no reason; in fact he knew it wasn't necessary. It was understood that Tom would comprehend exactly why the paper no longer required his services.

He was alone in the world now; no job, no apartment and no girlfriend. Intuitively he also understood that the apartment he had shared with Imogene would now be deserted.

He didn't know what to do and had no idea if he would ever see Imogene again. In a moment of clarity he recognised the irony of his situation; by admitting to his partner that he could not share his life without a sexual relationship, he had driven her away.

He trudged back to the Holiday Inn, tears streaming down his face, unaware of the passers by who stared at him with curiosity. He wasn't even sure where he could go to deal with this crisis in his life. One thing was for sure; he couldn't stay very long at the Holiday Inn, not at the prices they charged…

'*You summoned us, Imogene?*'

'*Yes. It is important we discuss the earthly situation.*'

'*You wish to discuss why you deserted that poor man?*'

'*Well, I assume you want to know what I've been doing.*'

A look of surprise came over the faces of the assembly.

'*Where are you, at the monastery?*'

'*Yes.*'

'*We know exactly what it is you've been doing, Imogene,*' *the Tribunal Chairman said.* '*What we want to know is why? Why did you decide to abandon that poor man? Why did you cast him to the wolves as if he were no longer of any consequence to you?*'

'*It isn't easy to explain – not to non-humans.*'

'*Are you suggesting that the driving force of your energy has now become human? Enlighten us, please. Assume that we will endeavour to understand, and if we misconstrue anything, then we are sure you will correct us. Well?*'

'*I realise that the position in which I find myself is of my own making – I would hate any of you to assume I am delegating responsibility. But the truth is, since you decided I had to inherit an earthly body in order to supervise the … well, let's just call him the survivor, shall we? It has placed me in an invidious position. You see, in order to retain any kind of contact with Tom Metzler I was forced to allow the human part of me to subjugate my spiritual side – that is, my natural essence –*'

'*Is this going someplace, Imogene?*' *The Chairman said disinterestedly.*

'*If you'll permit me, members, I do believe it is necessary to explain the motives behind my apparent abandonment of this young man. That is, if you genuinely wish to understand what lies behind it?*'

'Carry on. Please.'

'Well … where was I? Yes. As I was saying, I allowed my human part, under the circumstances I have described, to become dominant, an easy quarry to the temptations of the flesh I was confronted with.'

'But you were able to resist these temptations, where you not?'

'I was, yes, but not without a great deal of stress and torment. You see, Chairman, I love Tom Metzler, almost in the same way he loves me. At first it was relatively simple for me to resist his charms – it wasn't so much that he was sexually avaricious, it was really a case of his delightful charms that I found bewitching. And as time went on I discovered that my human part was gradually taking over, overpowering my spiritual side.

'I have to tell you, dear brethren that my body began to yearn for him. Time after time I was compelled to distance myself from his advances. It was then I went to worship at the altar for Divine Guidance. And when he met the other woman, the one whom he engaged in sexual copulation, I am forced to admit I felt envious.'

'And yet you continued to resist him?'

'I did, yes, but with increasing difficulty. When he finally confirmed he was planning to live with her, there was something in me that decided there was no way I could exist in that situation, him living with another woman and myself continuing to oversee him.

'So I spent that afternoon at the altar of St. Patrick's praying to my Archangel for guidance. I was told I was duty bound to continue my resistance, to let him go, but to allow myself time to adjust to the new conditions whilst staying at the monastery.

'And that is what I did and the reason why I did it. I hope you can understand this'

'So we are to believe you are suffering from the human condition of jealousy? For that is how it appears to us.'

'I don't know. I have questioned my reactions but I have been unable to find any satisfactory answers. So I suppose it could be argued that, yes, I was jealous.

There was silence for a moment before the Chairman responded.

'Imogene, we want you to remain where you are for the moment, in the monastery. We will consider the matter further and revert back to you in due course. Are you happy with that?'

'Thank you, Chairman,' said Imogene. 'Yes, I am happy with that arrangement and I will wait to hear from you.'

As Imogene finished her exchanges with the Tribunal, Abbot Mancini came in and sat beside her.

'Did you receive good news?' he asked.

'I don't know yet, Augusto. I am to remain here while the Tribunal consider the matter; when they've decided, they'll contact me again. Is that all right with you?'

Augusto sighed. He had never had to exchange any kind of pleasantries with an angel before, much less a dialogue of such a serious nature.

'My dear child, you may stay as long as it takes – forever if needs be. Come; let us take lunch with the others.'

CHAPTER TWENTY-NINE

Before checking out of the Holiday Inn, Tom tried Imogene's mobile but there was no reply. He thought about going down to the apartment and then changed his mind, knowing it would be a waste of time; she had already left. He was desperate to know why she had resigned from her job, and feeling distraught he rang his mother to put her in the picture.

Mary was shocked. 'I don't understand, Tom. She just resigned without giving you any warning?'

'No,' he replied truthfully. 'We had a... well, a disagreement. Molly was asking me to choose between her and Imogene... and I...'

'What, you chose Molly? Mary said, surprised. 'You opted out of the relationship with Imogene? Why?'

He sighed, 'Because I was sleeping with Molly and she issued me with an ultimatum; either her or Imogene.'

'And Imogene told you to pack your bag – is that it?'

'Worse – she packed it for me! Unfortunately she also packed in her job, which means I've lost mine too. I daren't tell Molly, she'll think I'm pathetic.'

There was silence for a moment before his mother said, 'I think you'd better come home. No... I don't mean come to the house; I mean come here to Wilmington. Let me know what time your train's arriving... I assume you'll be travelling by train? I'll meet you at the station and we can arrange something. Is that OK?'

'I guess so. I don't really have any alternative at the moment. I'll ring you from the train... Mary.'

As an afterthought she added, 'Have you any idea where Imogene's likely to be? Has she made contact with you?'

'Not a word. She mentioned before that she was spending time in some monastery here in New York; it's in the Bronx, I think, but I don't know where it is. Look, I'll ring you later – it'll probably be tonight, but if it's too late I can find a hotel and come to the hospital tomorrow.'

'All right, Tom. I'll be thinking of you.'

The trains to Wilmington departed more or less every hour from Penn Street. Tom caught the late afternoon departure, having been to the apartment and discovered his intuition was correct and it was empty. Tom couldn't understand how Imogene was able to achieve something like this; one minute she was behaving like a human being, the next she produced miracles as if they were common place.

He arrived at Wilmington station at around eight-o'clock in the evening. It was cold; the snow had turned to drizzle, but the temperature was falling rapidly so it wouldn't be too long before the snow returned. He telephoned his mother from the train to let her know his arrival time.

She was waiting at the Amtrak Station when he arrived. She hesitated, causing Tom to think she might be about to shake his hand, but then gave him a big bear hug.

'Have you reserved a hotel?' Tom asked.

She nodded. 'Just for tonight; I've booked you into the Du Pont on Market Street – you may remember it's just round the corner from the Hospital. But, from tomorrow, I have a surprise for you.'

'Really? What would that be, Mary?'

'Well, since I was last in New York I've been making enquiries in the local property market – and just over there,' she pointed to the other side of the Christina River, 'they are building a new development and I have leased a two-bedroom apartment. It will be ready in a few weeks' time, including furniture, for you to move into.' She looked into his face, expecting him to express some surprise. 'What do you think? Exciting, isn't it?'

He shook his head, at the same time frowning.

'Why didn't you tell me?'

'Because I wanted it to be a surprise; I knew you would have to return here at some point.'

'How could you possibly know that?'

'I... I... I don't really know. I had an intuition that something would happen that would make you come home ...' she rubbed her forehead as though her actions were puzzling her. 'Perhaps it was Imogene who told me?'

'That's crazy, Mary. We only separated yesterday. When did you begin negotiating for the apartment?'

'Six weeks ago.'

Oh Christ, he thought. That would be about the same time he had started sleeping with Molly.

'Look, I can't think about this at the moment, but I really don't see how I can possibly take up residence again in Wilmington.'

'How do you mean?' She frowned at him.

'Well, I'm not known here – I have no relatives or friends here, in fact the only contact I can possibly have is through you, and that's only because I was supposed to know Tom Metzler at Harvard. It would seem unlikely to people that I'd want to live her, unless they think I'm your toy boy or something!' He gave a mirthless laugh as Mary shook her head.

'Does it matter what people think?' she asked, her face expressing surprise.

'Yes it does; especially in such a small place like this. I feel we'd draw attention to ourselves.'

'But... but what will you do. Where will you go?'

'I'll stay tonight at the Du Pont, but tomorrow I intend to buy a car and take myself up to Philadelphia. I've saved nearly twelve thousand dollars in the last twelve months, thanks to Imogene. I can find an apartment there easily enough – somewhere where I can disappear. After a while I'll look for a job; who knows, with my experience maybe the Daily News will hire me? I'm sorry, moth… Mary,' he corrected himself, 'if you think about it I'm sure you'll agree it makes sense.'

'I don't know what to think,' she said in shock, a tear forming. 'This is so sudden… I was planning on your staying here for quite a while… that's why I leased the apartment. I suppose I can always cancel the lease and it won't cost too much. I can see what you're saying but… what will you do in Philadelphia? You won't have any friends there either.'

'I realise that, but I know the City pretty well, and I'm still young. I might even meet a gorgeous girl, get myself a good job, maybe as a legal secretary, settle down and then come and visit you!' He added, 'And you can visit me whenever you like – no one will know you're there, will they?'

'I suppose not, but I'm very disappointed, Tom. I really believed you would be home for good.' She let her head fall at the news.

He sighed. 'That isn't very realistic, is it? I know you don't like to be reminded, Mary, but your old son is dead. This is the new me, someone, who, if you think about it, you'd hardly have anything in common with. But don't worry you're not going to get rid of me so quickly.

'Have you eaten?' he enquired, suddenly remembering his manners.

'Y… yes,' she stumbled, unsure how to take the sudden change of direction in the conversation. 'I had supper with your father – he thinks I'm working tonight. But I'll join you for a drink.'

CHAPTER THIRTY

After checking in at the Du Pont, Tom joined his mother in the hotel bar. Decorated in cocoa brown and warm cream, the bar managed to look modern and cosy at the same time. The room was divided with brass rails into smaller seating areas on different levels, each space containing a couple of sofas below a huge abstract print. Tom looked about him; apart from a small group of business men and a young couple they were the only people in there. A bartender, dressed in matching dark brown, motioned for them to choose a booth and offered to come and take their order.

'What about you, Tom? Have you eaten yet?' Mary asked, raising her eyebrows as her words were nearly drowned by gusts of raucous laughter from the all-male table. 'Looks like they're having fun,' she gestured across to the men, taking off her heavy red wool coat and laying it across one of the cream chairs.

'Yes, lucky them,' Tom mused, his depression threatening to descend again.

'Food?' Mary asked, more gently this time, 'have you eaten?'

'No,' he shook his head, unconsciously underlining his words. 'I haven't been eating much lately. I just don't feel hungry, stress, I guess.'

'Well, I thought you might be able to unwind here,' she shrugged. 'How about a sandwich, you ought to eat something.'

'No, thanks, I'd rather not bother.'

'Do you think you'll hear from Molly?' she said, settling into the brown velour sofa and reverting back to her old topic.

He paused before answering. 'I don't see how, she doesn't know where I am. I told you – I daren't contact her because she will ridicule me.' He rolled his eyes back as if in embarrassment. 'I mean, I was supposed to be thinking about moving in with her, then, suddenly I lose my job, my home, my....'

'Your sweetheart?' Mary interrupted.

'Yeah, that too,' he said sardonically.

'What I don't understand is why Imogene just vanished.' Her shoulders rose in a gesture of anxiety. 'Surely she must have said something to you?'

He took a sip of his drink, avoiding answering. Looking around the room he tried to think of a way to change the subject.

'Well?' Mary asked, ignoring his avoidance tactics.

Tom took another sip still refusing to answer.

She leaned across to him and whispered. 'She's an angel, Tom. Angels don't simply disappear, at least not without warning.'

'Well, let's say that she didn't want to have sex with me.' He shrugged.

Mary laughed at his phraseology. 'What? Are you telling me that, because she wouldn't, you gave her an ultimatum? Oh, Tom, what did you expect? She's an angel!"

'Of course I didn't give her an ultimatum!' Tom started, looking outraged, and then more thoughtfully he continued, 'Well, not specifically. I did say that I'd only consider staying with her if we consummated our relationship, but it wasn't an ultimatum. Honestly,' he added, seeing the doubtful look on Mary's face. 'I thought she'd just reject my advances, allow me to move in with Molly, and continue our working relationship. Instead she just upped and left me!'

Seeing the look of anguish on his face Mary said quietly, 'Perhaps she's jealous? It sounds like it to me.'

'Jealous?' Tom exploded, 'Jealous? She's an angel – as you keep reminding me – and angels don't get jealous.' He looked at her steadfastly. 'Do they?'

'No. But this angel's spent over a year inhabiting a human body. How do you know that the spiritual part of her hasn't changed?'

'What are you saying? She's become human?'

'Only part of her,' Mary corrected him hurriedly. Her eyes locked on his, earnestly. 'Humans do get jealous, envious even. How do you know that she isn't suffering from these pangs of humanity?'

'I don't, but then how can you know?'

'Because she isn't merely a Guardian Angel. She's your own very special one, someone who has looked after you from childhood, and having met her I believe that as a human she is terribly innocent. She won't know how to negotiate with her peers; won't understand her feelings or have the experience to argue with you; she will simply allow her resistance to dominate her and… well, run away. That's what I believe she's done.'

She shook her, sadly. 'Oh, Tom, this is such a tragedy… I don't really know what to say… she's such a beautiful person.'

'Christ! You make it sound as though I'm the bad guy here. You have to bear in mind, Mary, that I'm only human too; I did everything she asked of me; including a vasectomy, and…'

This time she looked at him in horror. 'What? Did I hear you right? A vasectomy?'

He refused to meet her gaze, afraid that yet again he was guilty of his own indiscretion. 'Yes. She didn't want me to father any children as that could have been one of those paradoxes I told you about.'

'But you could have taken precautions – you didn't need to have a vasectomy.'

'Well, that's what she wanted. Anyway, I did it. She said it would be irreversible.'

'Yes, well a vasectomy should be considered permanent, but it is possible to reverse it, especially if it's done fairly soon after the original operation.' Mary cut in, unable to keep her thoughts to herself. 'I think the success rate is something like eight in ten men, so she's getting confused with her biology.'

He shrugged. 'OK, Mary, but as I was saying I did everything she wanted of me! Up until I met Molly I even kept away from women altogether! So you can argue as much you like about her innocence, but the truth is I was the one who was naive.

'I worshipped her – I followed her around like a pet spaniel, listening to her, doing whatever it was she asked of me. Until, finally, I was totally in love with her, and wanted to show her physical love as well as emotional. That's when things began to change between us.'

'I'm beginning to believe that,' she said, leaning forward and taking hold of his hands. 'Look, Tom. Why not stay here, just for a few days, let me organise something.'

'How do you mean?' he asked.

'Remember, I'm the doctor here, and I know a specialist surgeon who can restore your fertility. A vasectomy reversal is usually done as a day case under general anaesthetic. You can have it done in the Christiana Hospital, the clinic attached to the Du Pont; it's not very far from the main hospital.' Catching the look of horror on Tom's face, Mary swiftly reassured him, 'That means you'll be asleep during the procedure! You may have to spend a couple of days in hospital, but it has to be worth it.'

He looked surprised. 'You'd do that for me?'

'Don't be ridiculous,' she almost snorted. 'Of course I will! I think it's morally wrong to deprive a young man like you of the chance to become a father. Once the stitches have dissolved and the surgical clips removed, about two weeks later, you can go to Philadelphia.'

He stood up and went to the bar to order another drink, welcoming the opportunity for a few minutes to consider what she was offering.

'Can I think about this?' he asked, as he returned carrying two more glasses of wine. 'Overnight.'

'Of course you can. Although I don't see what there is to think about – but I'll leave it with you and I'll pop by in the morning.'

'Fine, and Mary, thank you.'

Leaving her fresh drink untouched she grabbed her coat and got up quickly from the table. 'It's OK, Tom. You don't have to give me a kiss!'

CHAPTER THIRTY-ONE

It was gone eleven the next morning when Mary arrived; Tom had long finished his breakfast, packed his bag and checked-out. He sat in the lobby, flicking through old copies of Condé Nast Traveller, waiting.

'Sorry I'm a bit late; it took longer than I thought,' she said as she bustled through the revolving doors.

'Were you able to make the arrangements?' he asked quietly.

'Yes, of course. I've arranged for you to check-in at the Christiana Hospital in…' she checked her watch, 'just under two hours, so don't eat anything else – I assume you've had breakfast?'

'Yes. About three hours ago.'

'Good. Because this afternoon you'll be anaesthetised and by late afternoon it'll be done; it only takes about an hour.'

Tom sighed, almost with relief. 'And then?'

'Well, you will need to rest until the effects of the general anaesthetic have worn off. Your scrotum will feel sore and you may need painkillers, but the nurses will sort this out and you will be wearing supportive underwear to help relieve any discomfort. As long as you don't have any bad reaction to the anaesthetic you should be fine to leave the next day. I'll have to come and get you though, you shouldn't drive, but don't worry, Tom, you're going to be fine.'

'I just hope it works out OK.' Tom muttered, suddenly apprehensive.

'It will. Trust me – I'm your… well, you know what I was going to say.'

They stayed at the Du Pont for a while; Mary had a coffee and allowed Tom to sip some water, until it was time for them to leave.

'Who's the surgeon?' he asked in the car.

'Mr Benskin, he's the consultant urologist. I don't think you ever met him, but he's a really nice man. I've known him for years and trust him completely.'

'Who does he think I am? I mean, does he think I'm a relative of yours?' Tom asked; keen to get the story straight in his own head before the anaesthetic clouded it.

'Obviously I couldn't tell him who you are really. I just mumbled something about you being a distant cousin of the family.'

'Well, I hope he's accepted that. Didn't he wonder what the hurry was? I don't want him asking me any awkward questions.'

Mary was right; Mr John Benskin was indeed a very nice man, as well as a renowned expert in his field. All the difficulties and embarrassment that Tom had envisaged melted away as he was shaken warmly by the hand in the surgeon's private office. A tall, slim man in a well-cut suit, he exuded professionalism and confidence. He was balding and didn't try to disguise it by combing his hair across the top of his head. Taking Tom's blood pressure and using the stethoscope around his neck, Tom felt more relaxed than he had since his mother had suggested it.

'So you're Tom,' John Benskin said, peering down over bi-focal spectacles that showed enough of his eyes for Tom to realise that he had a permanent twinkle in them. 'And you want me to reverse your vasectomy?'

Tom coughed. Not sure what to say. 'Well, yes. Is it possible? I was told it would be irreversible.'

'Yes. A lot of men are told that, and generally it could be true. However, before I go on to talk you through the procedure I would like to know a bit of background. You are awfully young to have undergone this type of surgery.' The surgeon flashed Tom a glimpse of perfect white teeth as he smiled encouragingly.

This was a question that hadn't occurred to Tom, so he decided to try and stick to the truth as much as possible.

'Well, I was in love with a fabulous girl who convinced me she never wanted to have children. We've split-up now, but I allowed her to persuade me at the time to have it.' It sounded quite plausible, Tom thought, but Benskin looked at him as though he didn't quite believe him.

'It was all over so quickly; I was in and out in the afternoon.' He waved his hand around. 'Now I think I was foolish to make such a big decision.'

John Benskin briskly clapped his hands together and rising from his seat said, 'I'm amazed a surgeon performed the operation without extensive counselling, but let's see if we can rectify it, shall we? Come along, let's get you checked in and someone will show you to your room. I'll send a nurse in to take a blood test and we should be all set to go later this afternoon!'

Two hours later, after signing a medical consent form, Tom was relieved to be anaesthetised and wheeled down for surgery.

'How was it?' Tom asked Mr Benskin groggily, realising he was back in his hospital room.

The beaming surgeon grinned at him. 'Very straightforward,' he confirmed. 'The procedure went well and I have every expectation that you'll be fertile again. We'll keep you here for the night and probably tomorrow for observation, and then we should be able to release you. How does that sound?'

'I'm very grateful,' he said, on the point of falling asleep again.

'I hope your children will think the same,' he chuckled.

By the evening Tom was starting to feel better, if a little sore as he had been warned. The anaesthetics had worn off and he was relieved to feel unexpectedly cheerful. Wanting to share his good mood with someone, he made a decision to call Molly.

'Where are you? I heard you lost your job.' Her familiar voice said after three rings.

'I'm in Wilmington. Having my vasectomy reversed.'

'What? Are you alright? What prompted that decision?' The words tumbled out of her mouth in astonishment. 'What the hell is going on, Tom?' she demanded. 'I mean, why on earth are you in Wilmington having it done instead of New York? Are you on your own? Or do you have friends or relatives there?'

'Hold on Molly!' Tom smiled, pleased that she hadn't hung up on him and seemed interested. 'I'm in Wilmington because I know the surgeon who did the reversal; it isn't easy to do, you know, and I wanted the best.'

'OK, I can accept that, but what made you decide to do it?'

So he told her the truth; at least the part he had told John Benskin, that it was Imogene's refusal to have children that had prompted his original decision. The more he recited the story the more he recognised just how stupid it all sounded. On the one hand he had convinced Molly that Imogene refused to have sex with him, and now he was trying to persuade her that he had made a life choice based on the possibility that one day they might. Even to his own ears it sounded nonsensical.

'You're kidding me, right?'

He coughed with embarrassment. 'I know it sounds crazy, but you would have to meet Imogene to understand just how easy it was for her to … well, to dominate me.'

'You're still losing me,' she said. 'I, I… I can't take this in at the moment. Why doesn't she want children?'

'Remember I told you she wasn't really interested in sex? Well, I think this was part of her fear: that she would become pregnant and she couldn't possibly cope with that.'

Unable to leave it Molly pressed him further, 'But what would have happened if you had got married? Presumably you would have had sex and surely she would have wanted children then?'

'Well, I truly believed she didn't want to have children – under any circumstances.'

'Really? So what's changed? You haven't told me why are you having it reversed?' Molly sounded less than convinced.

'Because she's dumped me.' Tom admitted.

'Fucking hell! That was sudden wasn't it? Did you have some kind of a bust-up?' Molly tried to keep the glee out of her voice.

He sighed, the pressure getting to him. 'I told her about our conversation, the choice I had to make between her and you.'

'In other words you offered to give me up if she would have sex with you?' the anger in her voice was evident.

Tom blushed, feeling ashamed when it was put so bluntly. 'Well, not exactly,' he lied. 'What I did say was that as she was persistent in her desire for celibacy it would be better if we were to separate. It had little or nothing to do with you, Molly.'

'How long are you going to be in hospital?' she asked, changing the subject, almost as though she was dismissing his explanation.

'Another day or so. For observation.'

He heard her sigh across the wire.

'Look, why don't I come down this evening and visit you – then you can tell me all about it.'

'Hell, yes. If you don't mind, Molly. It would be nice to see you and I'll gladly explain everything to you.'

He gave her the name of the hospital and its address and ended the conversation by expressing his desire to see her again.

CHAPTER THIRTY-TWO

'Scott Hardy', he announced.

'Scott – it's Molly. I've just had a call from Tom Heaton. He's in hospital down in Wilmington.'

There was silence for a moment before Hardy said, 'Strange, what's he doing there? That's where that woman I was following lives. So why is he in hospital? Has he tried to take his own life?'

He heard her gasp over the telephone. 'No, of course not! What made you think that? Actually, he's in a clinic and he's had his vasectomy reversed.'

There was silence before Scott said, 'I don't understand … unless it was his Guardian Angel that organised it in the first place. Am I right?'

'It would seem so; at least that's what he implied. Although he didn't mention she was his Guardian Angel.'

'So why is he reversing the procedure?'

'Er, possibly because she's dumped him and he doesn't think it will look that good to prospective lovers?? Look, Scott, I'm already on my way to Wilmington; he's agreed I can visit him in the hospital. So after I've spoken with him I'll ring you and let you know what's going on.'

'Did he mention Imogene to you?'

'Well, not as such; only that she is afraid of sex – or at least afraid of becoming pregnant - and that it was she who insisted he had the vasectomy. Frankly I don't buy it.'

'Yes. I see what you mean. Except it doesn't explain why he now wants the procedure reversed. The fact she's deserted him still doesn't mean he's allowed to have children – I've researched this, Molly, and it has something to do with a Time Paradox.'

'What the hell does that mean?' she asked irritably.

'It's where someone's life has ended but for some reason he or she lives on in a kind of different timeframe. If they were to do something that couldn't possibly happen because they were already dead – like having children – then a paradox happens and a piece of time becomes distorted. Evidently it could cause a monumental tear in history.'

This time it was Molly who was quiet before she added: 'I see what you're saying. But we're still going along with what he told you about Lockerbie and how it was Imogene who rescued him; I still haven't had any confirmation of this from him.

'I suppose the only thing I can do now is ask him. He has at least given me the ammunition for some loaded questions.'

'Are you going to ask him about his angel? Or what his intentions are? I'm talking about you two living together.'

'I don't know yet – I'll play it by ear and see how he reacts. I'll ring you later, Scott.'

'OK. But while you're there try to get a sample of DNA, a piece of hair should do the trick.'

'Are you sure that really works? I've heard of it, but no one's sure how valid it is.'

'Oh, it works OK; but it's damn expensive. We need to have quite a large sample for mitochondrial testing, which will trace the ancestry of his maternal line.' There was a further pause before he continued: 'I've thought about this, and it seems to me that if we're to confirm what we believe, then we need to prove that Tom Heaton is definitely the son of Mrs Metzler.'

'But won't we also need a sample of his mother's DNA?'

He sighed, exasperated. 'That's who I'm talking about. I've already had a sample of Heaton's DNA analysed so we're clear on that side. Now we need his mother's.'

'But how do you propose I go about getting hold of that?'

'I dunno. Wait around at the hospital – I'm sure she'll come and visit her son. Then it might be possible to get a strand of her hair. Where are you now?'

This time it was her turn to sigh; an exasperated one that let him know he was testing her patience. 'I'm in Wilmington. You don't make it easy, do you? OK. I'll try to get the sample. Talk to you later. By the way, it's snowing like hell here.'

Mr Benskin, fastening a blood pressure cuff around his arm, woke Tom from his slumber.

'Wha... what is it?'

'It's all right, young man. I'm completing my examination of you. That seems to be fine, no bleeding, and no real reaction. I am confident that the operation's been a success.'

'So when do I get outta here?' Tom asked, rubbing his eyes.

'Well, I need to check up on you tomorrow, but I would think we should discharge you after lunch. You OK with that?'

Tom smiled his gratitude and muttered his thanks.

'Doctor Metzler's waiting to see you. Shall I send her in?'

Tom nodded uneasily, aware that Molly should be arriving any minute.

'See. I told you it would be easy, didn't I?' she said as she took a seat at the side of his bed.

'Yeah. You were right... Mary. I really feel as if I should check out now.'

'I wouldn't think of doing that, Tom, if I were you.' She patted his arm. 'You just stay here tonight and John Benskin will check you out in the morning. Then we'll see. Have you heard anything, from Imogene, I mean?'

'No. But Molly's coming to see me later. In fact she should be here by now.'

Mary pursed her lips, trying to disguise the contempt she felt. 'It'll be nice to meet her. After all I've heard about her.'

'Well… I dunno… do you think that's a good idea?

'What time's she due to arrive?' she asked, ignoring the question.

He checked his watch. 'I'm not sure. Anytime now I should think.'

'Well, I think I'll take myself off to the coffee shop – I haven't had lunch today. I'll be back in about an hour.'

She was gone, her hand waving a see you later.

CHAPTER THIRTY-THREE

He was still feeling drowsy when Molly entered the room. She looked a bit grim as she came over to his bed and placed her arm on his shoulder.

'How are you feeling, Tom? You gave me quite a fright.'

He sat up in the bed. 'I'm fine, thanks. It was really good of you to come and see me, especially as I'm not actually an invalid.'

'Well, I could hardly refuse when you told me you were in hospital,' she grinned, 'although you look OK to me!' She patted his face affectionately. 'So, how long will you be out of action?'

Tom looked down at his groin. 'Oh, you mean this?'

'What else could I mean?' she laughed, bringing a chair to the side of the bed and taking hold of his hand.

He grinned, 'I wasn't sure if you were talking about my employment.'

Molly grimaced. 'Mmmm, I heard about that; it's all round New York – that and Imogene's disappearance. It's OK if you don't want to talk about it, but I knew something had happened when you didn't call me.' She shrugged. 'What I'm trying to say is that even if you'd decided not to move in with me, I knew at least you would have called to let me know. Why did you lose your job, Tom? Or even more to the point why did your... your girlfriend simply disappear?'

He shrugged. 'I've been trying to create some kind of a plausible excuse for you to accept, but I can't think of anything to say – except that after Imogene and I had the conversation I told you about on the phone it seemed the best way out for her was to... I don't know. Go away.'

'Well, that does seem to be logical. But why then did you lose your job?'

'I didn't actually lose my job; it was a joint decision between Andy, the Sub-Editor, and me, although, to be fair, it wouldn't have been the same without Imogene. I really did want to move in with you, Molly. Only I was afraid to ring you because I thought you might ridicule me for leaving The Times.'

Molly walked across to the window. The snow was starting to fall harder now; it was virtually sheeting down and the hardtop approaching the hospital was already covered in a thick white blanket. She already knew about Tom losing his job because Scott had told her, but composed her face into a picture of concern.

'I won't ridicule you, Tom – it was just a job. So what happened with Imogene? Did you have a row?'

'Not as such. No. I told Imogene what you had said to me and how I... well, how I couldn't live without a relationship with someone I felt something for... and she... well, she went up to Saint Patrick's for guidance, she goes up there quite frequently to pray.'

She put a hand up to hide the glee on her face, convinced he was about to start spilling the beans. 'I take it you were talking about a sexual relationship? Not just about me?' She moved closer to him and put her hand on the side of his face, stroking it gently. 'It's OK, Tom, you can tell me anything...'

He nodded. 'Yes, I know, and it's one of the things I like about you. But I'd hate you to think that sex is all we had between us, Molly. I care for you, deeply ...'

'But you'd have preferred it if Imogene had relaxed her virtuous stance and slept with you. Is that it?' She said frowning; trying to look offended and hurt.

He looked downcast, not sure what to say. 'If you want the truth, yes; but I realise that for someone like Imogene, by her own standards of morality, this can never happen.'

She looked at him, straining for a few tears to edge her eyes, convinced that he would feel sorry and tell her everything. She said nothing for a while, hoping he would continue but when he didn't she resumed, 'you know, Tom, I don't really know you, do I? Oh, I know we slept together and you're a marvellous fuck, but apart from that,' she shrugged sadly, 'well, I know nothing about you. You told me you worked for a Delaware newspaper, but why are you keeping it so secret? Was it one you made up in your head? You see, I've checked it out and none of the papers in this part of the world have ever heard of you.' She rose, and started to pace around the small area in front of his high hospital bed, deciding that as looking shy and sad hadn't worked she would try more aggressive tactics.

'There was a newspaper in Philadelphia, The Reporter, where I spoke to one of the sub-editors, and he asked me if I was confusing you with Tom Metzler, who he met at Harvard?

'So, lover boy, come on, let me hear your confession. Who are you Tom Heaton? Where do you come from? Which school did you attend?' She leaned across, gave him a direct look and lowering her voice confided, 'Come on, if we're to live together, babe, then we can't have any secrets.'

Tom turned away, avoiding her eyes. This was impossible for him; he needed someone in his life, Imogene had deserted him, and he was confused as to what he should do. The weight of the secrets he carried was too much and he longed to talk them through with someone special. In that moment he decided he should tell her the truth. She was right; if they were going to live together he had to put her in the picture. It was just a bit hard to know where to begin and which bits to leave out. Should he tell her about his miraculous rescue from the Pan Am disaster at the hands of his Guardian Angel? He mentally shook his head. It sounded as if he was delusional; Scott Hardy had not believed him, why should Molly?

'Why are you shaking your head, Tom?' asked Molly.

'I don't know… I suppose it's because I don't even know the starting point.'

'Try the beginning. Tell me, for instance, why you misled me about your newspaper career and how you were able to persuade the New York Times to hire you? It takes years for a beginner to get a job like that! Unless, of course, you have a Guardian Angel; is that it, Tom? Is that what Imogene is; your Guardian Angel? Is that what the big secret it?

'Come on, Tom, open up to me. You want me to be honest with you; aren't I entitled to some reciprocity?' Molly leant across the bed and took his face in her hands. 'I can't live like this – not knowing the truth or whether you're misleading me all the time. I can't share the rest of my life with someone I can't trust.'

Tom looked away, finding it hard to meet her eye. Seeing his torment and spotting a chink in his reserve, she continued, 'Do you need time to think about it? Or is it just that I'm not worthy of your trust?'

He shook his head. 'No… I mean, no, I don't need time to consider. I do trust you, Molly and you've already guessed the truth; strange though it may sound…'

'About your Guardian Angel?' she interrupted, trying to hide her triumphant smirk.

Tom fell silent, his face whitening.

'So I'm right!' exclaimed Molly, failing to fully conceal her glee.

'Well, yes… You are… But how the hell did you…' he mumbled.

'Call it women's intuition,' she chuckled. 'But seriously, I guess I did kinda have a feeling about this whole weird relationship of yours... So come on, tell me all about it!'

'Well, it's like this... You see, she rescued me from the Pan Am disaster a little over a year ago – I owe my life to her.'

'How did she do that?' Molly asked a little too quickly, then quickly cautioned herself – she was in danger of getting carried away. 'Sorry,' she said. 'Do you want to leave it until you're feeling better?'

He lay back in the bed, weary at this exchange, but trying to stay focused.

'She is, or was, my Guardian Angel - yes, the real deal. She saved me from what would've been certain death because she thought I was too young to die in that disaster. And then she got me the job at the New York Times...'

'Really!' Molly interjected, unable to hide her curiosity. 'So what did you do before she intervened?'

'I worked at a firm of lawyers in Lexington Avenue.'

'So why didn't you just go back there, or practice with another firm? I mean, why become a journalist at the New York Times, no less, without any training?'

He sighed, 'Because she thought that my father had coerced me into becoming a lawyer and that I really wanted to become a journalist. So she got me the job at The Times.'

'Christ! She must have been persuasive – arranging a job like that.' Molly cuddled closer to Tom, inviting his confidences with her body language.

'She was very persuasive. I know we shared an apartment together, Molly, but we never once had sex...'

'And it was she who convinced you to have the vasectomy?'

'Yes. One of the reasons she's here is to stop me creating a time paradox.' Seeing Molly's puzzled look he tried to explain further. 'That is, if I were to do something now, like having children, when I'm supposed to be dead, then it would create a distortion in time that might affect the whole universe.'

'Fucking hell, Tom, is this true? No, don't answer that. I know it has to be true; no one could come up with a story like that! So you turned to me? I was second choice because your Guardian Angel rejected you!'

'Molly, it wasn't like that.' He looked at her pleadingly. 'I really am fond of you, and I believe we could have a good life together.'

CHAPTER THIRTY-FOUR

Taking her hand in his he tried to explain, desperate not to hurt her feelings again. 'I'm not saying that I wasn't attracted to Imogene, Molly. There's something fascinating about her – some special kind of allure...' Seeing her look of disapproval he shook his head. 'I'm sorry, I know it doesn't make much sense but Imogene just captivated me. And she did save my life.'

'I guess. But you've got to admit it's a hell of a thing to take in. And what I still don't understand is why you're having it reversed?' She pointed towards his crotch. 'Or have you done it now that she's gone to prove she no longer has a hold over you?'

'I don't know,' he admitted. 'She's disappeared and the apartment's empty.' He shrugged. 'So where she is now is anyone's guess; all I do know is that I've been rejected.'

'And you still want to move in with me? Won't you miss her? You've been together for a long time now.'

'Yes. I'd be a liar if I said I won't miss her – she was part of my life, but not in the same sense as you are. She watched out for me, Molly, but I was never part of her life; I couldn't be.'

Her expression appeared so plaintive that Tom reached out to her, despite his pain.

'And, yes, I do seriously want to move in with you, but not in New York – it holds too many memories for me. I thought perhaps... well, if I get a job and an apartment in Philadelphia we could share the travelling between us. You know, one week I could come up to see you, the next you could come to Philly? I know it's not ideal, but it's only a couple of hours on Amtrak. What do you think?'

Molly was silent for several seconds until Tom nudged her. Taking his face in her hands she looked deeply into his eyes and sadly said, 'if what you're telling me is true, how can I possibly match up to… your angel?'

He nodded, as though considering her question, but failed to respond.

Well, well, well, she thought – the truth at last! But how do I handle it now he's told me almost exactly the same as he said to Scott? How the hell do I deal with that? And what am I going to do about moving in with him, even on a part time basis? Now it was her head that was spinning; she hadn't expected him to disclose quite so much and it was blowing her mind. Could she go the whole way and betray him? He was not exactly naïve, but there was an air of innocence about him and he had fallen willingly into her trap.

She tried to pull her thoughts together quickly; Scott had already found out that there was some doubt about the passengers on the Pan Am flight. Tom was definitely on the flight list, but no one seemed sure if he had actually boarded the plane. If that was so, then maybe Imogene was an angel; perhaps she really had managed to save him. The whole story was so ridiculous it almost had to be true. It also changed things; Scott wasn't just asking her to betray Tom, but to betray an angel too. Although she hadn't been to church in many years there was still a residue of the little girl who had taken her first communion, and this part wasn't at all sure about the whole idea.

She got up from the bed and walked to the window; the snow had become a blizzard. That's all I need, she thought, to get trapped in Wilmington. I really need to speak with Scott.

'I have to think about this Tom; it's asking a lot of me to just accept this convoluted story. I look at you now and it's almost like seeing a corpse.'

'I don't think it was a corpse who was fucking you,' he said simply. 'You don't have to decide today, Molly.'

'Yes, I do,' she said. 'It isn't that I don't want us to be together; I do. What I'm afraid of is that she'll suddenly emerge again and want to control us. Like insisting you have this vasectomy done again, or something. It's things like that; they scare me.'

She was opening the door when Tom's mother emerged. Mary's frown deepened when she saw Molly, but she took her arm and steered her back inside the room.

'So you're Molly? Tom's told me about you.' she said abruptly.

'And you're Doctor Metzler?'

Mary nodded. 'You work for CNN, don't you? I've seen you once or twice. Good of you to come all this way.'

Molly grinned. 'You mean especially when he isn't ill?'

'Humph!' she snorted abruptly. 'He's told you then.'

'About the operation? Yes, I know all about it.' She looked across at Tom and grinned. 'He doesn't look much like an invalid, does he?'

'When are you planning on returning?' Mary asked, her lips softening a little as a response to Molly's humour.

'Well, I'd like to get away tonight; I have a conference in the morning.'

Mary nodded towards the windows. 'Have you seen the weather?'

Molly moved over to the window again and made a show of looking out, grimacing when she saw the blizzard.

'Are the trains still running?' she asked.

'I'm afraid not. You won't get as far as Philly in this weather.'

'I suppose I'd better let the office know and arrange for hotel accommodation.'

'I doubt you'll find anything available – not now. The hotels are full up with commuters from out of town. I think you're stuck here for the night.'

Molly grinned again and pointed towards Tom. 'And he's not going to be much use, is he?'

This caused Mary to burst out laughing. 'Not for a while – no. But I can find you a bed for the night.' She acknowledged Molly's look of surprise, swiftly followed by a smile of gratitude, and continued, 'sorry to drag you away from him, but if we don't leave now I'm going to have a job getting anywhere. It really is dreadful weather and the forecast says it's going to get worse – the roads are becoming treacherous, almost impassable.'

Molly pulled on her snow boots and shrugged into her dark green parka, pulling up the hood so that the fur lining framed her pretty face. Collecting her purse she leant down and gave Tom a last goodnight kiss before leaving with Mary for the parking lot.

CHAPTER THIRTY-FIVE

Mary was right. The snow was already banking up in the middle of the road, as they drove out of the grounds of the Christiana. Peering into the dark night, Molly could see drifts accumulating either side of the road, right onto the sidewalk; it was like driving through a snow tunnel. On top of that, visibility was poor because of the snow beating an endless tattoo on the windscreen. Slightly unnerved, Molly began to question whether or not Mary had made a good decision.

'Are you sure this is sensible?' she asked.

'I'm not sure – I can't really see anything. We're OK with this four-wheeler, it can deal with almost any conditions, but if this blizzard gets any worse we're going to have to abandon the journey.' Mary admitted.

Molly gasped. 'What? You mean dump the vehicle and try to get to where we're going through this lot?'

'No, Molly, I'm not that stupid. If we have to I have a tank full of gas so we can keep the engine running with the heater on full blast and sit here waiting to be rescued. But what I have in mind is that we're not far from the Du Pont Hospital, where I work, and I'm sure they'll find us a couple of rooms for the night. Are you fine with that?'

'Hell, yes. Better than being stuck out in the snow; in these conditions we're likely to become frozen-up.'

There was no sign of snow ploughs, so the drifting accumulated at rapid speed until their vehicle was almost traversing the mounds spreading across the roads.

'We're turning here,' Mary said, struggling with the blinding conditions. Lights shone in front of them rather like beacons attracting them to safety. 'The Du Pont,' she said the relief evident in her voice.

'It's a children's hospital,' Molly stated, spotting the entrance sign.

'Yes. I'm a paediatrician. We do important work here.'

They left the car in front of the building and tried to shake off the snow from their boots before entering. There were crowds of people congregating around reception when they entered – no doubt parents who were stranded. One or two of them greeted Mary and asked if she were now stuck, as they were, in the drifts. She grinned at their humour, exchanged pleasantries, and then steered Molly away from reception after signing-in.

'I don't think we're going to get rooms, do you?' Molly asked.

'Don't worry, we will – I'm staff, we always have rooms available for night-stops. And anyway there's always the hotel - it's called the Du Pont too.'

Mary led them down a long corridor, past an open ward where one or two of the children waved as they saw her.

'Do you look after them all?' Molly enquired, impressed by seeing the older woman in her work environment and the respect she clearly inspired.

Mary shook her head. 'No. That isn't possible. I deal with those children who have respiratory problems – including the cystic fibrosis cases.'

'It must give you a great deal of pleasure.'

'Yes, and a great deal of heartache to go with it, but I'm a professional, Molly, it's what I do. Come on,' she said as they entered a small room off the corridor, 'we'll leave our things here and then we'll go and get something from the cafeteria. Hope you're not too hungry because at this time of night I guess they'll be reduced to a sandwich or two.'

'I don't mind what there is – I'm starving!'

Mary led them into a small room with twin beds and a shower room leading off it. It was rather basic but functional for the night staff. Curtains were drawn against a window and an old Van Gogh print hung from one of the walls.

'Hope you don't mind sharing,' she said, throwing her coat onto one of the beds.

'No, not at all.' Molly was too grateful to be inside in the warm to worry about sharing, 'but I don't have any change of clothes – not even a toothbrush.'

'Don't worry about that; you'll find what you need in the bathroom. You'll just have to make do with the clothes you're wearing, as we all will tonight. Come on. Let's go eat.'

They were lucky that night; the cafeteria had kept the soup going so they each a bowl with a sandwich. Once they were seated it was Molly who led the conversation.

'So how do you know Tom?' she asked innocently.

'I'm a distant relative of his,' replied Mary, without meeting her eye. 'It seems that after this girl bewitched him and persuaded him to have a vasectomy, she ditched him! So, he asked me if I could help, as I'm in the medical profession, I referred him to a colleague, who's a specialist, and now he's undergone a reversal.'

Molly pursed her lips, almost challenging. 'A distant relative? Tom never told me about you, although I know you visited him in New York some time ago, so I knew you were a doctor. What kind of distant are you, Mary?'

Mary turned her head as if she were afraid of being exposed. It wasn't difficult for Molly to spot the evasion.

'I'm a sort of distant cousin – it would be hard to explain. He lived here as a child so it was logical to contact me for the procedure.'

Molly held her gaze, suggesting the story was not plausible. But she said nothing.

'You should be able to get back to New York tomorrow,' Mary mentioned, anxious to change the subject.

'Will the tracks be cleared?'

'I would say so; they're pretty quick around here to restore civilisation.'

Molly smiled to herself. She had obviously embarrassed Mary, and although she would love to know what the truth was, decided she needed to be cautious. Before she could continue the discussion, Mary asked: 'Do you come from this part of the world?'

'Chicago. I took a degree course in media studies and then got a job with the local television company.'

'And how long have you been with CNN?'

Molly looked puzzled at the interrogation. 'Two years now. But I'm not yet on the front desk. I suppose I'm still what they call a "runner".'

'Does your family live in Chicago?'

'Yes.' She sighed this time. 'And before you ask, Mary, my parents are both well and I have two sisters.'

Mary coughed. 'Sorry about that. I get so used to asking the children these types of questions... it becomes natural for me.'

'That's OK. Has Tom told you he's asked me to move in with him?'

Mary turned her head away again to avoid glancing at Molly. 'Well, no. But then why should he? After all we're not exactly close.'

Molly smiled; it was obvious that Mary knew full well what Tom's intentions were.

'I don't suppose you are. But then he doesn't seem to have anyone else to talk to – at least not from what he's told me.'

'Have you decided what to do?'

'Not yet. I don't want to sound confusing but he's given me some bizarre story that I'm having difficulty getting my head round it.'

'Yes, but what does your heart tell you?'

Molly stroked her hair again, taking the question seriously. 'I'm not altogether sure. I mean, we get on OK, and he's fantastic in bed but …' she shrugged. 'I suppose if you ask me how I really feel about him then I'd have to say that I'm a bit sorry for him.'

'Why? Because you think he's lonely, perhaps because his girlfriend has unceremoniously dumped him?'

'I don't know that either. I agree he's very lonely and I do think he needs someone to confide in; that's probably where I fit in.'

'So you're still undecided?'

'Don't you really want to talk about Imogene?' said Molly, diverting the topic.

'Well, I suppose I am curious – you know, about where she came from. One minute she was with Tom and the next, she disappeared. Do you know anything about her?'

Molly said nothing for a few moments, as though she were considering how much of the story she could discuss with Mary.

'You're pretty quiet,' Mary commented.

'It's not that I'm trying to avoid the question; it's just that I was thinking about what Tom told me about his ex-girlfriend. I suppose if I were asked for an opinion I would have to say she was some kind of an angel.'

Mary's eyes opened wide. 'You're joking – right?'

Molly ran a hand through the red highlights in her hair. 'Crazy isn't it? But no, I'm not. I am absolutely serious.'

'God, Molly. You'll have to enlighten me. How on earth did you work that one out?'

'Well, it's pretty much as you said earlier. There is this mysterious woman who appears from out of nowhere, no one knows anything about her – and for some reason she captivates Tom, gets him a job at the New York Times, induces him to share a flat with her, then persuades him to have this… this vasectomy when she has no intention of having sex with him. What would you gather from that?'

Mary nodded her head thoughtfully. 'I don't know. I've never thought about it like that. I just assumed she was an enchanting female who captured his heart but who, for whatever reasons, is afraid to have sex or children. There are cases like that I've come across, you know.'

Molly looked doubtful at this statement. 'Really? But your area of expertise is children! I mean, how experienced are you with adults?'

Mary shrugged. 'Well, not very, I confess. But I've heard of people with intimacy issues, like this, from my colleagues.'

'So you don't believe she's an angel?'

Now Mary laughed. 'Hardly! What on earth would an angel want with Tom Heaton? He's hardly the next Messiah! He's just a very ordinary guy who became fascinated with an attractive female and was persuaded to go along with her wishes.' She got up from the table and collected her cutlery.

'Now, I don't know about you, but I'm tired and ready for bed. You coming – or do you want to hang around here for a while?'

'Do you have any children, Mary?'

'What? Where did that come from?' Seeing from Molly's face that she was unlikely to let it drop Mary sat down again. 'Yes. I had a son – Tom. He died in the Lockerbie disaster. He was only twenty-two; a lawyer from New York.'

'I'm sorry. It must have been terribly hard for you to lose someone so close to you.'

Mary frowned at her. 'What are you getting at, Molly?'

Molly held her gaze until it was Mary who turned away.

'I just feel sorry for you to have lost a son – especially in such tragic circumstances. It must have broken your heart?'

'Yes. I've shed a few tears. It isn't right that parents should have to bury their own children.'

'I agree with you. And if I can't convince you Tom's been going out with an angel then I'd better get some rest.'

In the small bedroom, as Molly waited for Mary to use the bathroom, she noticed a hairbrush left on a shelf by the sink. She extracted a couple of the longer hairs, folded them, and placed them in a handkerchief. At least she had achieved what Scott Hardy was after, although she did feel a little ashamed. Mary seemed to be a very nice woman, even though she had resisted her opportunity to explain Imogene's presence. Pushing her conscience to one side, Molly concentrated on the news she was taking back to New York.

CHAPTER THIRTY-SIX

By the next morning the snow ploughs had done their work, Amtrak confirmed that the lines were now open and Molly decided to drop in to see Tom on her way home.

Tom was sitting on his bed reading a newspaper when Molly entered the room. He looked great, she thought.

'Hi, Molly! Want some coffee?' his face lit up at the sight of her. 'Where did you spend the night?'

'Mary found me a bed in the Du Pont - the hospital, that is, not the hotel. Look, Tom, I'm only here for a few minutes, and then I'm catching the train to Manhattan.'

'So soon,' he said handing her the coffee.

'Yeah. I've already missed a meeting this morning.'

'Do you have any thoughts about our chat yesterday? You know, about moving in with me.'

She frowned and sat next to him on the bed. 'Tom. Please don't take this the wrong way, but I still feel I need more time. If you're moving to Philly, give me a ring when you're settled in, I'll come down and discuss it with you then. It'll give us both time to see how we really feel.'

Tom looked dismayed. 'So is that a "no"?'

She frowned. 'I don't think that's fair. I haven't made up my mind yet. Like I said last night I want to see if Imogene reappears – if she doesn't then, it's probably a yes. Can you wait for that?'

He grinned, satisfied with her reply.

'Yes, of course. And I don't think we'll see her again.'

Molly leaned over and kissed him. 'Take care of yourself, Tom. And ring me soon.'

Moments later she took a taxi from the hospital and caught the early morning train back to New York. On the way she rang Scott Hardy.

'It's me,' she announced.

'Where are you, Molly?'

'On the train – heading back to New York.'

'Good. We'll meet up for lunch and you can tell me all about it. Don't talk now; I've got someone with me.'

'Sure. Meet me about one outside CNN.'

Molly was feeling disturbed as she stepped from the train at Penn Station. Having spent time with Tom and listened to his story, then shared a room with his 'mother', a woman she found she responded to, it didn't stack up with her sense of moral values to now enter into a campaign to betray them both.

She was due to meet Scott outside the CNN Offices in about half-an-hour, so she just had time to change her clothes and visit the apartment where Tom used to live – really to enquire what had happened to the tenancy. After changing, she dodged the sleet that threatened to merge into a snowstorm, easing her way from shop-doorway to shop-doorway.

It was a beautiful old Georgian Brownstone in the heart of Greenwich Village. There was no concierge on the door but she had to press one or two of the bells before she could gain entry. She climbed the stairs, rather than take the lift, and on the first floor a tenant was waiting for her.

'You pressed my bell,' a middle aged woman demanded.

'Sorry. Yes, I did. I'm trying to find some information on the tenants who occupied an apartment on the second floor. Tom Heaton and ...'

'Oh yes. You mean Imogene?'

'Well... yes. Do you know what happened to them?'

The woman shook her head. 'No… I'm afraid I don't. I'm the caretaker of this building and I have a refund for them… that's if they ever appear.'

'I don't suppose you have the keys, do you?' Molly asked with her sweetest smile.

'Are you a relative?'

'No. But I'm an old friend of Tom's. He's in hospital at present and he's asked me to collect some clothes for him.'

The caretaker frowned. 'I don't know what he's expecting to find. I was in there the other day and it's completely empty.' She took some keys from her apron pocket. 'You can go ahead and look if you want – but if you don't mind I'll come with you.'

Molly had visions of racing down the stairs, like a thief in the night, with a television tucked under her arms. She turned her head away so the woman wouldn't see her smiling.

'Here we are – 2B,' she said opening the door.

It was a lavishly appointed apartment with wall-to-wall carpeting. They went into the spacious lounge; Tom had told her it was once beautifully furnished with luxurious sofa's, cushions that would grace a palace, antiques and works of art that Molly would have given a year's salary to have owned. Now it was completely empty, as though no one had lived in it for some months.

The caretaker pointed around the room: 'See? It's completely empty.'

'But I understood it was completely furnished,' Molly said in surprise.

'No. It was always unfurnished – aside from the carpets. They obviously brought their own furniture. Come with me – I'll show you the bedrooms.'

Two very large bedrooms, each with private facilities, were also empty; no beds; no bedside drawers. Molly opened the closet doors to be met with vacant hangers, but no clothes.

'I don't understand it,' she exclaimed. 'Tom was living here only a few days ago. Did Imogene give you notice?'

'No. But having paid six months in advance, plus the statutory deposit, it isn't really necessary to give the landlords notice. That's why they are due some kind of refund.'

'But are you able to rent out the apartment in the meantime?'

'That isn't for me to say, young lady. That will be up to the owners. But I wouldn't think so – I mean, they've been paid. I just reported to them that the place was now vacant.'

'Well thank you very much,' Molly said as they left the apartment and went down the stairs.

'If you speak with that gentleman… Tom… could you ask him if he has any intentions of returning? Maybe he could get in touch with Imogene – she probably has his clothes.'

'Yes. I'll do that.'

It was ten-minutes from one-o'clock. She would have to hurry.

She was five minutes late and Scott was already waiting.

'Where've you been?'

'I was looking into Imogene's old apartment. It's empty. In fact it looks as though no one has ever lived there!'

'Well, we knew she'd disappeared – why would an angel need an empty apartment?'

Molly tossed her hair. So he was still playing the same old tune, despite her misgivings. She said nothing as they entered the restaurant.

'Are you hungry,' asked Scott.

'Not really. And I have to say, Scott, I have some questions about this angel business.'

'Did you get hold of the sample I asked for?' he said, ignoring her.

She nodded. 'Yes. But I didn't like doing it.'

'Really?' He said as they were led to a table. 'Why would that be?'

'Because I quite liked Doctor Metzler – she's a very nice person. And I felt as though I was betraying her.'

Scott held out his hand. 'You were; let me have the sample. Then you can clear your conscience.'

She handed over her handkerchief with the hairs inside, again saying nothing.

After they had ordered Scott turned to her and said: 'Let me remind you, Molly, that however nice you think she is she's protecting her son by pretending her own Tom Metzler died in that air disaster. She also knows Imogene, including what she really is.'

Molly shrugged. 'I suppose. But she isn't doing any harm. I mean if it were my son and I discovered the truth I'm sure I'd do anything to protect him. So you can't blame her for that.'

'I'm not suggesting I blame her – however, what I am searching for, is the most sensational story this world has ever heard since the birth and crucifixion of Jesus Christ.'

There was silence as the waiter cleared their dishes. Molly ordered a coffee whilst Scott waved his hand to dismiss the waiter.

'So what will you do if the DNA confirms that Mary and Tom are mother and son? How will you announce that to the world?'

'That will be the evidence I'm seeking! After that I need to look into how Tom was able to check in for the Pan Am flight and then disappear. I told you what my informant says, didn't I? One minute there was some confusion, as though he weren't going to appear, the next it's all taken care of and they claim he was on-board.'

'Yes. You told me that; he simply checked in, with only hand baggage, and then failed to turn up when the flight was boarding?'

'They don't allow that these days. If a single passenger is missing, especially if any have checked in baggage, then they check out the terminal for him or her; it will be non-stop announcements till they find the passenger. So, someone got on that aircraft; either it was our Tom Metzler, or someone who took his place.'

'You mean like another angel?'

He frowned at her. 'This isn't funny, Molly.' He paused and then said, 'I think it's better if I don't say any more until I've checked the sample. It might not come to anything.'

'And if it does?'

'Then we'll have a sensational story to tell - one worth millions!'

'So tell me, if the samples match and we discover that Mary – Doctor Metzler – is the mother of Tom Heaton then so what? I mean, he told me more or less the same story he told you, that Imogene's an angel and, yes, she did rescue him from that tragedy, but surely, isn't that simply hearsay?'

'You surprise me. I never thought he'd go that far.'

'Why not? This is the man who wants to move in with me – why shouldn't he tell me the truth?'

'I guess so. But we'll have gone a long way to prove the story if the samples do match.'

She tossed her head. 'Really? Couldn't she say that this Tom Heaton was a mistake? You know, she'd had an affair, unknown to her husband, and this second son was the outcome?'

'Fucking hell! Now who's being naïve?' He held out his hands. 'Think about it? This second son you mention has exactly the same date of birth as Tom Metzler, and the so-called second son has no reliable background – in other words he simply doesn't exist. No schooling, not on any register, aside from the New York Times has never paid any taxes, is not on any voters register, has no driving licence -'

'All right' she interjected 'You've made your point. And Imogene? How will you explain her disappearance?'

He sighed, obviously frustrated. 'Oh, I'd love to find her – maybe have a chance to talk to her. See if she can describe the celestial body she obviously occupies.'

'How do you think you might find her?'

'I think I'll let Tom Heaton explain that one away. Come on – I've got work to do.'

'Before you go, Scott, There's something I would like to ask you.'

They were now outside the restaurant, trying to shelter from the rain.

'What is it,' he said irritation in his voice.

'Do you actually believe this story about Tom Heaton and the angel?'

'What? What the hell do you think I've been doing? Playing some game? Of course I believe it. Why? Don't you?'

'I'm not sure. It all seems so fucking bizarre to me. But if you genuinely believe it then aren't you missing the point?'

He sighed. God, women; they could be so irritating. 'And what point is that, Molly?'

'It's just that… well, shouldn't you be concentrating on the miraculous side of the story; that there is life after death? Isn't that the real essence of the story?'

'Of course it is. And it is that that I'm going to bring to the world as a whole. Come on, you're holding me up.'

An Angel's Kiss

CHAPTER THIRTY-SEVEN

Imogene stood in front of the assembly having been summoned to appear before them.

'You wanted to talk to me'

'Yes, Imogene. There is a matter of some urgency we should discuss with you.'

'Does it concern Tom?'

'Yes. We have been considering your withdrawal from your present engagement and we have to tell you that our sympathies are with you. We never expected that occupying a human body would have such a terrible effect on your senses; it is not a solution we will consider if we ever face another event like this one.

'However, there have been one or two developments we should bring to your attention, and then we will leave it to you to decide your actions.'

'Please, tell me.'

'Well, firstly, a few days ago, Tom Metzler had his vasectomy reversed, thanks to his mother. Now, whilst this in itself does not concern us too much, we have to tell you that Scott Hardy was given a sample of Doctor Metzler's hair by his partner, Molly Sinclair. He is now in the process of having this analysed through a DNA process, which will confirm that Doctor Metzler is, indeed, his mother.'

'I'm sorry; I was informed that the vasectomy was irreversible. But more importantly, why would Molly Sinclair hand over to Hardy a sample of Mary's hair?'

'Because she is his partner; they live together.'

'I see. I'm astounded. So this relationship between Tom and Molly Sinclair was merely a set-up to entice the truth from him?'

'Yes. We confirm.'

'Tom doesn't know this; he has to be informed! Why has he tried to have the vasectomy reversed? Oh dear… the complications I have caused.

What do you think I should do about this? And what should I do about Molly and Scott Hardy?'

'Discuss it with Abbott Augusto, see what he recommends, and when you do decide what your future holds, come back to us and let us know your decision, preferably over the next few days. Please bear in mind, Imogene, whatever you do decide we will support you - all of the way.'

'Thank you, Chairman.'

'Abbott Augusto, may I have a word with you?' Imogene asked.

The Abbott rose from his seat behind the enormous desk and came towards her, pointing her to a nearby seat.

'How may I help you my dear?'

'I have been asked to discuss my problems with you in the hope you may counsel me, perhaps give me the benefit of your wisdom.'

He smiled. 'I'm not sure who told you that, Imogene, but my wisdom is seriously diminished as I grow older.'

She looked at him, a serious expression on her face. 'You're too modest, Augusto… The tribunal know what they're talking about and it was they who recommended that I get your advice… but now I'm here, I don't know where to start.'

He smiled again. 'I usually say, try starting at the beginning.'

'Yes. I asked for that, didn't I?' She paused to clear her mind. 'Well, it's about Tom… You know, the one I rescued from an air crash. You know I was falling in love with him… but it's worse than that now. I've been struggling with the constant temptation, the lust, I suppose you'd call it…'

'Yes, yes, I remember. And didn't you leave him?' He rubbed his face with a hand.

'Yes, Abbott, I did, but not without some consternation. I still miss him even though he went off with his lover.'

'I can see you're not finding it easy without him, Imogene. So how may I help?'

'I'm not sure. I regret letting him go but I felt I didn't have any choice. Now it seems he's in the target of some kind of a conspiracy between his girlfriend and the lover she's kept secret from him. Worse than that, I've met this guy - he's Tom's superior at The Times - and I instantly sense that he's evil. I mean really, fundamentally evil.'

The abbot raised a concerned eyebrow.

'I see. Please, go on,' he murmured, deep in thought.

'Furthermore, having taken some DNA from the young man's mother they're intent on proving that they are mother and son. And if that were to happen then these people – both of whom work in the media – will have a spectacular story to tell the world.'

'You mean they would have some evidence to disclose of the supernatural world?'

'Yes. That's the real worry.'

The abbot's eyes widened as the he processed the enormity of what was at stake.

'But surely their story won't be credible unless they can interview the participants involved; including perhaps yourself?'

'No doubt - but right now there's not much stopping them doing that. Somehow I need to convince Tom that his intended partner is… well, that she's deceitful and manipulative; that she's already living with his former boss and they're planning to expose him - expose us, and the secrets of the afterlife - through the media.'

The Abbott paused for a while, then returned to his desk and began filling his pipe.

'Hope you don't mind,' he said. 'I think rather better if I'm alight. Aside from which this is the only place in the building I'm allowed to smoke!'

Chuckling, she nodded her head in acceptance.

Eventually he raised his head and regarded her contemplatively. 'The problem with that, my dear, is that, under the circumstances, he probably won't believe you. I think you'll have to provide him with unequivocal proof.'

Imogene shook her head. 'That sounds ideal, Abbot, but how do you propose I go about it? I can hardly get them to sign a confession, can I?'

Augusto grinned at her naivety. 'Why don't you buy one of those new camcorders? Then you can follow this man home from work, hoping his girlfriend will be with him, film them both entering the apartment, and again the following morning when they leave for work. Do you think you can you do this?'

'I guess; assuming someone will show me how to work the damn thing!'

'I wouldn't worry about that – they'll give you a demonstration at the shop. Now, if you can accomplish that, give him the evidence. Then I suggest that either you bring him here, where we can protect him, or else you consider leaving the country. In either case no one will be able to interview you and any story they may have will have a hollow note. In other words it will be full of conjecture - and easy target for all the doubting Thomases out there who'll be eager to refute the existence of the supernatural..'

'You make it sound so easy.'

'It shouldn't be too difficult. I might also suggest you visit your boyfriend's mother – who, as you informed me, knows you quite well, - and explain to her the situation. It is clearly in her interests to protect herself and her son.'

'I suppose – but how's she going to achieve that, Abbott?'

He shrugged. 'She should be able to convince him that he's in danger and urge him to go with you. Do you agree with that, my dear?'

Yes. And thank you so much, Augusto. I'm not sure if I'll be able to persuade Tom to stay here at the monastery though.'

Augusto placed his arm on her shoulder. 'Dear Imogene. You're so innocent. That's something you need to think about – either bring him here or take him somewhere overseas. Let me know, in due course what you decide, won't you?'

She nodded again, and then kissed him on the cheek.

'My,' he exclaimed. 'Again! I've just been kissed by an angel.'

Later that day, Imogene waited outside the office of the Times until she saw Scott Hardy emerge. Discreetly she followed him through the windswept streets, pausing only to watch him admire the expensive jewellery in an upmarket shop window before checking his appearance in the window. Finally, with urgency, he quickened his step until he reached a fairly modern apartment building where a concierge welcomed him. Shortly after, Molly Sinclair arrived and was also warmly welcomed by the concierge. Through the lens of camcorder Imogene had a clear shot of them both from her hiding place in a shop doorway.

Imogene waited until they had both disappeared before approaching the middle aged concierge. She looked deeply into his eyes and asked him for the number of Hardy's apartment, which he gave without blinking an eyelid. He also added Scott Hardy's home phone number in case she needed it.

Returning early the following morning, in case one or the other went to work at the crack of dawn, she watched as they emerged from the building, arm in arm. She was hardly able to contain her delight as Hardy gave Molly a sensuous kiss before she caught a cab. Now she had everything on camera.

An Angel's Kiss

An Angel's Kiss

CHAPTER THIRTY-EIGHT

Imogene made herself comfortable on the train, having booked herself into a first class compartment. She closed her eyes and ruminated on what the future might hold for both her and Tom. In effect she had been given carte blanche by the tribunal to deal with the matter as she saw fit. The only thing that occurred to her was that although Tom and Molly were now destined to separate; he might not want her back. She decided that she would tell Mary that she would be available to help him during this stressful situation, whatever his decision.

She wondered how he might handle this revelation. She shook her head; it really was something of a conflict. She didn't want to be the bearer of such bad news, but Tom had to know what was really going on behind Molly's enchanting smile. Next, was the question of how to deal with the potential publicity any revelations would create if Scott and Molly decided that they had sufficient data to go public. It might well be appropriate for both of them to disappear as Abbott Augusto had recommended. But where would they go? If they were already in the public eye she doubted there was anywhere in the world where they might be inconspicuous.

Imogene felt totally out of her depth; her own innocence of how the world worked seemed to overpower her. She had been told in the past by the people at the New York Times, and recently by Augusto, that her virtue made her vulnerably naive. She could agree with this, blaming it on her lack of knowledge of human nature and how the world worked. After all, she mused, she had been denied the umbilical bonding that babies have with their mother; she had never suckled at her mother's breast and she had never grown up with parents as a moral compass. Not that she lacked the morality that goes with being a human – that was intrinsic to her spirituality – she simply had no guidelines to direct her. The tribunal had launched her into a human frame, without the basic knowledge and experiences that are imperative to growing into a well balanced, mature adult. Sure, she possessed a woman's body, but in a way she was a newborn in an adult physique. It was interesting that the Tribunal had appeared to notice this during her last encounter. That was all very well, thought Imogene angrily, but it hardly helped her now.

She was still deep in thought as the train pulled into Wilmington. It was an overcast day with the sky threatening rain and the wind blowing off the river, making ripples race across the steel grey surface. Clutching her overnight bag, she pulled up the collar of her new cashmere as she alighted and searched for a taxi. It was only a short journey to the Du Pont Hospital where she asked for Doctor Metzler. After waiting impatiently at reception for some time Doctor Metzler finally arrived.

'Imogene,' she expressed her surprise. 'What on earth brings you to Wilmington? I thought you and Tom had … well, kind of split up.'

Imogene went over and kissed her on the cheek.

'Yes. We have, Mary, but something has come up that I feel you should know about. Do you have time for a coffee?'

'Of course,' said Mary, glancing at the clock behind reception, now showing that it was after twelve. 'I can take an early lunch. Come on, we can go to the cafeteria.'

'What I have to say has to remain confidential, is there somewhere else we can talk?'

Seeing the look of genuine worry on Imogene's face, Mary thought about it for a moment before announcing, 'Yes, there's a diner not too far away – it shouldn't be too busy at this time of day. Come on, we can walk it.'

'Where are you living now?' asked Mary, trying to make conversation as they battled through the still gusting breeze.

Imogene pressed a finger to her lips intimating she shouldn't ask her these types of questions. It was only when they were seated at an empty table, after ordering sandwiches and coffee that she elected to speak.

'Where's Tom?' she enquired.

'He has an apartment in Philadelphia. He only rented it a few days ago; I guess about now he's searching for a job. Look, I know it's personal, and I probably should wait but do you mind me asking why you broke up? I hope you forgive me, but I need to know before I can really talk anymore.' Mary smiled to soften her words.

Seeing Mary flush with embarrassment at her direct approach, Imogene nodded her head. 'Of course not; we separated because Tom was thinking of moving in with his girlfriend, Molly Sinclair, she works for CNN.'

'Yes, Tom told me,' Mary interrupted. 'But that's not the only reason is it? I know it may seem inappropriate, but Tom did confide in me about your reluctance to engage in a sexual relationship.'

'I hoped you might understand,' Imogene said, looking away.

'Oh, I do; I certainly didn't need it explained to me – it's Tom who seems to have the problem. So, did you want to contact him?'

'No, Mary. I want you to contact him - after I've left.'

Mary frowned. 'I don't understand.'

'Let me explain. Sometime ago, Tom told his boss at the Times, after repeated questions about his past, the truth. That is, that he'd been saved from the Lockerbie disaster by his Guardian Angel, had his appearance changed, and given, with no experience, the job as assistant reporter on the newspaper.

He also told him that I was the Guardian Angel, there to look after him.'

Not for the first time Mary's mouth fell open. 'Jesus! I don't believe it. When was this?'

'About six months ago. Look, I don't think Tom did it maliciously, it's just that Scott Hardy, that's his ex-boss's name, kept on and on at him and was making life really difficult. Tom thought that Scott had dismissed it as a joke, but he hadn't. In fact, since then he has been intent on proving that it is a true story. One day, he even followed you on the train after visiting Tom; I was only able to stop him by putting him to sleep until Washington.

'However, when Molly was here, visiting Tom, she took some of your hair as a DNA sample; this is now being examined at a laboratory and it will prove beyond doubt that you and Tom are mother and son.'

'Oh, dear God, how does she fit into this?' Mary cut in, dropping her sandwich back onto her plate in utter surprise.

'I'm sorry; but Molly's part of the plot to uncover the truth about Tom and me; she's actually Scott's girlfriend.'

'What? This is terrible! I thought she was my friend; I actually liked her! Now you're telling me she's betrayed us both? Why?' She hesitated, a shocked expression on her face. 'Poor Tom, what am I going to do?'

Imogene reached across the table and covered the older woman's hand, passing comfort and warmth from her own to help her digest the bad news. Smiling encouragingly, she started, 'Mary, you're not alone. I'll support both of you through this. First off, we have to expose them to Tom.'

'Yes. Of course he has to be told. How will you do that?' Mary sighed, wiping her free hand across her face in a gesture of weary acceptance.

'I won't. This is something you will do – with this.' She explained, handing over the camcorder to Mary, and switching it on. As Mary realised what she was watching her eyes grew wider and she nodded grimly at Imogene.

'What I suggest you do is see him today; tell him about the DNA sample, let him know that you and I have met, and show him the camcorder. He can see for himself that his girlfriend already has a lover, his former boss, and that they're setting him up. He needs to go to New York and ask them what they're planning; perhaps you could go with him?'

For a moment Mary looked distraught as she tried to absorb all the information. 'Look, Imogene, I can't go today,' she said after a while. 'I have some parents to talk to about their children. Could I go tonight?'

'Put them off,' Imogene said firmly. 'This is a matter of some urgency – I have no idea how far they've got with the sample. Who knows, Mary, they could already be on the point of making a news statement.'

Mary frowned at her. 'Well, say Tom does agree we should go to New York and confront these people in their apartment and confirm what you're saying…'

'Yes. That's the idea,' Imogene interrupted urgently.

'OK, but what then? Assuming they have the DNA results and I'm established as his mother? I mean, how's he going to get them to change their minds when they have the most sensational story in the history of the world since the birth and death of Jesus Christ? Can you imagine the headlines that proof exists of an afterlife, with the intervention of a Guardian Angel, who intercedes in Divine providence? You, in other words, Imogene. It's a licence to print money – they can command as much as they like, and that's without the fame and glory they will get for a scoop like this!'

Imogene was silent at this. In her own naivety it hadn't occurred to her that Tom, and everyone else involved, would be impotent to stop Scott and Molly revealing the news story of their career. Of course Mary was right; they would simply laugh at him, and probably ask him for a statement.

Finally she said, 'I'll have to think about this. What time are you expecting to finish for the day?'

'I'm off duty at four.'

'OK. Let's meet up again, but meanwhile, give me Tom's telephone number – I might give him a call this afternoon. Perhaps I can persuade him on my own.'

'I hope you're right,' said Mary.

CHAPTER THIRTY-NINE

Jennie - a colleague at the Times - seemed surprised when Imogene called her one afternoon out of the blue, asking for beauty and fashion advice. Something about Imogene's aura of unworldliness had filled the older woman with an urge to take her under her wing; to mother her, Jennie supposed if she was honest with herself. Until now, though, Imogene had seemed disinterested in her offers of beauty and fashion tips. Not that Imogene ever looked anything less than stunning - it was just that some of her fashion choices were questionable to say the least. When Imogene had turned up for work in a svelte evening gown teamed up with a baseball cap and trainers, Jennie's heart had gone out to her as junior staff stifled their derisory giggles. But it was when she noticed Imogene's singular choice of perfume (it was Paco Rabanne aftershave for men!) that she felt compelled to set the poor girl straight.

"So why the sudden need for a makeover, babe?' Jennie asked, genuinely curious.

There was a long silence on the line before Imogene replied, 'Let's just say I'm planning a hot date and I want to look my best!'

'OK, honey,' Jennie chuckled. 'Let's go shopping!'

A couple of hours later, Imogene was ensconced in a chair at a famous Fifth Avenue hair salon, her hair sprouting twists of foil and smeared in some noxious-smelling paste, while Jennie oversaw the stylist's work with motherly authority. Jennie's only concern was the cost - but although Imogene left the salon looking a million dollars, Jennie had noticed no money changing hands. Clearly the girl has a private income, Jennie thought with a shrug. Let's go for it!

Shrugging off her money worries, she took Imogene to a frighteningly expensive and chic Fifth Avenue boutique; when she left the shop she was almost unrecognizable, she was so beautiful.

Finally, Jennie took Imogene to her home in Queens where she taught her how to shave her legs; it was a strange phenomenon for her. And when she asked her to strip, including her panties, Imogene was shocked, but it was only because Jennie wanted to shave her pubic hairs.

'What are these hairs for, anyway?' she asked.

'That is a very strange question, my dear. They're here 'cos when a woman shaves them it makes her look more exotic when her lover sees her naked.'

It took the whole of the afternoon but when they were finished Imogene had had a complete makeover; she looked so beautiful both outside and in and it would be a revelation if Tom was ever to see her undressed. And Imogene had a feeling that revelation was imminent.

CHAPTER FORTY

Tom was sitting on a bench overlooking the Delaware River trying desperately hard not to feel sorry for himself. Already, he felt the symptoms of depression knocking quietly but persistently on the door of his mind, and it was making him heartily sick, of both himself and his life. Again and again he had gone through the traumas of the past fifteen months, and all that had happened was that his mind was now going round in circles as if he had had too much to drink.

Should he have caught the Pan Am Flight? He most certainly would not be here now, but according to Imogene, he might well be at peace in God's Kingdom. The one thing he did know was that he, and possibly only he, had proof of life after death. In a way he was another kind of resurrection. Every time this dawned on him he felt angry with his own ignorance; up to now he had totally ignored the miracle, concentrating simply on the sexual angle with Imogene.

By now he had spent a wasted couple of days seeking employment without success. The newspapers evidently didn't want him; it appeared that news of his dismissal from the Times had preceded him. When he introduced himself there was a kind of perfunctory shake of the head, as though they were expecting him and had rehearsed what to say. Trying to be honest, he conceded that his appearance might well have put them off. In the fortnight since he had separated from Imogene some of his standards had slipped; his suit badly needed pressing; his shirt was crumpled and dirty and he had done nothing to put a shine on his shoes. In short, he looked a mess, and he knew it.

Sighing and vowing to get his act together, he considered trying some of the law firms in the area. He realised that he couldn't prove he was a qualified lawyer, but he felt certain that he could make an impression as a legal assistant.

For now, though, he was content to stay slumped on the bench, gazing at the river in a kind of stupor. Winter was already fading allowing the brightness of spring, so at odds with his grey feelings, to emerge. He sighed, shrugged into his creased topcoat, and made his way back to the hotel. Since leaving the hospital in Wilmington he had booked into the Holiday Inn, on Walnut Street, close to the shopping arcade. It wasn't cheap, but as he had not yet purchased a car he decided the dent in his capital was justified.

Trudging back through the drizzle, he decided that he would have to make a move soon. He had already told his mother that he had found an apartment in East Philly, which wasn't exactly true, although he did have one earmarked, not too far from Fairmount Park. At the moment he simply didn't feel quite up to it. No doubt, he told himself, it was the depression stifling his energy.

Suddenly, the sun shone through the rain and a rainbow shone over the tall buildings. Tom looked up in wonder and felt instantly enlightened; it was if the rainbow, with its shining colours and message of hope had uplifted him - as if something fundamental had changed for the better. For God's sake, Tom, he told himself, you really are truly blessed! He had met his own angel, face to face; had lived with her; had worked with her; and she had kissed him – a beautiful angel's kiss. He wondered if he would ever see Imogene again – in his lifetime.

Thoughts of Imogene filled his head and stayed with him as the rainbow faded and he struggled through the ever increasing downpour. 'Wherever you are, Imogene,' he said aloud, 'thank you for empathising with my feelings.'

He felt quite alert as he entered the hotel and shook the water from his raincoat; his hair was drenched but he couldn't do anything about that. It was as if the depression had dissolved in the rain. He walked across to reception and got the shock of his life when he saw, what at first, seemed to be an apparition.

Imogene was sitting in one of the leather button back lounge chairs, looking as stunning as ever. She was wearing a soft Irish Green sweater over a long, dark fitted skirt that exemplified her femininity. Her hair, the colour indeterminable and spreading almost to her shoulders, underlined her beauty. She glanced over to him and smiled as her eyes sparkled, one of those moving smiles that brought tears to his eyes and made him fall in love with her all over again.

He went across to speak to her, but she placed her fingers over his lips.

'Not here,' she whispered. 'Let's go to your room.'

'You were thinking about me,' she said after the elevator doors had closed.

'Yes. Yes, I was. I was hoping you might pick up my thoughts. Jesus, Imogene, I never thought I would see you again. How did you find me?' He turned and held her hands, gazing at her in awe. Then, impulsively, he held her in his arms, and squeezed her tightly.

'I'm so glad to see you.'

'Have you been looking after yourself, Tom?' she enquired, ignoring his earlier question. She raised her eyebrows and looked him up and down, taking in his dishevelled appearance, but said nothing.

He didn't speak until they entered the room, then he said, 'Not really – but I guess you can tell that. I think my psychological defences came apart after … well, after we split up. But I'm beginning to feel better today. But why are you here? Is it because of my operation?'

She smiled again. 'No, Tom, I'm not here about that; although it has caused us some concern.' In that instant she decided not to tell him that the operation, however well performed, was pointless as the vasectomy he had in New York was irreversible. 'I'm here because something's come up that could cause us some serious problems.'

Tom sat down on the bed and gestured towards the one solitary chair in the room.

'Is it because of something I've done...' he started, looking downcast.

'No. It isn't,' she cut in. 'I've just been to see your mother – the original intention was for her to come to see you with me, but either you believe me or you don't.'

Tom shook his head. 'You're confusing me now. Why don't you start at the beginning?'

'Do you have any coffee?' she asked.

'What? Coffee? Yeah. Sure.' He picked up the phone and rang room service.

'They'll bring it.'

'OK. Well, I know Molly recently visited you in the hospital – supposedly to see how you were.'

'What does that mean, "supposedly"? You aren't going to start on about her again are you, Imogene? I don't want to talk about her; I'm too pleased to see you. I thought we'd been through all this...' Tom tried not to feel stressed.

'Please listen Tom, it's not easy to tell you, but I have to.' Drawing a deep breath she plunged on, knowing how hurt Tom would be, 'Molly's sharing an apartment with Scott Hardy in New York, and has been for some considerable time... Let me finish, Tom,' she said as he tried to interrupt. 'It was his idea for her to make contact with you and effectively seduce you. The purpose behind this was for her to investigate and establish if there was any truth behind your story to Hardy about the Pan Am accident.

'When she visited you at the hospital, Scott Hardy told her to get a sample of your mother's hair for DNA forensic testing. He already had your own DNA on file and now he wants to match up your mother with yourself. That would prove to him that you should have been on the aircraft; you should be deceased; and that as you had already informed him, I was indeed an angel.

'Can you imagine what would happen if that were to hit the headlines? There'd be an international outcry. Proof, that life after death does exist.'

Before he could reply there was a knock on the door. It was the coffee arriving.

Tom, once again, was shell-shocked. He couldn't speak for a while, the news was so devastating. He simply couldn't believe it – not after all he had shared with Molly. He felt angry and ashamed that he had confided in her that Imogene was indeed an angel and that, in truth she had rescued him from the Lockerbie Disaster. He sat there, drinking his coffee, unable to absorb what Imogene was saying. He had spoken to Molly several times since leaving hospital, she was loving and kind and interested in the new life he was trying to build. A life that she had led him to believe would include her too. Perhaps Imogene had got it wrong? Perhaps she was trying to split him and Molly up? He shook his head at the prospect.

'I take it you think I might be deceiving you, Tom?' Imogene's voice cut into his thoughts.

'No; I'm just having difficulty getting my head round it all. You see, I was honest with her; I've told her everything – especially about you being an angel and saving me. I haven't seen you, I don't know where you've been or what you've been doing, and now you turn up, out of the blue, to tip my life upside down.' His shoulders shook and he looked as if he were going to burst into tears. 'I really thought she was genuine – I had no idea anyone could be so duplicitous.'

'I don't think what you told her matters at present; not under the circumstances but that was one of the reasons I wanted your mother to see you today. To show you the film on the camcorder I shot outside their apartment, which will show you that I am telling the truth. After that I wanted you and her to go to New York and confront Molly and Scott.

'It isn't only that that worries me, Tom. It's the DNA sample Molly collected from your mother's hairbrush. Did you know she offered Molly a bed for the night because of the snowstorm?'

He nodded. Mary had informed him the following day.

'So, she took advantage of that, and stole some hair from your mother. Whatever you might feel about her living with another man and effectively misleading you with her emotions isn't really the problem. If we attract world headlines – and I believe this is their intention - can you imagine how your life would be affected? Me, I can simply vanish, evaporate into thin air, but you and your mum, your lives would have to exist under the banner of the headlines – throughout the world.' Imogene stopped; looking carefully to make sure he understood the implications of what she was saying.

'That scares the hell out of me! I don't want to be part of some world news story, forever! But what can we do to stop them? If they link Mary and me as mother and son…' He shook his head and looked crestfallen, 'I wouldn't have a clue how to persuade them to hold off their story. I'm really sorry, Imogene, I never thought for a second something like this could happen. Do you have any suggestions?'

'I suggested to Mary that you and I might just vanish from the face of the earth. There's an old friary in the Bronx – that's where I was staying – that's offered sanctuary to us both. Either that or we go abroad to some out of the way place.'

Tom looked even more forlorn. 'Isn't that what I've been doing the last fifteen months or so – running away? And if what you're saying's correct then surely the entire world will be after us? I doubt there'll be any place we could hide.' His shoulders fell as if his depression had returned with a vengeance. 'I'm sick of running, Imogene. In fact I'm sick of living this kind of life. I don't know who I am anymore, I can't come out into the open for fear of betrayal, and everything I do's a meaningless charade. Molly described me as a living corpse. I think she was right.'

'So what will you do? Let them publicise the story and then pressurise you both every day for interviews? Your mother still has a life to lead – she wasn't responsible for this disaster. Are you going to make her the subject of press hounding? She would have to give up medicine, forfeit her home and her husband, and sacrifice her friends? Is this what you'll allow?'

'I don't know,' he almost screamed. 'You're asking the impossible of me! If we go to this sanctuary, will my mother have to come too? Can you imagine how we'd both feel? It would be worse than a prison! Locked up in some forgotten monastery behind closeted walls! What do you think that will do to our lives, Imogene?'

She reached across the bed and held his hands. 'Well, at least you won't be hounded. I suggest that you stay in the friary until the heat has died down – and it will, believe me, if neither of you is contactable. What do you think the media is likely to do? They will have the essence of a seraphic story, but without any of the substance.'

He scowled, rather like a young boy who has been caught out in some minor mischief. 'Really? And how long will we have to stay there? Eons? We'll be the ones without substance – no family, no jobs, and no money. When and if we do emerge at some time in the future what do you suppose we will do? It will be impossible for us to take up our old lives again – mother and son, destitute, homeless, candidates for the shelters.'

Imogene got up from the bed and walked over to the window. The rain seemed to have stopped; even a hint of the sun was showing through a gap in the clouds. She thought of the comments that Tom had just made, and to some extent she agreed with him. It wasn't so much the effect it would have on him; it was the impact it would have on his mother.

She turned from the window and said, 'I said to your mother earlier today, that I'd need to think about this. I don't think that's changed; leave it with me, let me consider it overnight and I'll come back to you tomorrow?'

Tom nodded. There really wasn't anything to say.

'Where are you staying tonight?' he asked before she left.

'I'm not sure yet. I still have to speak with Mary, let her know how we've got on.'

'Why don't you stay here?'

She laughed. 'What? You mean share a room with you? I… I don't know.'

'No. I didn't mean that, Imogene.' He held out his hands by way of an apology. 'I was thinking if you took a room in this hotel we could perhaps have dinner together, and then talk. Maybe even ask Mary if she wants to discuss it.'

'I… I'm not sure. Look, I have to call Mary. I'll do it from reception and I can ask them if they have a spare room for tonight.'

CHAPTER FORTY-ONE

'What did Mary say?' asked Tom meeting Imogene in the lounge, on the way back from her call.

'She's coming over in the morning; we need to talk about what we're going to do with those two characters.'

'Is she coming to New York with us?'

Imogene shook her head. 'I don't think so. What she said was that I should go with you, but that you should confront them on your own.'

He frowned. 'Wonderful. And has she any suggestions as to what I might say to them?'

'No more than I have at the moment. I just feel that somehow we have to try to stop them investigating us. I know I keep saying this, but I do need to think about it – and so do you for that matter.'

'Yeah, right. Now, what about dinner?' he asked, changing the subject. 'Oh, and have they got a room for you?'

'Yes. I'll stay here tonight. And no, I'm not that hungry.'

'Yes, but, as you kept reminding me, you have to eat something. Come on, I'll order for you.'

Imogene quite surprised herself with her appetite, although on this occasion she was sadly disappointed with the food. They both started with the soup of the day; lukewarm Italian Minestrone that wouldn't have recognised Italy had you taken it to Sorrento. This was followed by an over-done fillet steak and a limp side-salad. Imogene had to laugh.

'You bring me to the best restaurants, don't you?' she exclaimed sarcastically.

'I thought you weren't hungry,' Tom reminded her playfully.

'Just as well, isn't it? Do you mind if we go to the bar? I really need a stronger drink than this diluted wine.'

'Really? You are surprising me tonight. What is it you fancy – a brandy?'

'No; a single malt, a large one! Something to take my mind off these worries.'

Tom signed the bill and followed her out to the bar. Despite being a gloomy, old-fashioned place, filled with oak panelling and decorated with vases of fake flowers, it was quite crowded. Somehow, even in this less than average hotel bar, with her customary ease, Imogene managed to find them a cosy, quiet corner where they wouldn't be disturbed. He noticed she had already ordered her drink and was sipping it rather hastily.

'You didn't waste any time,' Tom said, taking a seat next to her.

'I told you, I needed a drink,' she responded.

'Sure,' he said dubiously. She had never ever needed a drink in all the time he had known her. He wondered what this was all about.

She finished the whisky and held out her hand with the glass.

'Another?' he questioned.

'Please. A large one.'

'What's going on, Imogene? You've hardly drunk in the past; now you're knocking 'em back like there's no tomorrow.'

He went to the bar and repeated the order. When he returned, her eyes had a glassy look in them, as if she was already feeling the effects.

'Are you sure you want this?' Tom asked.

'Probably not. But all this is really getting to me now... I need something to take my mind off it all.'

She took the glass from him and then placed it on the table.

'Shall we go to bed?' she said simply.

'I'm not really tired,'

'I meant you - with me. Shall we go to bed together?'

'What?' His mouth fell open. 'Are you sure?'

She squeezed his hand. 'Come on, before I change my mind.'

He hesitated, unsure as to what he should do. As if sensing his dilemma, Imogene took him by the hand and led him from the table.

'Are we going to your room?' he asked.

'I didn't book a room. I just presumed we'd spend the night together.'

His heart was in his mouth at this declaration. He didn't dare speak. This was something he had longed for and now it seemed as if it were about to come true. As they entered the room he asked, 'What about your divinity, Imogene?'

'Let me worry about that,' she replied.

She slipped off her skirt as he unbuttoned her blouse.

'You're so beautiful,' he gasped, stroking her soft skin, which gleamed in the shafts of moonlight that streamed through gaps in the thin curtains.

'Do you love me, Tom? Truly love me?'

'More than anything in my life. I worship you.'

'Please be gentle with me, won't you. I never thought it would come to this but now I feel helpless.'

She helped him off with his clothes and naked they lay on the bed together, wondering at each other's bodies and feeling delight in the closeness of finally being together after all this time.

He kissed her, gently at first, then, like a man drowning, he plunged into the depths of her embrace. The sweet aroma of roses filled his senses and as he breathed in the fragrance he was suddenly lost. The passion and the love for Imogene that he had repressed for so many months was now released to consume him; it was as if she had breathed into him a spiritual essence he thought belonged only to the divine. Never in his life had he experienced such happiness and bliss.

They made love for most of the night, unable to get enough of each other. In between bouts of lovemaking they dozed fitfully; Imogene clung on to him, frightened to let him go in case he somehow deserted her. In the morning she gave him the sweetest smile he had ever seen. It both consumed him and devastated him.

'I love you so very much,' was all he could say.

'Not as much as I love you,' she smiled ecstatically, kissing him, that scent of roses still lingering on her lips.

'Let me use the bathroom first,' she said, 'then we'll have breakfast with Mary.'

'How d'you feel?' he asked, hesitatingly.

'I don't know. At the moment I feel exalted, as if I've been lifted up to Heaven, but I don't know how long that will last. I'll let you know. In the meantime, we have to work out what we should do about our old boss.' She shook his shoulder jokingly. 'Come on, lazybones. Let me borrow your toothbrush.'

Mary was in the restaurant when they entered. She was a little surprised, albeit pleasantly, to see them both together.

'Are you back together,' she asked, tentatively.

Imogene leaned across and gave her a kiss on the cheek.

'What do you think, Mary?'

Discarding her usual reserve Mary clapped her hands with excitement. 'Oh, I'm so glad; now we can act as a team!'

'Have you had any thoughts, Mary,' Tom asked.

'Not really, no, but I have brought along the camcorder. Do you want to have a look at it, Tom?'

'Not now. I think we should save it as ammunition, in case they argue with us.'

'I have a suggestion,' Imogene announced. 'Maybe Augusto - that's Friar Mancini, in the Bronx… Maybe he can help us…'

'No disrespect,' Tom interjected, 'but don't you think we need a hard-nosed detective type - not a sweet and gentle old monk!'

Imogene laughed.

'I take your point - but trust me, there's a lot more to old Augusto than meets the eye! And anyway, I think we need that insight of his - and his contacts in the Catholic Church could really help us find out about Hardy's background,' she enthused.

'But what makes you think Hardy's a Catholic?'

'Don't ask me how - I just do. Anyway, I'm dead sure he went to a Catholic school, which would still make Augusto's contacts valuable.'

'Well, OK - but I hope your friar can move quickly,' Tom pointed out. 'We don't know how long we have before this story breaks.' He hesitated for a moment, adding, 'So, you're not averse to a bit of blackmail then?'

Imogene laughed, looking delighted.

'This isn't blackmail! This is, hopefully, a way to prevent two wicked people ruining our lives and destroying God's will. We cannot allow that to happen.'

'Well, since you put like that, I'm sorry. I take it all back!' he grinned and within the hour they were on the fast train back to New York.

CHAPTER FORTY-TWO

The journey back was spent in silence. Tom was wondering what had changed Imogene's mind about taking their relationship further; not that he was about to start complaining. Imogene was worried.

Have I done something terrible? On the other hand, in fairness to myself, she thought, I am feeling euphoric. Maybe the tribunal will accept the limitations of my flesh.

Finally, to break the silence, Tom asked the question that was starting to burn inside him.

'Where are we going to stay, Imogene?'

'I'm not sure!' she responded, looking genuinely surprised. 'I haven't thought about it yet. We could always go back to the apartment.'

'But won't we be easier to find there?'

'Probably, but I'm not sure the monastery's the right place; especially after we ... well, after we... you know what I mean.' She blushed, unable to say the words yet.

He smiled; so last night wasn't merely a one off! That was something of a relief to him.

'Yes. I know what you mean.' He squeezed her hand. 'You're not sorry are you... about last night I mean?'

'No, but maybe I should be... Now I guess I'll have to consider myself truly human.'

She leaned over and gave him a kiss. 'It was wonderful,' she said.

'Do you mind my asking what changed your mind?'

She shook her head.

'I'm not altogether sure. I suppose I just missed you – we hadn't been together for two or three weeks and I couldn't bear the thought of never seeing you again. Are you happy, Tom?'

'Unbelievably. I can't find the words to describe the feelings I have for you, and I shouldn't worry too much about losing your divinity; what happened to me last night was truly divine.'

He hesitated for a moment before saying, 'Can I ask you a question?'

'Sure,' she said, nuzzling up to him.

'Well, it occurs to me that if there is anything to find out about these guys past then… well, couldn't you simply ask the Tribunal?'

'It's a good question, but the truth is that the past of every person in the world has already been passed to a higher authority; even the Tribunal has no knowledge of that.'

He placed his arm around her shoulders, allowing her to doze and luxuriating in the feeling of having her close. She was at peace.

When they arrived at New York he shook her gently awake.

'We've arrived,' he said to her.

'Good. The sooner we get this started the better,' she replied, blinking sleepily.

They met Augusto at what Tom described as their 'newly-furnished apartment' because last time he had seen it the place had been empty. The Friar gazed with approval at his surroundings and said, 'Was this your idea, Imogene. Or Tom's?

'It was mine to tell the truth. I thought he might be more comfortable in these surroundings.'

'And were you, Tom?'

'Not at first, no. But even I can get used to luxury like this.'

They smiled as Augusto took out his notebook.

'So, you're already aware that Scott Hardy was enrolled at a Catholic School?'

Imogene nodded.

'And you'd like me to investigate his background further?'

'I thought it was a better idea than effectively becoming hermits hiding out at the monastery.'

'You may well be right. But I'm not sure I can help you, Imogene. I'm not a detective and I have no idea how these people work.'

Imogene smiled at his naivety.

'It's quite simply really, Augusto. First, you fly to Chicago, then you contact the headmaster of Hardy's old school – you'll find he's retired now, and he's living in one of the church's retirement homes. And then you talk to him, ask him what he remembers about Hardy's schooldays.'

'Listen, my dear, I have a better idea - why don't you fly to Chicago and you talk to him?' he replied with a grin.

This made Imogene giggle.

'We shouldn't laugh, you know, this is serious,' Tom said.

'Yes. You're right,' apologised Augusto. 'OK, Imogene, I talk to the headmaster, and what do I say?'

'For God's sake,' Tom almost shouted, 'you ask him does he remember Hardy, and what kind of problems did he cause when he was in school; either Lower School, or even High School.'

'Right,' Augusto muttered, 'you've made your point, Tom. So now I'm well briefed. Except, just how far have these two characters gotten with their so-called exposure? I mean, they do have any real evidence, or is all of this merely hearsay?'

'I'm afraid they've managed to steal a sample of Mary's DNA - and Hardy already had Tom's - so as soon as they get the test results and match them they'll have real evidence, if not exactly proof,' Imogene intoned ruefully.

'Why? Doesn't she have any other children? What I mean is that Tom could well be Mary's son, but not the one who's missing... just a brother.'

'I am still here, you know' Tom muttered, feeling a bit left out.

'Sorry about that,' Augusto apologised, turning to him. 'I'll try to include you in the conversation; I just want to get it totally clear in my mind. You were about to say, Imogene?'

'After the crash it was well publicised that Tom was her only child so there's no way we can suggest there was a brother - and certainly not one with exactly the same birthdate! All we can do is find some dirt on Hardy - and we know there's plenty. We've got to get something to use against him. Something he just can't afford to have exposed - and we only have the time it takes for him to get those DNA matching results. After that, it's too late - he'll take his story to the world the moment he has it in the bag!'

She fell silent, her gaze settling on the abbot as the full weight of the challenge sank in.

'So can you help us, Augusto?' she pressed quietly.

He finished his coffee without saying a word. Then he said, 'I don't see why not. But I'm not sure there'll be anything to discover about Hardy. It's rather like fishing in a lake for a shark; sometimes they don't exist...'

'Oh they exist all right. I think I mentioned before, Augusto, the moment I met that man I knew instinctively that he's inherently evil. That's why he's immune to my influence - and that's why I know he'll have done some terrible things in his life. You just have to find out what they are.'

'Oh is that all?' Augusto twinkled ironically, then sighed. OK, leave it with me and I'll do everything I can. Can I contact you here?'

'Yes. But Tom's due to start a new job in a couple of days.'

'Which is pretty much all the time we have! I'll be as quick as I can.'

He stood up and gave Imogene a kiss on the cheek. Then he stretched out a hand to shake hands with Tom.

'What'll you do if I don't find anything?'

Imogene shrugged. 'Don't know. Maybe we'll have to take you up on your offer and stay at the monastery. One thing's for sure, we can't stay here in New York.'

After he'd left Imogene asked Tom the question, 'What did you think of him?'

'I'm not sure. At first he seemed to be... taciturn. In the end I rather liked him, though. His concern for you came across - he's sincere, I can see that. But whether he can uncover anything about Hardy remains to be seen.'

'If there's anything there to uncover you can bet your life Augusto will find it. He's got amazing insight; a way of understanding people… In any case he really is our last hope.'

'Did you mean what you said before, about falling in love with me?'

'Of course I did. It isn't something you joke about. Come on, Tom, I'm hungry.'

'You soon got your appetite back.'

'I know. Let's go to that Italian – I could do with some pasta.'

Tom shook his head. She was constantly bewildering him with her spontaneous tactics and for a moment he gazed at her, silently contemplating their future together. It was true, as Augusto had tried to point out, that he was truly blessed; the entire world would give anything to meet their Guardian Angel and witness an insight into an eternal life. And this angel he loved with all of his being; he would do anything for her, even die for her.

Even so, he couldn't dismiss what might lie ahead. Where would they go with headlines around the world chasing them? There would be no place to hide. Imogene would become a kind of shrine that people would want to worship, and the media of the world would demand interviews. He shuddered at the thought, 'I was just thinking about the future. What it might hold for us.'

'You don't believe the Friar will find anything do you?'

He looked into her eyes. 'I'm not sure. Perhaps he will. But my worry is what if he doesn't? Where will we go? There won't be a place in the world where we will be safe.'

She snuggled up to him. 'Why don't you let me worry about that?'

Tom bent across and kissed her.

CHAPTER FORTY-THREE

It is not for nothing that monks are called brothers. Once he had the bare facts of Hardy's background it did not take the wit of Sherlock Holmes to phone around the Catholic fraternity in the Chicago area with some vague questions about one Scott Hardy. It was not long before he came up trumps with the name of Hardy's old school headmaster. He could hardly believe his luck when the name of Father Patrick O'Brien… Could it really be his old friend Patrick? It was! The aging priest and retired headmaster was still in Chicago - but now living in a small retirement flat close to his church. Framed by the remaining wisps of grey hair, his face was heavily lined as though he had experienced all the worries of the world. At one time he had been a heavily built man but time and ill health had evidently collected collateral against his body and the repayment took the shape of a considerably wasted man. However, his eyes still had a sparkle and his thoughts were still very clear.

Father O'Brian welcomed Augusto and ushered him into the lounge of the small but very comfortable apartment. It had a number of seating areas positioned around an artificial coal fire; there was one fairly large bedroom and a small but functional kitchen off the lounge.

'It's so delightful to see you, Augusto.' he sighed. 'It's been so long - and I believe that Father Time has now become my partner; it sits here talking to me and reminding me that he won't be here much longer.'

'Mother of God, dear Patrick, are you always this despondent?'

Patrick laughed. 'I suppose I'm looking for sympathy but I've picked the wrong person. Anyway, it's so good to see you after all this time, but tell me,

Augusto, are you just here to check on my health or is there something else you need to discuss with me?'

Augusto chuckled.

'I see you haven't lost your sense of humour. First. Let's have tea together. Do you have a housekeeper?'

'Of course. She's in the kitchen preparing the tea. Mrs Dyson. She's been with me since I retired.'

A middle-aged lady brought the tea in on a tray.

'Shall I pour, father?' she enquired.

'No, but thanks anyway. Mrs Dyson this is an old friend of mine, Friar Mancini. He's come all the way from New York to visit me.'

She bowed her head graciously.

'Nice to meet you, sir. I think any visitor he gets these days is very welcome. And you've come such a long way!' She turned to father Patrick. 'Shall I make some lunch, Father?'

'Excellent idea, Margaret. Something light will do me, but of course I can't speak for Friar Mancini here.'

'Thank you so much. Something light will also do for me.'

They settled down after Patrick poured the tea, and then he said, 'So, Augusto, you've come all this way so it must be something important. Do you want to begin.'

'Well I don't know how far back your memory goes, Patrick, but I'm here to ask about one of your former pupils: a Scott Hardy. It must have been around twelve years ago when he was at the High School, after which he got a job at the Chicago Tribune. Since then he's moved on to the New York Times.'

'Quite an achievement. Especially for someone who, as I remember, was such a violent pupil.'

'You obviously do remember him then. What can you tell me about him?'

'It's a long story, Augusto. I remember when he was just a youngster, his father was stabbed to death. Evidently he was a drug dealer and he got involved with some of the big boys.'

'You mean he crossed them?'

'Yes - although there was no conclusive evidence... The police arrested a man the drug gang had apparently used for the stabbing. Anyway, the culprit was sentenced for manslaughter and he got... Sorry, I can't remember his sentence. But what I do remember is that a few days after the man was released from prison some years later, he also was attacked; stabbed in the same way as his victim. They found his body in an alleyway.'

'Strange. But what had this to do with Hardy?'

'Oh, right. Well, by then he was about nineteen-years of age – I recall, as you mentioned, he was working for the Chicago Tribune; it was Father Murphy who got him that job - and again, although there was no proof, the police were convinced Hardy was the killer. But if you want any of the case details you'll have to talk to one of the detectives involved, a Bob Connors. 'Course he's retired now, living by the lake, but I'm sure he'll remember Hardy.

He and another detective named Albertini were on the case. They talked to me a couple of times, asking me about Hardy but I could hardly disclose his background to them now could I?'

'His background? What do you mean by that, Patrick? Is there something you haven't told me?'

'Well, yes, there was a serious incident when Hardy was just a teenager. Actually, he was more into his late teens. Anyhow, there was some kind of a scuffle during one of the breaks with a fellow student called Bruce Wearing - they were either about sixteen or seventeen at the time. Anyway, the argument was about Alison Wright, a pretty young teacher here at the school. Evidently, Wearing was having an affair with her and Hardy wanted to impose…'

'You mean he fancied her?'

'Well, if you put it like that, yes. And Wearing, in the vernacular, told Hardy to fuck off. At least that's how it was explained to me.'

'And what did Hardy do?'

'Do? He pulled out a knife and took a chunk out of Wearing's right shoulder. He was hospitalized for quite a while. In fact, he'd have been dead if he hadn't ducked!'

'Jesus. And were the police called?'

'That's where it got a bit tricky. You see Wearing and Alison were… how can I put it?'

'Copulating?'

'Yes. That's a good way of expressing it. And what Hardy had done was to take a Polaroid photo of the couple… well, naked and copulating, in one of the classrooms. When I threatened to call the police, Hardy showed me a copy of the photo. What he was saying was that if I called the police, Alison would be exposed and prosecuted for having sex with a minor; I believe they call it statutory rape. Certainly she'd have gone to prison.'

'I see. So you allowed Hardy effectively to blackmail you? Am I right, Patrick?'

With a big sigh, the priest got up and went to the window. He was silent for a moment before he said, 'What else could I have done, Augusto? What they did was, I suppose, a natural act, and they both told me they were in love - and I felt she certainly didn't deserve to go to jail. What would you have done?'

'I suppose if she were a perfectly respectable woman, and possibly this was the first time it had happened, then, well. I guess I'd have agreed with you; she certainly didn't deserve to go to prison, especially if they were serious about being in love. However, it put Hardy in a very dangerous position. We're talking here about grievous bodily harm here - and I'm not sure how I'd have dealt with him. In my opinion this guy deserved a very serious prison sentence.

'Tell me, Patrick, what was his background like. Where did he live? What was his mother like, especially after the death of her husband? Did you know anything about that?'

'Of course I did. His mother was a peasant from Romania. She hardly spoke any English and more often than not she scrubbed floors. She was also a devout Catholic; I believe she went to Church almost every day.'

'How were they able to manage after her husband was killed?'

'My own view is that her son looked after her with some of the money from his drug dealings - and I guess he paid her a reward for giving him an alibi.'

'An alibi for what?'

'For the killing of Lewinski, the guy who murdered his father.'

'Are you telling me that that's how he escaped from the police? Because his mother gave him an alibi?'

'I guess so. So what did you expect me to do, Augusto? Challenge her and tell her she was a liar.' He sighed again. 'I'm not a policeman my dear friend. And it's all very well your arriving here out of the blue and digging up old ground almost as though it's the resurrection but you haven't even told me yet what all this is about?'

'Sorry, Patrick, you're right. I should've put you in the picture. Let me tell you my own story and how Hardy fits into the background.

'First off, there are two people working at the Times, one is a young man called Thomas Heaton. He's there with his, shall we call her his girlfriend? Her name 's Imogene and she is, or was, his Guardian Angel; now, because she rescued him from the Lockerbie disaster, she's compelled to watch over him as a human being for the rest of his natural life...'

'Christ, Augusto, is this some kind of a joke?'

'No. It isn't. And will you please stop interrupting me. Coming back to this Hardy character, he has some suspicion that Imogene and Tom are tied up together, and that Imogene really is a Guardian Angel. So what he's trying to do is to expose her and make a fortune in the deal by publishing a sensational story in the nationals that proves there's a life after death. And I'm here, Patrick, to try and stop him.'

Patrick observed him in silence, as if all this information were spinning round in his head. For a while he couldn't speak until Augusto said, 'Well, what do you think?'

'Think? Dear Mother of God, Augusto, you come along here, out of the blue, not having seen you in so many years, and you start telling me a story about angels and a soul who was rescued from an air disaster and now, how this angel's been forced to become human... Fuck me, Augusto, if you'll pardon my language, what the hell d'you expect me to think?'

Augusto grunted. 'Not like you to cuss, Patrick. However, it matters not to me if you believe me or not - it won't stop me intervening. What I'm dealing with here is something very serious and it has to be stopped, with or without your help.'

'OK, OK, let's assume what you're telling me's true... and please believe me, Augusto, I'm not doubting that you positively believe the story. I'm just questioning whether or not you're dealing with reality here. Do you understand?'

Augusto laughed. He rose from his chair and looked out of the window.

'It must be very nice here in the summer time, with the flowers opening and the sun shining on the window. I can imagine you sitting outdoors taking in the sun and getting a nice tan...'

'You're doing it again, aren't you? Patrick interrupted. 'Changing the subject.

Why are you avoiding my question? Have I embarrassed you in some way?'

Augusto shook his head. 'No, not in the least. Nothing about this case embarrasses me; I agree it's so bizarre it defies explanation. But what I'm dealing with here, Patrick, is neither myth nor a figment of my imagination. It might surprise you to learn that I've had a vision concerning this matter. Not a material vision but a mystical voice telling me what's happened to Imogene and the trouble she and a man called Thomas Heaton are in and why, as a kind of penalty, she was transformed into a human. The voice then asked me to give her sanctuary. A couple of days later she was knocking at the door of the monastery and she refused to explain how she managed to find us in the Bronx. I gave her refuge and looked after her as if she were my own daughter. She's a lovely girl, Patrick, and were you to meet her then I'm sure your doubts would simply disappear. I hope that answers your question, Patrick, and why I'm here is to find some evidence that might conceivably destroy Hardy and prevent him from writing his sensational headline. And in this regard I believe it's incumbent on you, Patrick to help me in any way you can.'

Before Patrick was able to give his answer, Mrs Dyson appeared from the kitchen with sandwiches and tea. Although she didn't speak it was natural that, given the closeness of the kitchen, she must have overheard their conversation.

'You don't have to worry about Margaret, Augusto, most of the time she's not really with us - although she does an admirable job around the apartment and she's quite a good cook.'

He handed out the sandwiches and then poured the tea.

'I envy you, Augusto, most of my life I've prayed for a visitation but I'm not worthy, it seems. And yes, I'll help you in any way I can. I'm not able to walk very far with my artery problems, as you no doubt have noticed, but if you a have a rental then I'm sure we can manage. I think, first we should go and visit Bob Connors, the retired detective. I know where he lives.'

'Can he add to what you've told me?' Augusto asked.

'Probably not, but I'm sure he can amplify what the detectives were thinking at that time. It'll be worth talking to him, Augusto.'

They pulled up in front of a two-storey block of apartments facing Lake Michigan. Augusto noticed that this was a high-class building that must have cost the detective a small fortune.

'Good morning, Bob,' Patrick greeted his old friend as the door was opened by a middle-aged thick-set man, balding and with a stomach that was too familiar with the booze.

'Father Patrick? Jesus, it's good to see you after all this time. Come in, please. And who's your colleague?'

'This is Friar Mancini – he's come all the way from New York to see me.'

Bob pointed to the seats. 'Please. Sit.'

'What a wonderful view,' Patrick announced as he wandered across to look out of the wide picture window with a panoramic view of the lake. He then indicated the expanse of the lounge with a sweep of the hand. 'This must have set you back a few bucks, Bob.'

Bob laughed. 'This is where most of my retirement went. Nice isn't? So, Patrick,

tell me, why are you here? Not merely a social call, is it?'

'No, Bob, it isn't. Friar Mancini –'

'Call me Augusto, please.'

'Yes, sorry. Well Augusto here has come all this way to investigate the background of an old school pupil of mine, name of Scott Hardy. Do you remember him?'

'How could I forget him?' He snapped. 'He's a nasty piece of work who, in my opinion, got away with murder.'

'Want to tell us about it, Bob?' Augusto asked.

'Sure. Some years back, Hardy's father was murdered. He must have fallen out with some drug gang. Anyway, he was knifed to death. The assailant, a character called Lewinski, was arrested and finally sentenced to fifteen years for manslaughter, but with parole. We couldn't make the charge of murder stick. He was released on parole after serving some seven years and was accommodated in a halfway house hostel. One night, only a few days after his release, he must have hit the bottle and, as he was walking home… perhaps I should say staggering… he was attacked, thrown into an alley, where his head was split open on the concrete and then he was knifed viciously as he lay on the ground…'

'How would you define "viciously?" Bob,' Augusto asked.

'He had multiple stab wounds; the ME estimated there were some forty stab wounds all over his body. We concluded this was a revenge attack and that's where our investigations took us. We looked at his prison records, to see if there was someone he could have upset, but he'd led a fairly innocuous life as a prisoner. If there were someone outside waiting for him then that would be somewhat inconsistent; in other words, if someone were after him they could have killed him while he was inside.

'So, finally, we arrived at Hardy. He was nineteen years of age and he had a monumental grudge against Lewinski. Albertini and I – he was my young partner at the time – remember this very clearly. We questioned him and he was furtive, avoiding looking into our eyes. He then declared that he had an alibi from his mother. So we questioned her; she spoke very little English but she did confirm that Hardy never left the apartment that night.

'So we were stuck. We tried everything possible to get her to withdraw her alibi but she was resolute. We had no weapon and no other suspect but Hardy. So, in our view, he got away with murder.'

'What if she withdrew her alibi at this stage?' Augusto asked.

Bob shrugged, 'There's no statute of limitations on a murder charge, so if for some reason you can get her to change her mind then we would probably have a clear case to prosecute Hardy. Is that something you might achieve?'

'Who knows, Bob. It's something we might try, but anyway many thanks for the insight. It'll certainly help me.

'Well, I hope you resolve the young lady's problems. If I can do any more to help you, let me know.'

They said their goodbyes at the door and Father Patrick gave Bob a hug.

'It's lovely to see you, Father. Next time I'll visit you.' He shook hands with Augusto and wished him well in his endeavours.

CHAPTER FORTY-FOUR

There was a heated exchange between Imogene and Tom. Sick to death of Hardy and his deviousness, he was determined to visit him at his apartment and have it out with him; Imogene was urging caution and begged him to wait until Augusto came back from Chicago.

'No. I don't want to wait,' Tom insisted. 'What the hell for? We know he isn't going to turn up any more than we know already – if there were anything substantial against Hardy then surely the police would already have prosecuted him! We are just wasting precious time!'

She placed a hand gently on his shoulder trying to calm him down. 'You may possibly be right, but…' she trailed off, shrugging and wishing he hadn't come to the same conclusion she had reached earlier.

'Even if you are right, how is visiting Hardy going to rectify things? What is it you're planning? Going to threaten him; what with, Tom, what with?'

They were in the kitchen trying to eat a takeaway that Tom had ordered. His was left virtually uneaten whilst Imogene had wolfed hers down. His face coloured at her remarks.

'I don't know,' he confirmed. 'It might not make any difference but at least I'll be able to let him know I'm aware of his relationship with Molly; and if that bitch is there, then so much the better.'

'So, it's satisfaction you're after, is it? And do you think that's going to stop him? Do you really believe that having confronted him he's then going to go away? Fuck me, Tom; sometimes you can be so infuriating!'

He grinned. 'You do have a wonderful way of expressing yourself, Imogene, for an angel!' He leaned across the table and kissed her. 'And I do love you, so very much.'

'You haven't answered my question.'

He sighed, hoping he might have changed the subject. 'Let's say that you are right and it won't change anything; so he won't go away and maybe he'll be indifferent that I know all about him and Molly. OK. So what? At least I'll have frightened him that I'm not prepared to sit back and do nothing. And it will give her something to think about.'

Her lips tightened at this somewhat naïve remark. 'So how will you frighten him?'

'I'll tell him about the abbot and his old headmaster. I'll tell him that he's under investigation and we already know things that could affect his career.'

'You're determined, aren't you? She said quietly, a nervous note in her voice.

'Yes. I am. If we're both right and nothing comes out of the abbot's enquiries in Chicago then Hardy won't know that. He might suspect that matters have emerged which he has been trying to keep undercover.'

He took her hand in his. 'Come on, Imogene, let's give it a whirl.'

Later that evening they rang the bell at Hardy's apartment; the doormen had let them him without questioning their intentions.

It was Molly who answered the bell. Evidently she was stuck for words because she simply stood there expressionless. Her face went quite red when she saw them.

After a few moments silence Tom said, 'Aren't you going to say something, Molly? Like how pleased you are to see me. Or you could just say, yes, you'd be glad to share an apartment with me in Delaware.'

She stood there, shocked. Still unable to say anything, her face had gone from red to the white of a ghost, until Imogene said, 'Are you going to invite us in, Molly? It really isn't you we wanted to speak with – it's Scott Hardy.'

Molly stood back and allowed them to enter – still not saying a word. Tom gave her a sickly grin as he passed her; then patted her on the cheek. 'I've never known you to be stuck for words,' he said. 'No doubt you'll think of some plausible excuse later.'

'There's nothing I can say, Tom. The fact that you're here speaks volumes.' She shrugged philosophically. 'You've obviously found out what it is we're planning to do, so I suggest you take it up with Scott; after all, it is his idea.'

Hardy's face showed no reflection of his reaction to Tom and Imogene turning up; it was almost as though he were expecting them. He didn't get up from his chair either, he just pointed to some nearby seats and gestured they should sit down.

'So, why are you here, you two? Have you come for your jobs back?'

'Your facetiousness isn't very impressive,' Imogene remarked. 'Tom, perhaps you'd better tell him why we're here?'

'We're here, Hardy, to let you know that, for some time now, we've been aware of your plans. Including your little ruse with Molly...'

'It fooled you though,' interrupted Molly. 'You were quite convinced we were going to move in together – you even had it planned so we could share apartments here and in Delaware, pathetic really.'

'Well for your information, darling, you were found out some time back, but Imogene and I were waiting to discover exactly what it was you had in mind.' He paused for a moment, almost as though he were trying to recover his breath. Then he said, 'Oh, and by the way, if you think we don't know about your little trick taking a sample of Mary's DNA, you're also mistaken.'

'So, you're up to date with events,' Hardy said evenly. 'But what do you think you can do about it? You can hardly stop the headlines. Especially after we have collected the evidence. You two are going to become International Celebrities. In fact, I have an idea, why don't you now give us an interview now! You know - a world exclusive!' Hardy's sarcastic laughter rang out, 'Tell us, Imogene, how you managed to save this poor sod's skin, how you came down to earth to rescue him from the Lockerbie explosion and then assumed an earthly body to take care of him. Tell us how you have managed during the last fifteen or sixteen months to look after this pathetic creature. Why did you split up? Why did you get back together?

'Christ – if you'll pardon the expression – I could go on forever asking you these questions! So, are you willing to be interviewed?'

'Fuck you, Hardy.' It was Tom who intervened. 'There will be no interview; nor any headlines.'

'Oh, yeah? How d'you work that one out?' Hardy sneered.

'Because in a matter of days we'll have the evidence of your own tainted background; one of our investigators is already looking into all of the misfeasance's you've committed.'

'What? What the fuck are you talking about, my background? My misfeasance?'

'You surely didn't think we'd just sit back and do nothing, did you? We've had you under investigation now for quite some time. Already we know about your drug dealings...' Tom stopped speaking, afraid he might be giving something away.

Hardy laughed. 'Is that so? And who's this character who's investigating me?'

'A dear friend of mine,' Imogene explained. 'But I don't see why I should let you know his identity. Let's just say, he's extremely well-connected!'

Hardy stood. He was absolutely furious. 'Get out. The pair of you. And don't believe you can stop us because this headline will be far bigger than anything your private eye can uncover!'

It was Molly who showed them to the door.

'Tom – I am so sorry,' she murmured.

He looked at her and saw the embarrassment in her eyes.

'Sure you are,' he almost snorted. 'That's why you're still with him.'

They left without saying another word.

'So, are you satisfied?' Imogene wanted to know.

'Too fucking right I am. Did you see his face when we told him about Augusto? I thought he was going to explode!'

'Yes, well I just hope he comes up with something material and evidentiary.'

Tom laughed at her expression. 'Come on, sweetheart – it was fun, wasn't it?'

The both left the area laughing at Hardy's discomfort; the fact it might not have achieved anything was almost irrelevant.

CHAPTER FORTY-FIVE

It took them forever to find the South Side apartment blocks. It wasn't so much they were difficult to find, they stood towering above almost everything in Chicago, but it was the particular tower block that Patrick had problems in finding. Augusto was about to give up when Patrick breathed a sigh of relief and announced their arrival.

Augusto gazed around him in disgust. The precinct was like a used car dump; hordes of burnt out cars littered the streets; drug needles fragmented the sidewalks; used condoms festooned the ground whilst huge skips overflowed with debris. Everywhere they stepped they had to avoid the empty cans flung out from the balconies. Augusto shuddered when he witnessed the sights.

'Are you sure this where Mrs Hardy lives, Patrick.'

'Disgraceful isn't it? I've only ever been here the once. That was enough.'

Augusto looked up at the old, decrepit tower blacks, rising upwards of ten stories, reaching for the sky as if they were desperately trying to escape the cancer eating away in the fabric.

As was customary, the elevators were out of commission and the priests had to trudge-up six flights of stairs before they reached the two hundred numbers. Halfway up Augusto had to stop and help Patrick whose legs were screaming out at him. In the end he to grasp Augusto's arm to assist him. He shuddered at the desolation surrounding him; it was almost as though no one was living there. Fortunately, behind a strong safety lock, Mrs Hardy was at home. She was a woman in her mid-sixties with Slavic features and a heavy scowl on her face. Maybe at one time she might have been described as pretty, but now, she was heavily built, especially around the middle. Her legs were swollen, more so around the ankles, but it was the deepening scowl on her face that discouraged Augusto.

'Whadda yer want?' Her heavily accented voice growled at him, as her face peered through the gap between the battered door and the safety chain. He heard a dog snarling in the background.

'Mrs Hardy? My name is Friar Mancini. And this is …'

'Father Patrick?' It was almost as though she was going to bow. 'I thought you were…'

'Dead? No, I'm sorry, Mrs Hardy. I'm still here, waiting for the sun to set one final time. How are you by the way?'

She looked shocked to see him. 'Good,' she muttered. 'Why you both here? And you, sir. A Friar?' She couldn't think of anything else to say.

'Do you mind if we come in, Mrs Hardy?' Patrick asked. 'We can explain why we're here.'

She opened the door and Augusto almost gasped with the aroma of sour cabbage, mixed with the smell of cheap cigarettes. They followed her into a small apartment, although he reckoned it was sufficient for a single woman, except for the squalor.

'Yer lucky you two – is me day off. Want a seat?' she said pointing at hard backed chairs in the sitting room. The two priests eased themselves down careful to avoid any dog hairs – much less the fleas. The dog was still snarling until she shouted, 'Piss of Bruno. So, what yer want, sirs?'

'We're here, Mrs Hardy, to talk about your son Scott.'

She sat herself down on an old sofa, wrapped her threadbare cardigan around her shoulders, and lit a cigarette.

'Why yer want to talk about Scott?' She sniffed, then coughed, a real smokers cough.

'When did you last see your son?' Patrick wanted to know.

'Dunno. 'Bout five years I guess.' Ain't seen nowt of him since he went to New York. Why? Has he done summat wrong?'

'Not necessarily. At least not that we know of.' Patrick said.

Augusto frowned at him dismayed with his response. 'There was trouble at his school.' He remarked. I believe many years ago, when Scott was just a teenager. Something to do with a knife.'

'Yer can't hold that against 'im! I mean, he were just a youngster, and it were just a prank.'

'Yes. Except Father Patrick here tells me he almost killed one of the pupils.'

'Yeah. But he didn't though, did he? The other kid dodged and the knife took a bit outta 's shoulder. It weren't 'is fault anyhow! The boy came at 'im with a baseball bat.'

Father Patrick replied, 'That's what you were told, Mrs Hardy. But the truth was that Scott was jealous because the guy he stabbed was having an affair with one of the teachers. Your son also fancied her, some might say he was even in love with her; Scott had taken a photo of the two of them, naked, and had I called the police the young woman ... you can guess the rest? You didn't know any of that, did you?'

She shook her head. 'If you say so father then it 'as ter be true. I'm sorry.'

'Mrs Hardy,' Augusto picked up the conversation. 'I believe you're a devout Catholic?'

'What's that mean?'

'It means, my dear woman, that you visit the church regularly, almost every day when you're not working.'

She nodded. 'I love me church. Couldn't live without it.'

Augusto sighed and brought from his pocket a lengthy document. 'I believe that Scott has never even visited you in the last five years? So you tell us. He doesn't even come home for Christmas. Is that right?'

'No, but as long as he's OK I don't mind. 'E has a good job.' She glanced around the room. 'Anyhow, who the hell would want to live 'ere?'

'But you're his mother? Surely any son would want to spend time with his mother, especially as Christmas time?'

She shrugged again and a tear glistened in the corner of her eye. Patrick felt an enormous sympathy for her.

'Well, we have some disturbing news for you, Mrs Hardy. Do you remember all those years ago when you gave your son an alibi? After Mister Lewinski, the man who killed your husband, was murdered and the police were convinced your son was the guilty party?'

'I think I do yeah, but it were long ago. And I didn't mind, that bastard was a so and so.'

'Be that as it may, the fact remains that you gave false witness against your neighbour –'

'Wat's 'e talking about, Father Patrick? I don't know what 'ees saying,'

'He's saying, Mrs Hardy, that the alibi you gave your son was a lie; without it he might have gone to jail for a long time. Do you understands?'

She sniffed and lit another cigarette. Then she went over to a nearby cabinet and brought out a bottle of vodka.

'Yer want some?' she asked them both. They refused.

'So wot 'appens now?' she said taking a long drink.

'What happens now, Mrs Hardy, is that I have to give you this document; as you will see it sealed by the Vatican and conveys to you your Ex-Communication from the Church. From here on in you will not be allowed to enter any Catholic Church, you will not be able to partake of communion, nor will you allowed the sacraments, especially those of Extreme Unction.

'Do you understand, Mrs Hardy?'

She sat there shaking. She might not have learned much English but she certainly understood what Augusto was saying. She was banished. No Church. No Communion. No Sacraments. She felt faint and as in danger of passing out when Patrick grabbed her and held on tight.

'Did you have to do this, Augusto? Don't you think it's cruel?'

'That may be so, Patrick, but, under the circumstances, it is entirely necessary.'

'But where did you get the Document? And how did the Vatican seal it? I thought you knew nothing about Hardy's background until you came to Chicago?'

'That is what I led you to believe. However, you were needed as a witness, so was Bob, the detective. It is because of you two that the endorsement of the Vatican now becomes valid.

'I was informed about Hardy and his misdemeanours, by the visitation I received; I was pretty well given everything I needed for the visit. And I do hope, Patrick, you will forgive me if I seemed a little devious, but I was under instructions not to reveal anything until I had first hand knowledge. That is what you and Bob gave me.'

'So the Ex-Communication order is valid?' Patrick asked, still gripping on to Mrs Hardy who looked as if she might have passed out.

'Absolutely.'

'But what does she have to do to recant?'

Augusto shrugged. 'Nothing, as far as I can see. We are not here, Patrick, to play detective; what she does with her alibi is entirely up to her. Even if she withdraws it there is no promise of forgiveness, or redemption; this is not a confessional box.

'Shall we go, Father? I believe our work here is finished.'

'Sorry, Augusto. You go ahead without me. I really can't leave her like this, she could have a heart attack.'

'As you wish. I will wait for you at your apartment – if that is all right?'

'Of course. I'll be there whenever.'

Father Patrick emerged some half-an-hour later, feeling distraught. It had not been a nice experience to watch Mrs Hardy in tears. She was inconsolable at having lost her Catholic rights. Patrick made her a cup of tea and put the vodka away. 'You don't need that,' he assured her. He spent more time with her explaining the ramifications of her ex-communication but left when her tears had dried and she was feeling much better,

He joined Augusto who was waiting for him in his car some two hundred yards outside the South Side Apartments – a safe distance he felt.

'So,' he said when Patrick got in the car. 'Did it work?'

'Like a treat.' He answered, 'But I never realised you could be so cruel. Don't you think it was a bit heartless?'

Augusto grunted. 'Did it work or not?'

'I just said it did. Here is her signed affidavit withdrawing her alibi for Hardy. Are you restoring her Catholic rights?'

'Actually, I never withdrew them. The paper was a fake, but since she couldn't read it didn't make much difference.'

'But if she had shown it one of the neighbours? Who could in fact read English.'

'You don't seriously think she'll do that, do you? Allow the neighbours to realise she's been ex-communicated?'

Patrick sighed. He was entirely out of his depth.

'Are you going to show the confession to the police?'

'Not necessarily. It depends how Hardy reacts when we confront him. If he sticks to his story then, yes, the Chicago police will get it.'

'And if he backs down? What if he drops his big headline story?'

'Then we'll let him walk away. But that'll be the operative word – he'll have to walk away. From the paper. From everything. I'll let you know how we get on, and Patrick, thank you so much for all your help. I couldn't have done it without you.'

'So, have we finished, Augusto?'

'No. Not quite. I'd like to contact Mr and Mrs Wearing.'

'But they live in Springfield. That's two hours at least on the train.'

'I know, Patrick. Do you think I haven't researched this?'

'But I thought you had enough with Mrs Hardy's retraction.'

'No. Not nearly enough. If Hardy once tried to kill Wearing then I'd like some kind of affidavit to this effect. And the retraction might not be enough; they could argue coercion.'

'So, I'll have to book into a hotel.'

Patrick let out a huge sigh; this was going from bad to worse.

'You can stay with me, Augusto. You'll have to sleep on the couch but I'll ask Mrs Dyson to bring some blankets and a pillow.'

'That's very kind of you, old boy. And don't worry, I'll be off early in the morning.'

CHAPTER FORTY-SIX

Some days went by and Imogene was tired of waiting for news – news of any kind. She thought at least that Augusto might have contacted her before now. But nothing and the silence, as she remembered, was deafening.

She jumped up from the kitchen table and declared to Tom, 'When do you start your new job?'

'What? Next week, Why?'

''Cos I'm sick and tired of waiting for Augusto. So, let's have some fun. Let's go to Disney World.'

'What, now? I thought we were waiting for news from Augusto?'

'We've waited long enough. It will drive me crazy sitting here waiting for news; we've been here now for two whole days.'

'Christ, Imogene, it's not that long. Can't we wait for another day?'

'No. I've made up my mind. Pack a bag, we don't need much in the way clothes, and I'll book the flights to Orlando.'

Some hours later they were in the air en-route to Orlando.

'Do we have accommodation?' Tom asked.

'Don't worry, Tom, I'll book somewhere when we get there.'

At the airport they hired a car – Tom wasn't even sure whether Imogene had a licence or not, he knew, under his new name, he didn't. And, as was customary, no money exchanged hands. They parked the car as close as was possible to the entrance to Disney World, and Imogene clutched a book of all day tickets.

'Where shall we start?' She asked rhetorically. 'I know, the Haunted House.' She grasped Tom by the hand, gave him a loving kiss, and set off for the attractions. It was a delight, she thought. Having a day off from all of the worries; she felt almost carefree as if the weights had been lifted from her shoulders.

The Haunted House scared the living daylights out of Tom and he was relieved when they went on a love boat, just the two of them, and they kissed all of the way round. Later they had lunch, it was Imogene who was organising things today, Tom was just a helpless soul, but he loved it.

In the afternoon they boarded the Finding Nemo submarine and admired the underwater sights; it dazzled Imogene, who had never been underwater before.

By late afternoon Tom was becoming quite tired; it had been an endless day, attraction after attraction, with Imogene bursting with energy. At one stage he said, 'Do you think we could go to the hotel, sweetheart, I'm absolutely beat?'

She gave him a curious look. 'Are you sure? I was thinking we could go to the Epcot Centre, neither of us has seen it before and I believe it's wonderful.'

He groaned. 'No, please, not more sights and scenes? I can't speak for you, Imogene, but I've really had enough for one day.'

'We could come back tomorrow,' she suggested. 'The flight isn't till the afternoon.'

'OK,' he said at last. 'If you insist? Tell me, what hotel have we reserved for tonight?'

'I've reserved a villa at St. Petersburg – on the beach. Should be nice.'

Tom shrugged. This was history repeating itself. 'I don't suppose you're going to tell me how you were able to do that. I mean… Oh forget it.'

And she was right. The villa was exquisite. It was a luxury three-bedroom villa right on the beach and the taxi dropped them off at the door – almost as though he knew where they were going. Tom got out before any money for the fare changed hands. Not that he expected any such transaction to happen.

'I told you you'd like it,' she said. 'Come on, Tom, let's change and we can go for a swim.

Inside Tom was too tired to describe the house except it was enormous with a wide hall entering on to a sweeping lounge with Italian marbled tiles on the floor and a superfluous fireplace at one end with sofas and lounge chairs scattered all over the lounge. It was more like the lounge of a luxury hotel than a villa and Tom could only guess as to how much this would cost. Imogene led them into a spacious bedroom with a dressing room and an en suite leading off it. 'Come on, Tom,' she said, pulling out a bikini from the holdall.

'I don't have a costume,' he said.

'You do now,' she answered handing him a pair of light blue shorts.

Imogene went for a swim, amazing Tom that she even knew how to swim. There were very few other people about so he lay down on the sands, watching the turquoise sea until finally he fell asleep. He was woken by a nudge on his shoulder. 'Tom. Tom. Wake up. You'll get sunburnt.'

She was right. He could feel his chest was burning, not quite on fire but enough to be grateful Imogene had roused him.

Then they both went into the shower together. It was an incredible experience as she soaked his back, then washed his genitals before she bent down and took him in her mouth. He shuddered with delight, that was until she said, 'Is this love, Tom, or is it merely lust?'

He held her closely, his arms hugging her to him. 'I don't know the name for it, my darling, but to me it's all love.' Then he kissed her, long and sensuously, and carried her to the bed.

After dozing for a while he came to and Imogene was stroking his wet hair.

'Hungry?' She asked.

'Hmm. I think so. Where shall we go? I mean, do you know any good restaurants around here?'

'I'm sure we'll find one.'

As was her habit she was right. Shortly a taxi turned up at the door, greetings were exchanged, and they were whisked off to a delightful fish food restaurant overlooking the coast.

Imogene had never felt so happy, certain that Tom loved her with all of his life.

The next morning, after a long swim in the sea, Imogene decided to give the Epcot centre a miss. They spent the day lazing around, hired a boat and went fishing; Tom caught a small barracuda, not big enough to eat but a catch anyway. Dinner was spent at a small but intimate Italian restaurant where they dined on squid and pasta.

She hugged Tom in the taxi to the airport almost afraid to let him go. The previous night was spent in love- making that she felt should go on forever; she was delirious with happiness. They arrived back in New York in the drizzling rain, there was a forecast of snow but that didn't concern them; in a way Imogene was glad to be back wondering if there was any news from Augusto.

CHAPTER FORTY-SEVEN

Patrick was wrong; it didn't take two hours to travel from Chicago to Springfield; Augusto caught the slow train and it took over three hours. The train took him through Dwight, a traditional town that was part of the old homesteaders, and then on to Pontiac. Finally, the train sped on to Lexington and Bloomington, arriving in Springfield late afternoon.

Springfield was the original Capital City of Illinois and the birthplace of Abraham Lincoln. It was a lovely place to visit and Augusto was met off the train by Father Gavin.

'Good day to you, Friar Mancini.' Father Gavin was a lot younger than Father Patrick; he was slim with a full head of hair; had he not been a priest, Augusto was sure he would have caught the eye of a number of girls, he was so good-looking.

'Please, call me Augusto,' he said. 'And good day to you...?'

'Phillip,' he said, but you can call me Phil.'

'Nice to meet you, Phil. Tell me, have we heard anything from the Wearings?'

'Yes. I received a message that the two of them – Mr and Mrs Wearing – will meet us at the Hyatt Regency. I've booked a room for you tonight.'

'Oh, I was hoping I might fly back to New York.'

Father Gavin grinned. 'That would asking the impossible, Augusto. You'll have missed the last train and there are no flights from here to New York.'

'Oh well, that's life I suppose.'

Augusto sat down in the lounge and ordered coffee. Shortly afterwards, a youngish man came across.

'Friar Mancini, I presume?'

Augusto stood and shook his hand. 'Glad I could meet you, Mr Wearing.'

'Yes. Well. You've come a long way – New York, isn't it?'

Augusto nodded as Wearing ordered coffee. When the waiter brought two over Augusto said, 'I've already got mine, thanks.'

'It isn't for you, Friar - it's for my wife. She'll be in shortly.'

She was still a beautiful young woman; early thirties, dark hair coiffed, slim features with bud-like lips that were enticing, and overall a woman one would have to save from prison. She was dressed in a blue skirt that fell just above her knees, a white blouse and a loose-fitting dark jacket that hung casually on her narrow shoulders; Augusto reckoned it was cashmere and he could well understand why Hardy had fancied her.

'I'm so pleased to meet you Mrs Wearing.' Augusto said.

'Alison,' she said. 'And this is Bruce, my husband.'

'Well, I'm really glad you came. What I want to talk to you about is...'

'Scott Hardy,' Bruce interrupted.

'You obviously remember him,' he said.

Wearing held out his left arm, 'You're kidding me, right? I'd have a problem forgetting this, wouldn't I?'

'Was this from the knife wound?'

Wearing looked at Augusto as if he were being deliberately obtuse. He then said quietly, 'You know he tried to kill me. It was only because I managed to sidestep that he missed my heart.'

'So how did he manage to get away with it?'

Augusto knew the answer of course, Patrick had told him.

Bruce sipped his coffee without responding. Then his wife said, 'I think you'd better tell us what this is all about Augusto. This is all very puzzling after all this time.'

'I'm sorry. I've been asked to investigate Hardy's background; currently he's a senior reporter at the New York Times and he's threatening to expose a very good friend of mine with a hugely damaging international story. Please don't ask me to clarify this Alison because I'm subject to a vow of confidentiality. Were he allowed to continue, then Hardy would destroy a very decent young woman who's done nothing wrong except to harbour and protect ancient secrets of the Catholic Church. It's Hardy's intention to publicise these and create a crisis within the Church - and worse.'

'It all sounds very mysterious, Augusto,' Bruce said, 'but I can't see how his attack on me could help.'

There was a moment of silence before Augusto said, 'Bruce, I want to collect evidence that could destroy Hardy's career, or at the very least discredit his professional integrity. Your stories, both of you, could very well provide me with what I am looking for, and that is, affidavits from each of you describing what happened during this altercation.

'I was told by his mother that you tried to attack him with a baseball bat and he retaliated with a knife,

'However,' he said holding up his hand to prevent interruption, 'I do know from Father Patrick that this was grossly untrue. But Patrick had to cover it up because Hardy had photos of the two of you in... well... I'm sure you understand, and you, Alison, would have gone to prison on a charge of statutory rape. There was no way Patrick could have allowed that to happen. So that's why Hardy got away with attempted murder - literally.'

'I see,' Bruce said, contemplatively, sounding exactly as a lawyer should sound. 'And what do you expect from us now?'

'I'd like to take a statement from each of you, rather I suppose, like an affidavit, testifying to exactly what happened.'

Bruce nodded his head, almost in agreement, and took a deep breath before continuing. 'What happened at school was that, well, Alison and I were together... I mean we were lovers. I know that may seem wrong to you, as a priest, but I'm not going to justify anything; all I will say is that we've loved each other ever since then. Hardy obviously must have spotted us in one of the classrooms... he took a Polaroid photo of the two of us... well, copulating describes it better. He kept that to himself until he was ready to tackle me about our affair; he told me, one day outside the classroom that he fancied Alison and I should back off or else he'd use the photo against us both. I told him to fuck off, so he came at me with a knife. There was no baseball bat - only his knife. At first I wrestled it away from him by gripping his arm and hitting him across the face. But he jumped and then stabbed me; had I not moved a fraction of an inch he'd have stabbed me in the heart.' He again showed Augusto his arm. 'This is what he did. A number of pupils came to help and someone reported it to Father Patrick. Evidently he was brought in front of him before the police were summoned. He showed Patrick the photo and made it clear that if the Headmaster were to call the police then he'd show them the photo; Alison would be arrested and no doubt charged with statutory rape.'

With a flush of embarrassment on her face, Alison said defiantly, 'That's all true, but what Hardy didn't understand, and I guess neither did Father Patrick, was that Bruce and I were very much in love, despite the difference in our ages...'

'It isn't that much of a difference,' Bruce said.

'Anyway, after that incident, Bruce was forced to confess that he came after Hardy with a baseball bat and he stabbed him in self-defence. I resigned from the school, but we didn't split up. In fact, after Bruce graduated from law school we were married and now we have a little boy. I believe both of us made the right choice.'

Bruce instinctively grasped her hand and they exchanged a look of love and contentment.

'And that's what happened,' he said. 'Does it help you at all?'

'Yes. Thanks for being so honest, I appreciate it can't have been easy. But as a lawyer, Bruce, you know that the statute of limitations has passed so there is nothing to fear from that circumstance. Now, I'm hoping you might give me a statement to that effect, so I can nail Hardy.'

'Yes, I would do everything I can to expose Hardy, but I have to tell you, Augusto, that if we do that then there can be no publicity. It isn't so much ourselves we're nervous about but we don't wish to attract publicity to the family. I hope you can accept that?'

'You needn't worry about that,' he said. 'I want to use the instruments as a threat to make Hardy resign from the paper; or maybe, hopefully, he might get the sack. Look, there's an office here we can use, if that's all right with you two; I can type it down and you both can sign it.

It took the best part of an hour to alter the transcription and finally, to sign it. Augusto gave them a signed copy, on the headed notepaper of the monastery, with the assurance that he would not use the testimony for publication.

'What will you do now?' Bruce asked.

'Well, I'll stay the night and tomorrow I'll have to go back to Chicago to see Father Patrick again. It will help if he also gives me a signed affidavit supporting all that you've told me.'

'I don't know if anyone's told you this, Augusto, but you're behaving more and more like a private detective,' Bruce said, with a twinkle in his eyes.

Augusto blushed. 'You're so kind – both of you. And thank you so much for all your help; I'm sure it will prove very useful in dealing with Hardy.'

'Will you let us know how you get on?' Alison wanted to know.

'Of course I will. As soon as something breaks,'

They all shook hands and Augusto retired early.

CHAPTER FORTY-EIGHT

Arriving in Chicago, Augusto phoned Imogene and put her in the picture about the latest developments with Hardy's background.

'Do you think that will help?' she asked.

'I don't want to get your hopes up, Imogene, but it's looking promising. I have one or two things to finish up here in Chicago and I should be flying back to New York later tonight. I'll let you know when I arrive, but please, don't say anything to Tom, will you?'

He took a taxi from the station to Patrick's home. He was still sitting in the same chair as when he had left him.

'Coffee?' he announced.

'Great idea, Patrick.'

'So, how did you get on in Springfield? Did you get a glimpse of Abraham Lincoln's home?'

'I saw nothing, Patrick. Other than Mr and Mrs Wearing.'

'Oh, right. Did they give you what you wanted?'

'Yes. They were very helpful. So much so that I've come back here to see you because...'

'You wanted another signed affidavit from me?' Patrick interjected.

'You've got it. Are you agreeable?'

'I don't see why not. But I'll have to insist on the same conditions as the Wearings. This statement's not to be publicised.'

'You've obviously been talking to them. I didn't realise you were so close. Anyway, Patrick, if you want to keep it secret then so be it. But tell me, is it because of your own position? Or something I don't know about?'

He smiled. 'You must think I'm either foolhardy or egotistical, Augusto. Actually, it has nothing to do with me. If you've given an undertaking to the Wearings not to publicise their statement then, self-evidently you'll have to give me the same order to protect them. Are you agreeable with that?'

'Sure. What I want from you now is a statement setting out everything that happened that day and in particular, why you weren't able to call on the police, even though Bruce Wearing spent some time in hospital. Didn't it occur to you, Patrick, that in reality you had no choice but to call them in; after all a knife was involved and that's a dangerous weapon.'

Patrick sighed as he poured out the coffee. 'Black with two sugars? Right?'

Augusto nodded.

'I believe I've told you why I wasn't able to call in the police. No doubt they'd have charged Hardy, he was a murderous little scumbag. But what could I do, Augusto? Allow Alison to go to jail in exchange for Hardy's imprisonment? Would that have been equitable?'

'I don't want to argue with you, except that even if Hardy had shown the photo to the police couldn't it have been argued that it was two completely different people?'

'Now you're the one being naïve. The photo, for your information, clearly showed Bruce and Alison's faces; I've seen it, remember.

'So, Augusto. Tell me what you need now.'

Augusto pulled out a paper from his holdall. 'I wrote this on the train. You'll find it quite concise, Patrick. And if you're agreeable I'd like you to sign it and then I'll be on my way.'

'Don't be in such a hurry, my friend. I'll read it at my leisure.'

Augusto scowled at him. 'You do realise, Patrick, that time's of the essence here? We're dealing with an out and out sociopath and if he has his way then Imogene, and possibly the Catholic Church, we'll be subject to the most sensational headlines across the world. And it will be largely of your making.'

'Sorry. Sorry. I just wanted some company. Here, I've signed it.'

'But you haven't even read it.'

Patrick sighed. 'Why would I want to read it, Augusto? I'm perfectly sure it's all in order.'

Augusto hesitated before he said. 'Patrick, why don't you come back with me to the monastery? You'd be very welcome there and there'll always be someone to take care of you.'

Patrick rose from his chair and gave Augusto a deep smile. 'That's so kind of you, Augusto. Maybe in the summer I'll take you up on that but for now…' he glanced down at his legs… 'Well, I can hardly walk until the sun shines on me. But pray for me please, and I'll pray for Imogene.'

He then gave Augusto a hug and he left with tears in his eyes.

CHAPTER FORTY-NINE

When Augusto landed in New York the rain had turned to a late spring snow; he knew it would not last but it was still a nuisance as he was wearing summer clothes. Rather than take a taxi he took the bus to downtown Manhattan and then caught a cab to Imogene's place.

She was anxiously waiting for him and started to speak when she opened the door.

In response he pulled some papers from his briefcase. 'These are the signed affidavits from the three parties who were involved that day – other, of course, than Mr Hardy. As I mentioned on the phone, Imogene, they tell a completely different story from the one I was first led to believe.'

'Do you think it might persuade Hardy to change his plans?'

'I'm not sure. We have to understand that he's a man without any conscience. He may decide that although this will reflect badly on him, he won't let it deter from his big moneymaking scheme.'

'Are you going to help me with this, Augusto? I mean confront him with this evidence?'

'Yes. I think that might be better. It might also help if I discuss this with his editor – I'm sure he won't be too happy. But I do know him well.'

'Great. So when do we go and talk to him?'

'We don't, Imogene. This is something only I can deal with; I'll make an appointment to see him tomorrow.'

He sipped on the coffee she had brought him, reflecting on his dramatic visit to Illinois. Right now he was tired and needed rest.

'Do you want to stay the night here, Augusto? You look exhausted and there's a spare bedroom now.'

He smiled, 'I don't think so, Imogene. I have to get back to the monastery and change; I also have the cat to feed otherwise it will feel neglected. Listen; bring Tom up to date, won't you? I'll make the appointment for tomorrow and when I have some news for you I'll ring.'

She led him out and kissed him on the cheek. 'Take care, and get some rest. We'll speak tomorrow.'

When Tom arrived at the apartment he was overwhelmed with the news from Augusto.

'Does this mean we're in the clear?'

'I don't know, Tom. Augusto isn't sure. He's arranging to meet with the editor, Andy Clarke, tomorrow to discuss it with him; all I do know is it's too early to celebrate.'

Across town, Augusto let himself into the monastery where he was greeted by a group of monks who wanted to know where he had been and what he had been doing.

'Brothers, I was out on an errand of mercy. I can't tell you precisely what happened but believe me if I'm right then I may well have saved the future of the Church.'

'Have you eaten?' Brother Peter wanted to know.

Augusto looked at his watch and saw how late it was. 'Tell the truth I am rather hungry, Brother Peter. Is there any food left?'

'I'm sure we can conjure up something for you, Friar. Come, I'll serve it in your study.'

Augusto was very grateful for the food and the service; he had never realised before how popular he was, but then it occurred to him that he was in charge of the order.

At his desk, he reflected on the events of the past few days; he also wondered where on earth Imogene had obtained her tan. She looked positively gorgeous. He hadn't shown her the copies of the affidavits; he doubted they would have meant anything to her except to confuse her. Then he felt so sorry for Father Patrick; he had such a lonely existence and it was a shame he couldn't have come back with him to New York.

He sighed. Sometimes life seemed to be full of worries - even for a friar. Time for bed, he thought.

The next morning there was still some snow about and it was very cold. Augusto had arranged to meet up with Andy Clarke towards lunchtime; they were old friends who had helped each other out on occasions. His first duty was to go into his office, check the mail, and then chair a team meeting of the senior brothers. Grateful that there was nothing terribly urgent that couldn't wait, he quickly photocopied the affidavits.

He met up with Andy Clarke late morning.

'So, how're you doing, Augusto?' Andy greeted him cheerfully.

'Fine, thanks. How are you, Andy?'

'Good. So, what can I do for you this morning?'

'This is somewhat delicate,' said Augusto.'

'Oh, come on, Augusto, it isn't like you to draw back. Spit it out.'

'Well, it's about one of your former employees. Imogene,'

'Hell. Yes. I remember her,' he interrupted, and then laughed. 'She's not after her job back, is she? I mean, I can cope with her, it's her partner I had a problem with.'

'No, no, no, nothing like that. It's just that she's being threatened by one of your senior reporters.'

Andy leaned back in his chair, looking troubled. 'Hey, buddy, that's a very serious accusation, I think you'd better start at the beginning.'

So Augusto began at the beginning, trying to be as concise as possible as he relayed what he knew was an amazing story, even if it was true.

'Wait a minute,' Andy said, intervening. 'You come here this morning with some convoluted story about a mythical angel that Hardy is convinced will make a headline. Either he's become disturbed or you're stretching our friendship. Don't you think you should tell me the truth, Friar?' Whenever Andy was serious he always referred to Augusto as the Friar.

Augusto almost bit his lip. This was not going the way he had believed; he was overlooking the experience of Andy Clarke, and the stories he had been told by countless people seeking their fifteen minutes of fame.

'Augusto, how long have we been friends? Twenty years? Twenty-five years? You were a young priest and I was a junior reporter when we first met; we have almost grown up together and we have helped each other out on many occasions; we have trusted each other. And I'm sorry to say this is not the case now.'

'I'm truly sorry, Andy – it isn't that I can't rely on you, it's… this matter's so sensitive that I'd be betraying confidences if I were to tell you the full story.' He shrugged. 'Apart from which I doubt you'd believe me anyway.'

Andy gazed at him for a long time, his eyes levelling with him. 'Try me,' he said sharply.

Augusto stood up from his seat and walked around the room. 'You'll have to accept that what I'm going to tell you remains "off the record", forever. What I said earlier about Hardy believing that Imogene was an angel, well, it happens to be true…'

'I knew it,' Andy cut in. 'I guessed, after she left the paper, that there was something mysterious about her – the way she made me give Heaton a job when I didn't know him from Adam – if you'll pardon the pun. So how's Hardy trying to prove it? Surely she can prevent that from happening? I mean, if she is an angel.'

'Oh, she's an angel all right. But the problem she has at present is, because she saved Heaton from the Lockerbie disaster, she's now obliged to live her life in a human form; a kind of spiritual admonition from the Higher Authorities.'

'What? As a punishment, you mean?'

'I knew you would have trouble in believing me. The reason is because "They" are trying to avoid a time paradox.'

'What the fuck is that?'

He sighed. For the love of the Lord how the hell did he get himself involved in this situation? So he talked an increasingly incredulous Andy through the whole story from the air crash to the present day.

'I know, I know. It's all so bizarre. But the fact remains, that Hardy's trying to prove that Tom Heaton's the real Tom Metzler and that his life was saved by Imogene the angel.'

'So how did you get involved in this?' a goggle-eyed Andy asked.

'Oh, Lord, Andy, please don't ask me to explain. That would take the rest of the morning. Let's just say Imogene asked me to investigate Hardy's background. So I tried to become a private detective, to see if there was anything to uncover that might dissuade him from going to the press.'

Andy pursed his lips. Augusto was right, he concluded. This was so fucking bizarre. Especially with him, a monk, for God's sake, trying to behave like a private dick.

'And did you uncover anything untoward?' There was a harshness to his tone that caused Augusto to recoil.

'I take it you don't like this?' he asked.

'Well, I'm not too happy about a Friar trying to behave like a private investigator looking into one of my senior reporters. No. I'm decidedly unhappy.'

'You mean if I proved he was guilty of attempted murder? And the Chicago police are convinced he did murder his father's killer after he was released from prison? Would you still be unhappy then?'

The editor had gone pale, with tightened lips he said, 'Prove it.'

Augusto drew the affidavit papers from his briefcase and showed them to Andy before excusing himself to go to the loo. It had been a very stressful morning and Andy needed time to read over them; Augusto couldn't imagine how he would react.

When he returned, Andy was staring out of the window looking a shadow of the man who had met Augusto earlier this morning. Nothing was said between them. Augusto picked up the documents from the desk and was on the point of walking out when the editor said, 'You might not realise it but this does confirm some thoughts I've had about Hardy.'

Again Augusto didn't say a word. He waited for Andy to continue.

'You know how Hardy got the job as head of the crime desk? I'll tell you. His predecessor was killed in a car accident – a hit and run.' He sighed heavily. 'The same thing happened when he worked at the Chicago Tribune; I was Sub-Editor at the time. We found a picture of the victim in the car and it appeared patently obvious that Hardy must have contrived the crash. But it was difficult to prove. So, I invited him to come with me to The Times, hoping I could keep my eye on him before he caused any more damage.

'He's proved to be a remarkable reporter. Did you know that in one case he was shot in the side chasing a drug dealer; evidently he killed the dealer but he spent a few weeks in hospital. And until his predecessor was killed I thought he was behaving himself. Except he wasn't, even though he denied any involvement.

'Now you give me this,' he pointed to the desk. 'Affidavit proof that he attempted to murder a fellow student because he had designs on the teacher; and supporting evidence now from the headmaster.' He shrugged and then sighed heavily. 'I'm not sure what to do about this, Augusto. I only know I can't do nothing and neither can I leave Hardy in his job. But if I dismiss him, how will we able to stop him from publishing the story?'

At last, Augusto thought. He's on our side!

'How much time do we have?' Andy carried on.

'I'm not sure. It depends on when the DNA test is available. I'm sure we have time to think about it.'

'Then let me do that. I'll consider how I should treat this. Are you OK with that?'

'Sure. Can we meet up tomorrow; same time?'

'Yeah, but give me a ring first – make sure there's no other crisis heading my way.'

The shook hands and Augusto caught a cab to visit Imogene.

CHAPTER FIFTY

After Augusto relayed the outcome of his meeting with Andy Clarke, Imogene was quietly subdued.

'Does this mean he's unlikely to do anything?' she asked, somewhat tentatively.

He shrugged and took a bite of the sandwich she had prepared. 'I'm not sure. Andy says he wants to consider it overnight. I'm due to see him again tomorrow.'

'Was he shocked?'

'Yes. His face lost colour. I'm not sure if he was more shocked about you or the fact that Hardy's a treacherous, lying bastard. The one thing he did say is that the affidavits confirmed something he'd had suspicions about for some time.'

'You mean about Hardy?'

'Yes. Do you mind if I change the subject for a minute?'

When she nodded, he went on, 'There was something I meant to ask you about. I would have spoken about it the other day but it didn't seem appropriate.'

She looked at him quizzically, but said nothing.

'It was a dream I had the other night; one of those vivid dreams where it's almost as though it were happening in real time. Do you know what I mean?'

'I'm afraid I don't,' said Imogene. 'I haven't lived long enough to know about dreams. What was it about?'

'It was all about Hardy. It was as though he were… well, kind of making a confession. He told me all about himself. How he had gotten into drug dealing; how he attacked a boy at school because he'd discovered he was sleeping with a teacher who he fancied; and how he'd murdered the man who had killed his father. There was that and more. I wondered if you were responsible for it.'

She laughed. 'Now you're being ridiculous. Like I said, Augusto, I know nothing about dreams, much less have the ability to plant them into someone's consciousness!'

'Then perhaps it was the Tribunal; they must have planted Hardy's confession in my mind. Anyway, it was real and it gave me an insight into what his intentions are.'

'You mean whatever he's done before he's planning to do again?' she cut in.

'Possibly. One thing I do remember is that, at the end, Hardy said that he was interested in gaining the Sub-Editor's job. Perhaps I should warn Andy?'

'I wouldn't if I were you. Leave him to his deliberations. But what will we do if he refuses to do anything?'

Augusto paused, wondering if he should say anything. 'Then the affidavits will be sent to the police in Chicago. On a charge of murder there's no statute of limitations; my belief is they'll arrest him. But I'd rather Andy just fired him.'

'But I thought you'd given assurances that the affidavits won't be publicised?'

'I have. But Andrew hasn't. And it will be he who sends off the affidavits; in other words, Imogene, it won't be any of my doing. The other as well is I have the signed confession of Mrs. Hardy's withdrawal of the alibi she gave for her son; this will certainly be enough for the Chicago police to arrest Hardy.'

'Will that stop him from releasing the story?'

'It will if we show Hardy the affidavits. We'll threaten to send them to the police if he makes a move.'

'But surely, shouldn't he be arrested if he's guilty of murder?'

'You may well be right, Imogene, except I don't believe we want to go through that trauma.'

'So, doesn't that mean that we've won?' asked Imogene.

Augusto nodded. 'I'll let you know tomorrow. Characters like these have all sorts of tricks up their sleeves. Let's sleep on it, Imogene, shall we?'

'Sure. But I'll be there with you tomorrow.'

That stopped him in his tracks. 'Do you think that's a good idea? If you're there won't it wind up Hardy? He might well go into a rage.'

'So let him. Tom and I have seen his childish tantrums before – he threw us out of his apartment earlier last week. And we did tell him that you were investigating him.'

He frowned. Sometimes he couldn't understand how this woman was able to get him into so much trouble. Then he remembered as a friar he was almost duty bound to help the unfortunate.

'OK,' he said, somewhat reluctantly. 'I'll pick you up when I've arranged the meeting – but I'll have to let Andy know you're coming.'

She smiled and led him to the door.

'What are you doing tonight, Augusto?'

'That's a strange question to ask a monk. Did you think I might have a date? See you tomorrow, Imogene. And don't worry, some good will come out of this.'

It was blowing a strong wind as he made his way back to the monastery; perhaps the last of the winter snow might disappear before dawn. He pulled the collar of his coat up and dismissed his thoughts.

CHAPTER FIFTY-ONE

The next morning it was still a cold day with the wind blowing off the East River, but at least the snow had faded away. Augusto collected Imogene in a cab quickly ushering her into the warmth of the car, and accepting her apologies from Tom, who couldn't take the day off. He had already phoned ahead to notify Andy that she would be joining them, and he hadn't objected.

Andy had company when they arrived, a middle-aged man with a portly stomach and bulging cheeks, dressed quite elegantly in a pinstriped suit. Andy introduced him as Graham Carlisle, the company lawyer, and he gave Imogene a warm welcome.

'I've asked Graham to attend because this might get very tricky. Shortly, I'll ask Hardy to join us – I've had to change his routine for the day, so I guess he's already suspicious.'

'What have you decided to do,' asked Augusto.

'I'll give him three options. He voluntarily resigns and commits not to follow up the story, which I doubt he'll accept. Failing that, he'll be sacked and I'll make it clear that I'll notify all of the country's nationals that he's been dismissed for malfeasance. Finally, if he should still resist then I'll forward on to the Chicago police the affidavits for their consideration; he'll know full well that he's not relieved from the Statute of Limitations, especially after he was accused of murdering Lewinski and especially now that his mother's withdrawn her alibi. No doubt he'll be charged. Graham will outline that for him in case there's any misunderstanding.

'Have you anything to add, Augusto?'

'I don't think so, no. You seem to have covered everything, and I regret this has to happen but… well, he's brought it on himself.'

'Right. I'll bring him in.' He picked up the receiver.

Hardy breezed into the office carrying a file under one arm; he was bright and cheerful until he saw the assembly, which stopped him in his tracks. He scowled when he saw Imogene, almost dropping the file.

'You know Imogene, don't you?' said Andy, 'and I believe you already know Graham Carlisle?'

Hardy nodded – the scowl hadn't left his face.

'And this is Friar Mancini. He's just returned from Chicago where he's been investigating your background.'

'What's this all about, Andy? Investigating my background? What the hell has that to do with anyone, especially a Friar?'

'We had some complaints, Scott, that you were intending to disclose information about Imogene here, and that it would be, using your own words, sensational and headline press. I presume you're not denying this, are you?'

Hardy sat down; the scowl had by now left his face and was replaced by a shocked expression. He couldn't speak. His face was ashen.

'I assume from your silence that you're confirming this. Now, the Friar here was commissioned by Imogene to carry out an investigation to try to establish if there was something in your background that might… shall we say, discourage you from proceeding.

'Are we clear so far, Hardy?'

Again there was no response.

'Then I'll continue. It's been confirmed – and I have a full report here,' he motioned to his desk, 'that at one stage in your juvenile years you attempted the murder of a fellow pupil,

Bruce Wearing, because, and again these are his words, not mine, he was having an affair with a teacher who obviously took your own fancy. This story was covered up because you blackmailed the headmaster of your school by informing him about the affair, showing him a photo you'd obtained, and threatening to tell the police. The headmaster had no alternative but to go along with your threats otherwise, aside from the teacher going to prison, the High School would've been brought into disgrace and could well have been closed.

'This is not hearsay, Mr Hardy, I have here affidavits from each of the parties involved, including the ex-teacher, Wearing, and the headmaster, each one confirming what I have outlined.

'There's also a further notice that your mother has now withdrawn an alibi she gave you, for the police, that you were at home the night a convict, named Lewinski, was pushed into an alleyway and knifed to death. I'm sure the police would be very interested in that since you were their number one suspect for the murder, more so, because this man was convicted of murdering your father.

'Now, this is a serious situation, as you are aware, and we have to decide what we should do about it. You may also be aware that the statute of limitations does not apply to cases of murder or attempted murder. Mr Carlisle is of the view that we should report these findings to the police. If that were to happen you'd be arrested and taken back to Chicago.

'Do you have anything to say in your defence before we proceed?'

Hardy's lips curled up and he took a deep breath. 'Before I say anything, or try to deny these outrageous accusations, perhaps you might enlighten me as to what the story is that I am planning to publish? Does it have anything to do with my theory that Imogene here is, in actual fact, a Guardian Angel?'

'Do you mind if I say something?' asked Graham Carlisle.

'Go ahead.'

He pointed a finger at Hardy. 'It seems to me that if you're questioning these affidavits the simplest solution will be to hand them over to the authorities and leave it to them to decide if they're genuine or not. Shall we do that, Mr Hardy?'

'Well, I'm not suggesting you do that.' Hardy's attitude had suddenly changed. 'Perhaps we should talk about it. I mean, you're referring back to something that happened when I was only a juvenile, and regardless of the statute of limitations I doubt the police would be very interested in prosecuting a case that happened all those years ago, especially against another juvenile. Also, you have to bear in mind that whatever happened between Wearing and myself at the very most could only be considered second degree murder, and I doubt that that's within the province of the statute of limitations.'

'There, I think you're wrong,' said Mr Carlisle. 'In the report it specifies that the Chicago police are convinced – albeit without evidence – that you were the killer of the man who murdered your father. They've never forgotten the case and it remains open; their conclusion is that if anything ever came to light that might indict you they will arrest you. It seems to me that it will go to court - more so when you consider that you partly disabled Bruce Wearing. His left arm is seriously disabled. Even if they're unsuccessful with the case, it'll destroy your career.

'Oh, by the way, did you know that he married that teacher he was having an affair with?'

'So you see,' continued Andy, 'there is a case to answer. What I want from you is your resignation and a commitment that you'll never pursue Imogene or any story about her.'

'Just one second,' said Hardy, somewhat indignantly. 'Why don't we ask Imogene what she thinks of a national headline; can you imagine the world's reaction when I disclose to them that an afterlife actually exists? That Imogene's a Guardian Angel who rescued Heaton… or should I call him Metzler… from the carnage of the Lockerbie disaster. Hmm? Do you believe they'll deny it, as you are? I don't doubt it for a second; they'll welcome the news as if it were the second coming. I'm willing to share the spoils with you – equal parts, but I get the exclusive. And my name on the by-line. So, what do you think?' He gave Imogene a suggestive glance.

'You're a very evil man, Scott Hardy,' she responded. 'You'll do anything, hurt anyone, even destroy anyone, to get a headline and further your career. Do you think I really don't know what you and Molly Sinclair are planning?' She said this in a calm voice, almost as though it were ordained in Heaven.

Hardy looked stupefied.

'Even if what you allege is true, then this newspaper will not be a party to your headline.' Andy said. 'And whatever you try to prove there'll always be doubt in the minds of the world; always the suspicion that this is merely a confidence trick. I will not allow you to destroy this woman's good name with your duplicity.

'You haven't answered my question,' Andy continued. 'Are you willing to resign?'

'You're all so fucking stupid,' he snarled. 'And yeah. If you make me, I'll have to. But don't be surprised if the story emerges from a different source.'

'If that were to happen, Hardy, then we'll know that you're the originator, and in such circumstance Graham Carlisle will pass on to the authorities the appropriate affidavits. Your papers and settlement will be sent on to you in due course.'

Hardy rose from his chair as two security guards entered.

'Please escort Mr Hardy from the premises,' Andy said. 'And remember, won't you, everything we have discussed.'

Hardy looked as if he might explode as he was held by his arms and led from the office.

'I'm so sorry you had to do that, Andy,' said Augusto. 'But I don't think you had any alternative.'

'No, I didn't, particularly after his reply. It was quite brutal. He didn't even try to challenge the accusations; his excuse that he was simply a juvenile who couldn't be held responsible for his actions are beyond redemption. Still… now I need a new senior crime reporter.' He turned to Imogene grinning and said,. 'Do you fancy your job back, Imogene?'

She smiled. 'I don't think so, Andy. But I would like to thank you for your understanding and especially for your compassion. I promise I'll say a prayer for you that will go straight to Heaven.'

She went across to his desk and gave him a kiss on the cheek and, together with Augusto, she left the office.

CHAPTER FIFTY-TWO

Imogene had decided to implement one final sequel to this adventure. She waited for Molly Sinclair outside the CNN Studios, who was duly shocked when she spotted Imogene.

'What do you want, Imogene? I thought you were now free of Scott Hardy?'

'So we are, Molly. But I'm not so sure about you. I suppose what I really want is your affirmation that the matter's over.'

'What, you think I might take over from Hardy and try to get this big story out myself? It was made clear to me that if the story were to appear, the Times' lawyer would know who the originator was, and the appropriate action would be taken. So, my dear, how the hell can I pursue this without damaging Hardy?'

'And what if you break up? What if you have a disagreement, go your separate ways, and you decide there's still a story that CNN might exploit? Has that occurred to you?'

'Do you want to go for a coffee? I'm fucking freezing out here.'

Imogene hesitated before replying, 'OK, why not.'

'There's a sandwich bar close to here, we can discuss this in private.'

When they were settled and sipping their coffee Molly said, her voice shaking with tears, 'I let Hardy to use me as a whore. I did enjoy sex with Tom, but it was manipulative; its only objective was to source information out of him. I'm sure you know all this now, but what you don't know is how I allowed Hardy to exploit me, and my body, to achieve his big story.' Overwhelmed, she bowed her head and covered her face with her hands. 'Do you think I'm proud of that?' she whispered, 'do you think I can sleep peacefully each night?'

'Does that mean you're ashamed of what you did, Molly?'

She nodded. 'Yes. I still have guilty feelings about the way I behaved, and I'd like to apologise, not so much for Hardy's deviousness, but for the part I was coerced into playing. I'm truly sorry for having hurt you.'

Imogene was nonplussed. Catching the bemused look on her face, Molly continued, 'I imagine you're wondering why, after all this time, I want to say sorry. There are two reasons, Imogene. The first is that I was too ashamed to confront you, and the second is that Scott Hardy and I have already split. Anyway, I never actually subscribed to the theory that you're a Guardian Angel. I still don't. So, you see, there's nothing for me to pursue.

'Imogene, please, will you accept my apology?'

Imogene leaned across the table and gave her a hug. 'Of course I will.'

CHAPTER FIFTY-THREE

After that, life became a voyage of blissful happiness, and Tom was sure that he was living his own perfect happy ending. He carried on working as a legal assistant, even though financially Imogene could support all their needs. He was happy in his work, and it felt good to come home to his sweetheart. They made love exhaustively, never tiring of each other's passion and enjoying the comfort of sleeping close together each night. Every month they made a point of seeing Mary; either in New York, or in Delaware.

Imogene decided that she didn't want to work; a lifetime in Paradise had effectively made her unqualified for arduous duties. She decided to take it easy and explore some of the more relaxing bits of human life. It was a simple task for her to arrange for the apartment to be cleaned and their clothes laundered. As she assured Tom, it was better to get this done by someone else as she found all housework a boring and irksome task. Occasionally she would pick up some groceries, but only if there was a grocery store near to wherever she was indulging her new passion for clothes, shoes and handbags. Aware that she was in danger of becoming vacuous and desperate not to bore Tom, she also developed a love of books, especially those that explored the human psyche.

It was a wonderful existence; they were enchanted with each other and life coursed along into spring. As the first rays of sunshine warmed the streets of New York, they made plans for summer, dreaming of lying on the grass in Central Park and having dinner at outside restaurants. It was all so magical, and so very different from the stress and strain of the previous summer. Tom's despair had lifted and, as Imogene had predicted, he now found joy in his existence.

Later on in the spring they took a holiday, away from the hustle of New York. Tom had always wanted to go to the Caribbean, so they flew off to Jamaica and stayed at a luxury hotel just outside of Montego Bay. It was almost like paradise. They had a one-bedroom villa on the beach and when they opened their front door they stepped right on to the sands and into the warm Caribbean Ocean. The food was magnificent with unlimited fresh lobster, jerk chicken with rice and peas, and beach BBQ's – all with the most delicious cocktails that Imogene had ever tasted.

On their third day at the resort, another couple in the hotel invited them on an excursion to the top of the Rio Grande; which was an unbelievable journey on a raft down the river. As the sun set, and the two young couples sat sipping rum based punch and listening to a steel band, Imogene and Tom learnt that this holiday was actually Paul and Alice's honeymoon.

It was later that night, as they walked back along the beach arm in arm, Imogene's hair blowing in the warm, gentle breeze, that Tom asked her to marry him.

'I hate to disappoint you, darling, but you must realise that's impossible - we will create a Time Paradox. It hasn't gone away, Tom, as happy as we are now; it is still a threat that hangs over us. I thought we were all right as we are?'

'Yes. I suppose we are. I just thought that it would be perfect if we were married – you know, like Paul and Alice, they seem so happy.'

She squeezed his hand. 'I love you, Tom, but we can't interfere with time.'

Tom smiled, slightly sadly then taking her in his arms said, 'I do understand; nobody can have everything, and I have almost everything.'

That was until Imogene got an urgent summons to appear before the Tribunal.

'*You asked to see me, Chairman.*'

'*Yes. I did. And I wanted the whole of the assembly gathered together to hear what I have to say. You may not realise it yet, Imogene, but you are in danger of triggering the time paradox.*'

'*Why? I know Tom asked me to marry him, but I said no, so what else have I done to upset you?*'

'*Imogene, you are now pregnant – something that is irrevocably forbidden.*'

'*How on earth did that happen? You told me that the vasectomy was irreversible!*'

'*Evidently not; you are three months pregnant. Surely, your body clock must have told something was amiss? How could you not know?*'

'*I'm sorry, Chairman, but I didn't realise. I just thought my periods had become irregular.*'

'*What worries us is that perhaps you do know, and are planning to go ahead regardless of the consequences?*'

'*That's so unfair! I've told you the truth.*'

'*Be that as it may, I have asked the assembly here today to inform you what you must do now.*'

'*Surely, there must be another alternative? What if I were to lose the baby?*'

'*You mean have an abortion?*'

'*No, of course not - but something could go wrong and I could lose the child.*'

'*We cannot look into the future; we can only deal with the present circumstances.*'

'*Well, why don't we wait and see? There is nothing to lose if we wait another month, is there?*'

There was moment of quiescence. Imogene thought they were giving due consideration to her request and prayed that it would be approved. Finally the Chairman spoke. '*We will give you another two weeks; after that your pregnancy will show and it will be too late. You have to understand, Imogene, this is something that originates from a Higher Order; we have to act swiftly, before disaster overtakes you.'*

After the hearing, Imogene lay on their bed, where so much love and joy manifested itself, and wept tears of sadness. She was a spiritual being, so abortion was out of the question and she abhorred the prospect of doing that to an earthly body. Yes, she could wait two weeks, but what was going to happen? She asked herself. Nothing. She was a young woman, fit and certainly healthy enough to carry a baby to full term. The worse thing was that there was no way she could share her conundrum with Tom. She loved him so much and in so many ways it was a blessing she was having his baby, but there could be no future for them now in this world.

The next two weeks went by in an atmosphere of great sadness. From time to time, as the days passed, Imogene began sobbing in private; she was inconsolable and no matter how Tom tried to press her she wouldn't explain her torment. She would sit at the kitchen table and suddenly burst into tears.

'What has happened?' he asked one morning when she wept at the table.

'I can't tell you, Tom.'

'Is this something I have to trust you with?' he said sardonically. 'Do you want me to take the day off work? They won't miss me, you know,' he offered, seeing the true misery clouding her beautiful face.

She thought about it. There were only three days left and she dearly wanted to spend them with him, but she daren't; it might give the game away.

'Are you going to tell me what the matter is now?' Tom begged her, as they met for a drink that evening.

'I can't, Tom.'

'Oh, come on, Imogene, whatever the secret is, surely you can share it with me? I mean we're practically engaged.' He threw his hands out, almost an act of desperation. 'Yeah, I know, we can't get married for all the reasons you've said. But we're as good as. So, why can't you trust me?'

'Let's go eat, shall we?'

'You're changing the subject again. You simply don't want to answer me.'

'I've told you. I can't. Now, are you hungry?'

'No, I feel like getting drunk. How about you? You wanna join me?'

'Good idea. Let's go to the bar by the apartment. Then I'll carry you home.'

The next two days sped by until the penultimate day arrived. Needing comfort and support, Imogene crossed the city to visit Augusto at the Friary. He was very upset when she told him what the plan was and how it would involve her and Tom.

'Does he know?' he asked.

'No. I am duty bound not to tell him.'

'Is this from the Tribunal?'

'Yes, Augusto. It is a direct command from the Chairman. I dare not refuse, nor dare I inform Tom what is about to happen.'

'Imogene, I don't know what to say. You came into my life at a very special time for me and there is no way I can thank you except to carry out God's work here in the Friary and in the community. May God bless you, Imogene, and thank you for everything.'

She kissed him again on the cheek. 'I hope you will always remember this Angel's Kiss. Goodbye, Augusto.'

There was little else she could do. The last thing she did was to phone Mary at the hospital and wish her goodbye, begging her not to repeat their conversation to Tom.

'But will I see you again, Imogene?' Mary said, sounding confused and frightened.

'No; but after tomorrow I promise you will not have heard of me. Goodbye, Mary, may God be with you.'

Finally, the last day arrived and she wiped the tears away from her eyes, forcing a cheerful smile for Tom as she kissed him goodbye for work. Finally, she made contact with Molly who was surprised to see her. She didn't go into the CNN building but met her downstairs in the large hallway.

'What on earth's the matter?' Molly enquired seeing troubled Imogene. 'You look terrible.'

'I'm so sorry to appear like this but I've had my share of worries.'

Molly squeezed her arm 'How can I help you, my dear? Is there anything I can do?'

'Just give me a hug, please. That will definitely help me.'

Molly obliged and stroked her back at the same time.

'Goodbye Molly, dearest one. Think of me when you open the present.'

She kissed her quickly on the cheek and left a confused and bewildered Molly watching her depart from the building.

The Tribunal had already warned her about any delay. She readied herself for what lay ahead.

EPILOGUE

Terminal Three at Heathrow was very busy as Tom arrived for the flight to New York. There were lots of passengers hustling about, as though they were about to miss their plane. He ignored them.

He checked in at the Pan Am desk, thanking his lucky stars again for the priority service that flying business class afforded him.

'Have a good flight,' the attendant wished him.

'Yes. Thank you.'

'You know where the Pan Am executive lounge is, sir?'

He nodded. He had seen the sign earlier, which he now followed.

He was feeling decidedly peculiar; it was as if he hadn't slept all night. He remembered being at the Natural History Museum ... was it yesterday, or today. He went into the executive lounge and stood in line for the young flight attendant to take his boarding pass. She checked him off in row five seat two b, and he noticed that someone else had already taken the window seat. There was no name, just a title; Imogene, which meant nothing to him. Just then a strikingly beautiful woman came and sat beside him.

'Do you mind if I join you?' she asked.

Tom could hardly speak, he was so overcome by her beauty and the fact she had chosen to sit next to him.

'I ... I'd be delighted,' he stammered, glancing around at the large number of empty seats available in the lounge. Looking again, he thought she looked faintly familiar, as if he'd met her somewhere before.

'Hi,' she said. 'My name is Imogene. And you are?'

'Tom,' he stuttered. 'Tom Metzler. Have we met before? It's just that you look familiar.'

She smiled. 'We haven't met, but I think we did see each other yesterday in the Natural History Museum.'

Of course, he thought to himself, that's where I've seen her before. She had looked at him directly as if she were trying to give him a message, but he was so overwhelmed by her beauty he couldn't actually challenge her. Now he absorbed the sweet smell of roses that overcame him, almost like an aphrodisiac, and he shuddered. She was so incredibly beautiful that words could not describe her.

'Is this a coincidence – I mean you sitting here? Or do you have something to say to me? I thought that was the case yesterday but we didn't exchange messages.'

'Well, as we're sitting next to each other on the aircraft I thought we should get to know each other. What do you do for a living, Tom?'

'I'm a lawyer, with Freeman's in New York. Well, a junior lawyer really; I'm over here to bring an affidavit.'

'And have you found it interesting – visiting London I mean?'

Tom had a vaguely uneasy feeling sitting next to this gorgeous beautiful girl. Somewhere, somehow, he had met her before but his mind wasn't working. Then he looked into her eyes, which appeared to change colour as he gazed into them.

In the blink of an eye he knew. This was his Imogene from another lifetime. This was the girl whom he had fallen in love with, whom he had lived with, whom he had shared a bed with; but what was she doing here? And what was he doing here about to board this Pan Am aircraft? Didn't they live together in New York? Yet again his mind was whirling. He had no idea what was happening to him, or why she was here, but he knew she was foretelling of a disaster about to happen.

'Why are we here Imogene?'

She sighed as if she was expecting this to happen. Then she said, 'It had to happen and I am very sorry that I allowed it.'

'Sorry. Allowed what?'

'I became pregnant and you were the father.'

'Pregnant? How was this possible?'

Just then the flight was called and they had to vacate their seats and move on to the aircraft. It took a while before they were settled; she had an orange juice, he had another coffee. The seat belts were fastened, the engines started up and they slowly made their way to the runway.

'Could you explain this pregnancy to me?' he asked astonished.

She sat back in her seat as the engines roared and they sped down the runway; a few seconds later they were airborne.

'It's rather simple really,' she said, 'I guess it was nature playing tricks on us. You had a vasectomy in New York that I thought was irreversible; but I was mistaken. Even after I surrendered to my human side I never believed we could have children. In fact you were incredibly fertile, and without knowing I became pregnant.'

'But why didn't you tell me? Why go to all these extremes? Why couldn't you just have the baby?'

Then it came to him; the Time Paradox. She was forced to bring him back here, aboard the same aircraft he should have been on all those months ago. She took hold of his hand and held it to her face as he shivered at the thought of what the outcome would be.

'Tom, I will never stop loving you, but the only way for the baby to disappear is to go back in time so it ceases to exist; it never happened. Please will you put your arm around me – tell me you still love me.'

'My dear sweetheart, I always said I would die for you and it seems that is what I am about to do.'

'Are you afraid?' she asked.

His face was ashen, 'terrified. I'm trembling, look at me?' He placed her hand on his heart so she could feel it beating faster. 'I don't know what to do.' He spread his free hand around the aircraft as a gesture to the other passengers. 'Did we really have to do this? Surely there must be another way?'

'I'm afraid not. I have been ordered by the Tribunal to go back in time to avoid the Paradox. I am so sorry, Tom, there was nothing I could do.'

He squeezed her shoulder and placed her head against his chest.

'I am so afraid. Please, Imogene, don't ever leave me, will you.'

'Darling, I will be with you forever.'

Suddenly, there was a rumble of thunder throughout the aircraft, as though they were being hit by a bout of severe turbulence; followed microseconds later, by a booming explosion, which tore the aircraft apart.

Imogene looked on in horror at the disaster unfolding around her, and unable to do anything other than watch, she closed her eyes as the resonance of screams bombarded her. Body parts flew past her through the cloud of terror. Parts of the plane fell to the ground and hit houses below, no doubt killing the innocent residents.

Finally, and tearfully, as the cloud of smoke started to thin and the wail of sirens could be heard on earth, she gathered the soul of Tom Metzler in her arms, turned, and headed for home …

The Tribunal was satisfied. Heavenly order was restored.

Testimonials:

Vanessa Rodgers for her professional and editing.

Carla Stockton for her American skills at editing

Kevin Saunders for his brilliant updates on re-writing

Jonathan Miller for his marketing skills in promoting this novel.

And the (Sorry can't remember his full name) artist for the front cover design

PREVIOUS NOVELS BY THE SAME AUTHOR:

Non-fiction:
> The Package Tour

Semi-fiction:
> Leave a Light on for Jesus

Tri-parte novels with Angela Crossley the psychic detective:
> 1) Nemesis
> 2) Contrition
> 3) Revelation

Play:
> The Retreat

www.ingramcontent.com/pod-product-compliance
Lightning Source LLC
Chambersburg PA
CBHW020907200626
46814CB00001BA/214